falling
for
finn

A MAPLEWOOD FALLS NOVEL
BROOKE FOX

AUTHOR'S NOTE

Falling for Finn was previously published as "The Fall of Us" by Kennedy Fox. It's been revised and includes a bonus chapter with a never-before-released bonus scene.

You're killing me in that tank top
　　You're flooring me in that dress
　　You're taking up all my Fridays
　　Taking away my breath
　　You're gonna drive me crazy
　　With the heaven you put me through
　　Baby, I love the way you push my buttons night and day
　　It's always something with you

Always Something With You
Mitchell Tenpenny

PLAYLIST

Listen to the full *Falling for Finn* playlist on Spotify

Cold As You | Luke Combs
Woke Up in Love | Kygo, Gryffin, Calum Scott
Kiss Me | Dermot Kennedy
Whiskey On You | Nate Smith
Always Something With You | Mitchell Tenpenny
Wish You Were Here | Lukas Graham, Khalid
Held by You | Abby Wolfe
More Than Whiskey Does | Mitchell Tenpenny
Do You | Mitchell Tenpenny
Something in the Orange | Zach Bryan
Midnight Crisis | Jordan Davis, Danielle Bradbery

CHAPTER ONE
OAKLEY

DAY 1

A BLUE RUSTIC Chevy truck that looks like it fell straight from an old film slows down in front of me. My brows rise when I see the Bennett Orchard Farms logo on the door and then meet the deep-brown eyes of the man driving.

Whoever he is couldn't look less thrilled about being here if he tried. Deep frown lines and a tense jaw. He could model for a constipation ad.

I flew from Northern California to Maplewood Falls, Vermont, and after two connecting flights, several coffees and bathroom breaks, I'm finally here. The Bennetts insisted they drive me to the farm from the airport, and after pricing a rental car, I agreed.

His gaze moves up and down my curves before he leans out the window.

"Oakley Benson?" he barks in a smooth, deep voice.

"Yep, that's me," I say politely.

He jerks his head. "Great. Get in."

I lift my carry-on and duffel to put them in the back but

struggle with my oversized suitcase. Although it's in the lower sixties and I'm wearing light clothing, I'm breaking into a sweat trying to deadlift it. After two minutes of failing, the guy who couldn't look less excited to be here gets out.

He's tall, wearing a plaid flannel shirt, jeans, and boots. Scruff grows along his chin and jawline, and when his tongue darts out to lick his plump bottom lip, I have to force myself to look away.

I take a step back, and he grabs my hard-shell suitcase, then tosses it into the back of the truck with a heavy thud. Based on his body language, he's not thrilled about being my ride. This isn't the reaction I expected after he drank me in a few moments ago.

"Hey! Things in there could break." I scoff, but he ignores me.

"We don't have time to stand around all day. Get in." He taps his knuckles against the roof of the truck before climbing in and slamming the door. No hello, nice to meet you or even a friendly introduction. Not even the hint of a smile. First impressions are important to me, and he failed. He's a grump who's acting like someone pissed in his apple cinnamon oatmeal this morning.

One of my biggest pet peeves is being rushed, but I'll give him the benefit of the doubt. I try to push my annoyance aside because I'll have to deal with this guy for the next hour.

After we drive for a few minutes in silence, I open my purse and grab some gum. "Want a piece?"

He looks at the package, then at me before returning his gaze to the road.

"Okay, guess not," I mutter, shoving one into my mouth. I keep my eyes focused away from him, but then I remember I need to text my sister so she knows I made it okay.

OAKLEY

I'm alive in Vermont!

TIERNAN

Oh good! Don't forget to send me pictures of all the pretty leaves! I need to live vicariously through you since I don't know what fall looks like anymore.

I snicker. My sister's sixteen years older than me and lives in Florida with her husband, Everett. She's told me it's either warm, hot, or scorching, and the four seasons we were used to in the Midwest don't exist down there.

After snapping several pictures of the gorgeous trees, I send them her way.

Now that I've seen the bright oranges and burnt reds, I'm even more excited to paint the Bennetts' orchard farm for their centennial celebration in ten days.

OAKLEY

The guy who picked me up from the airport is a jerk. And of course he's hot. All the hot ones are rude.

TIERNAN

Damn, that sucks. Scale from 1-10, how hot are we talking?

OAKLEY

He's a ten, but his shitty personality brings him down eight notches.

TIERNAN

Maybe he's married, and that's how he makes sure no women flirt with him?

I peek over the top of my phone and look at his left hand resting on his thigh.

OAKLEY

Nope. No ring. But I guess that doesn't always mean anything. I know plenty of men who purposely don't wear theirs.

TIERNAN

It's times like that I'm glad I'm not single or searching.

OAKLEY

Who says I'm searching?

TIERNAN

Oh please. You've always been my boy-crazy little sister and that hasn't changed.

I chuckle, and that's when Mr. Grumpy glances in my direction.

OAKLEY

Fair enough. But this farm guy ain't it, sis. Even if he looks like a Greek god. I'll be happy when we get there, and I never have to speak to him again.

I pretend I'm taking a picture of the barn we're passing on his side but zoom in on his forearm. Holding back my laughter, I hit send.

TIERNAN

Muscular, nice. How old does he look?

OAKLEY

Early to mid-thirties. But you know age doesn't matter to me. I'd be a baddie and date a Daddy.

TIERNAN

Oakley Jane!

I snicker, knowing how much she cringes when I talk about dating older men. She's nine years older than her husband, so she's one to talk.

After I send her three kiss emojis, I lock my phone. My sister is my rock and best friend, and I tell her everything. We vowed to have no secrets after she ended things with her abusive ex-husband. I knew something was wrong before she left, but she didn't want me to worry and lied about how bad things were.

"So how long have you lived in Vermont?" I ask, trying once more to strike up a conversation.

He keeps his eyes focused on the road. "All my life."

"Do you like it here?" I ask.

"Yeah."

Reba McEntire sings in the background, but other than that and road noise, it's quiet and awkward.

"Are you shy or something?" I ask because I've never experienced someone treating me like I'm a nuisance before they even get to know me. I literally said three words, and I was on his shit list.

"No."

He doesn't give any more explanation, and I take the hint—he doesn't want to talk to *me*. I could have a more enjoyable discussion with a rock. Instead of trying again, I keep to myself. It's obvious he has nothing to say, and I'm too tired from traveling three thousand miles to care. I hope this is the last time I have to deal with him.

I concentrate on filming the passing farms and the different shades of leaves as the sunlight hits them. While his company isn't the best, Vermont's beauty is everything I expected it to be and more.

Before accepting the job, I did a lot of research about what to expect once I was here, but the photos didn't do it justice. Colorful leaves hang from the tree branches, and some are even scattered on the ground and road. I'm more of a summer girl, but Vermont's cooler temps and scenery are quickly winning me over.

After forty-five minutes of silence, the truck turns down a gravel road, and I see the historic inn in the distance. I read online that it has twelve rooms and is known for its homemade food and hospitality. My jaw drops at how it looks in person, and I continue staring as we come to a complete stop. The rocking chairs on the large front porch have the perfect view of the surrounding apple orchards.

"Your meeting will be through those doors," he says, pointing toward the entrance.

"Great. Do I tip you?" I ask.

He scowls. "I'm not an Uber."

"Sorry, I didn't mean to…"

"Don't worry about it."

"Do I need to grab my things?"

"I'll drop your stuff off where you'll be staying. I'll be back to take you there once you're finished inside."

"Alright. Has anyone ever told you this place looks like it fell straight out of a Hallmark movie?" The hues have me itching to pull out my paints.

"Yeah, just every tourist who's ever visited."

My cheeks heat at how stupid he's made me feel, and I'm ready to escape inside. After this embarrassing exchange, I'd almost prefer him not to talk to me ever again. Thankfully, once I hop out, he drives away without giving me a backward glance.

"Asshole," I whisper under my breath and nervously walk inside. I'm greeted with the smell of fresh-baked cookies, and I instantly crave a dozen.

I walk through a common area with chairs and a fireplace to the hallway. The bay windows allow the afternoon light to cast a warm glow inside.

As I look around, an older woman with white-gray hair comes toward me from around a counter. She's got an oven mitt on one hand as she sweeps loose strands with the back of her free one.

"You must be Ms. Benson," she says kindly. Her warm and inviting demeanor is like the cozy inn, and I immediately like her.

"Yes, but please call me Oakley."

"Perfect. I've been expecting you, dear. I'm Willa Bennett, the innkeeper and owner you spoke to." She pulls me in for a hug. I'm not used to people being this friendly. Especially after the driver basically dumped me at the front door like a soaking wet newspaper.

Willa leads me into a dining area with a large table and chairs that look hand-carved. An older man is busy scribbling a mile-long to-do list in a Moleskine notebook.

"James, this is Oakley." She grabs his attention and then looks at me. "This is my husband."

He gives me a warm smile and outstretches his hand to shake mine. "The painter. We're so happy you're here. Thank you again for agreeing to do this. Once my wife showed me your portfolio, we knew you were the *only* one in the world who could do the farm justice. I'm still in shock you were available."

I blush. "Thank you. I'm very excited to be here."

That's an understatement, but I keep that to myself.

"Have a seat. I'm sure you're tired from your flight," Willa offers, then pulls the oven mitt off her hand. "I baked some cookies for the guests. Would you like a few?"

"Sure, thank you." I smile.

She walks away and quickly returns with a tray of milk and a stacked plate. We each grab one and dig in.

"Your painting supplies arrived early last week, so the boxes are at the cottage, waiting for you. We're looking forward to seeing your vision come to life. Well, when you decide what you'll paint for us," Willa says.

When we talked on the phone, they were very clear that I had complete creative control and wanted me to tour the farm to get an idea of its history. That was another reason I accepted the job. Not only are they comping the entire trip, but the piece they're paying for will also be one of my highest-paid commissions. However, it puts a lot of pressure on me to present something worthy of the occasion.

"Perfect. I'm glad everything arrived okay. I've never shipped my supplies across the country before." I smile, wanting to pop the entire cookie into my mouth but refrain. Considering this is my first big freelance job, I'm shocked by how smoothly the process has gone so far. I've heard a handful of horror stories from friends who were given unrealistic deadlines and underpaid offers as well as worked with unbearable clients. Other than the tight deadline I've set for myself, the Bennetts have allowed me to call the shots.

As I take a sip of milk, James speaks up. "We've also ensured that you'll get a proper tour of the farm. You'll visit different areas over the next few days. We want you to take your time seeing it all and get the full experience of the orchard."

I let out a relieved breath. My art takes time, and I don't like being rushed. "Thank you. From the drive here alone, I'm eager to start painting the trees."

"We've asked our grandson Finn to show you around, and he'll be your main point of contact. He has expert knowledge of all the different areas of the orchard and is passionate about the farm. You'll learn a lot from him," Willa tells me with a smile.

"That sounds perfect." I smile. "I can't wait to meet him."

"Oh, you already have. He picked you up from the airport," James explains.

My smile drops, and I have to stop the four-letter words from escaping my mouth. Not excited to be touring the place with a man incapable of holding a conversation.

Fan-fucking-tastic.

CHAPTER TWO

FINN

O<small>NCE</small> I'<small>M</small> at the cottage, I unload Oakley's bags while she chats with my grandparents. I wanted to give them privacy and also needed time to clear my head.

When I'm inside, I walk by the six boxes she shipped. They all weigh a ton, like her suitcases. Not sure why a painter needs this much shit for one project. Seems like overkill to me.

I'm already counting down the days until she leaves so I can go back to focusing on my shit instead of being her damn babysitter. It's only been a couple of hours, and her snarky attitude is already making her a major pain in my ass.

After everything is settled, I lock up, then drive the five miles back to the inn. I was gone for thirty minutes, which should be plenty of time. However, my grandparents could talk for hours if you let them.

When I walk inside, I find Grandma and Oakley chatting at the dining room table while Grandpa writes in his notebook. Oakley glances over her shoulder, and the smile melts off her face when she sees me.

"Speak of the devil," Grandpa says.

"Nice to meet you, *Finn*." She stresses my name, something I didn't share with her earlier. Not necessarily on purpose, but she never asked.

I grin, but her sarcasm isn't lost on me. This celebration is important to my family and me. Still, I'm stuck dealing with her because they know I'm as dependable as the old truck I drive.

My younger cousins Sebastian and Jessa would be more than capable of escorting Little Miss City Girl around, but my grandparents insisted I do it since I know how everything works around here. They want her to get the true orchard experience, but she's only going to slow me down during a time when I'll be busier than ever getting things ready for the celebration.

"We told Oakley you'd be showing her around," Grandpa tells me.

"Right. Well, speaking of…" I look at my watch, hoping someone gets the hint.

"Looking forward to learning all about the farm from you," Oakley says sincerely, but I hear the hint of amusement in her tone. She knows I'm not happy about it.

Spending time with her is going to be torture. I hate that I find her attractive when I shouldn't. Not only because she's at least a decade younger than me but also because she's only here for a week and a half. I also can't imagine we have anything in common. She's sunshine on a winter day, and I'm too coldhearted to give her the time of day. Shitty relationships with even shittier breakups will do that to a man.

"Would you like to take a quick tour of the inn?" Grandma asks her, ignoring my eagerness to leave.

"Absolutely," Oakley says, and it feels like she did that just to piss me off. As they move toward the stairs, her long, flowery skirt sways when she walks. The bracelets on her wrists clank together as she swings her arms, and she flashes a knowing smirk when she looks at me over her shoulder.

Once they're out of sight, Grandpa stands and gives me a pointed look. "Be nice. She seems sweet."

I glare in response. "This is business. I'm not here to be her friend."

He pats my shoulder. "I know how rough around the edges you can be, so remember you're representing the family, and she's our special guest."

"I told Grandma *several times* that I wasn't the right person for this job. I'm swamped. Jessa would've been better at chauffeuring her around. They could exchange beauty tips or whatever. We have nothing to talk about."

"You'll talk about the farm," he states matter-of-factly. "Plus, your grandmother is *never* wrong. She picked you for a reason." Grandpa shoots me a wink just as the phone rings. He goes to answer it, and I take the opportunity to step outside for some fresh air.

My phone vibrates in my pocket, and I pull it out to see a text from my best friend.

LEVI

I'll make it to the celebration, so save me some of your mom's apple pie!

Of course that's all he'd be excited for.

FINN

Great. Mom will be happy to see you.

LEVI

If you need any help getting anything together, let me know. I have some free time next week.

FINN

Appreciate that, man.

LEVI

So how are things going with the painter?

I told Levi earlier I had to drive to the airport to pick her up, and I've been dreading doing it all week with my already busy schedule.

FINN

Don't even ask.

LEVI

That bad, huh?

FINN

Yes. She talks a lot and dresses like a hippie. I'm surprised she doesn't go by the name Sunflower or some shit.

Levi sends me a laughing emoji.

LEVI

Is she pretty?

I roll my eyes because I'm not even surprised he'd ask that.

FINN

Yeah, I guess. If weird clothing and makeup are your type.

LEVI

Sounds to me like you already have a crush.

FINN

Shut the fuck up.

LEVI

Looking forward to meeting her next weekend. That's if you haven't run her off by then.

That makes me laugh. Levi's known for being a bucket of happiness, and I'm his opposite. But I'm more of a realist and prefer structure. Levi's always been more adventurous and a risk-taker.

However, after my nightmare breakup last fall, I've been working more days and longer hours to avoid thinking about it.

My ex and I dated for five years. I believed I'd spend the rest of my life with her until she blindsided me. Whenever I brought up marriage and our future, she'd change the subject. She eventually confessed she wasn't ready to settle down, and when she did, she wanted to move to the city.

She knew the farm was my home and livelihood. I never want to leave.

But then she wasted years of my life hoping I'd change my mind.

And now, I'm *done* trying.

Being single isn't the worst thing. I have the farm and my family, and that's enough for me.

After another fifteen minutes, Oakley and my grandma come outside. Oakley meets my eyes with a smirk, and my traitorous heart hammers in my chest. A weird underlying current streams between us, but I ignore it and turn my head.

My grandma continues talking her ear off, and Oakley politely listens to every word. "You'll be staying at a small cottage behind Finn's house. He'll drive you here for meals. There's a bakery on-site, and the fridge and pantry are stocked with plenty of food as well. Please feel free to help yourself to anything you'd like."

"Thank you so much," Oakley says, making Grandma smile wide.

"If you find that you need anything once you get settled, please let us know. Finn will be more than happy to help you, too."

I resist the urge to scoff at my grandmother volunteering me.

"Will do. Thanks again for this opportunity. I hope I can do the farm justice. What I've seen so far has been awe-inspiring."

"Oh, I have no doubt your creation will be incredible."

"Ready?" I ask, knowing if I don't pull her away now, Grandma will talk until the sun sets.

Oakley nods, and we walk to my truck.

"Do you want to stop by the bakery?" I ask as we open our doors. It's within walking distance, so it wouldn't take long.

"Nah. I'm pretty tired and need to unpack so I can set up my supplies tomorrow."

"Yeah, you'll want to rest up. We start bright and early around here."

She takes her phone out and snaps pictures of the scenery and buildings between yawning and fighting the urge to close her eyes. The three-hour time difference between California and Vermont will catch up to her by morning.

Soon, I'm driving down the road where she'll be staying. The cottage is close to my place but far enough away to give us each some privacy. It's set out from the hustle and bustle of the orchard for a reason. When business partners or family friends visit, this is where they usually stay if the inn is booked.

"This is it," I say, pulling up to the one-bedroom cabin filled with all her shit.

"It looks lovely," she tells me. "Nice and quiet too."

I unlock the front door for her, then hand over the key. "Don't lose this."

"I won't."

I turn to leave once she steps inside.

"That's it? You're not even going to say good night?" she asks with a bite in her voice.

Spinning around to face her, I shrug. "Did you expect me to stay and read you a bedtime story?"

She crosses her arms. "It'd be the most I've heard you talk all day."

I ignore what she says. "We've got a lot of ground to cover tomorrow, so don't keep me waiting in the morning. Six o'clock comes quickly."

Oakley places her hand on her hip, her bracelets clinking as they slide down her arm. "Getting up that early isn't my vibe, and I don't like being rushed."

"And I don't like being late or behind. Not all of us are on vacation for ten days."

"Vacation? This is *far* from that." She shoots me a death glare as if I've offended her. Without waiting for a response, Oakley walks inside and slams the door.

I'm not here to entertain Miss Sunshine, and she needs to know if she's following me around, I'm sticking to my schedule. There needs to be boundaries between us, and they need to stay strictly professional. It wasn't lost on me how she eye-fucked me at the airport. Smart and confident women are my kryptonite, and Oakley Benson is no exception.

CHAPTER THREE
OAKLEY

DAY 2

A HARD POUNDING on the door jolts me awake. I look around, noticing it's still dark outside, then check the time—6:00 a.m.

"I'm coming!" I shout as the pounding grows louder. Stumbling, I trip over my duffel bag on the way to the door. I crack it open to see Finn glaring at me.

"What are you wearing?" he asks, and I notice his eyes slide down my body. I'm wearing nothing but a T-shirt and panties.

"I think it's called *clothes*," I snap, followed by a yawn. It's brisk outside, and I shiver. These cool temperatures aren't something I'm used to.

"Meet me in the truck in five minutes, or you're walking." He turns around and storms off.

"That's not enough time to get dressed!"

"Shoulda set your alarm." His boots crunch on the gravel as he escapes into the darkness. Seconds later, he crosses the headlights of the truck, and the metal door slams.

"God, I *hate* him," I seethe as I turn on the lights, then rush toward my suitcase. I haul it on the bed and rustle through my clothes.

I was so damn exhausted after I settled in last night that I forgot to set my alarm. But he could give me a break, knowing I haven't adjusted to the time difference. Jet lag is going to kick my ass today.

After I use the bathroom and pin my hair out of my face, I brush my teeth. My body is sore, and if I weren't on a job, I'd crawl in bed and sleep another twelve hours.

The mornings are usually my oasis. I like to wake up quietly with Mother Nature. Most times, I meditate or stretch while brewing some tea, and then I spend an hour planning the rest of my day.

My thoughts are in complete chaos when I hear him laying on the horn.

I throw on a hoodie and some leggings, then slip on my sandals. After I shove my phone in my pocket, I grab my sketch pad and pencils. I'm annoyed and hungry, but mostly I wish I didn't have to depend on *Mr. Big Grumpy Jerk* to take me everywhere.

When I slide into the truck and buckle up, he roughly shifts into drive and speeds off. I'm going to need a mountain of caffeine to get through today.

The headlights lead the way, and low rolling fog billows along the road. I close my eyes and lean my head back, wishing for five more minutes of sleep.

"We're here," he mutters, killing the engine. I blink open my eyes, and he's already hopping out. The jerk doesn't even wait for me, and I have to rush after him as he enters the inn.

The smell of bacon, fresh-baked bread, and roasting coffee fills the place. We move toward the kitchen, where silver trays of perfectly folded turnovers rest on the counter.

"Good morning," Willa singsongs, gently placing her hand on my back. "How'd you sleep?"

"Great," I admit, although it took a while for me to settle down and fall asleep. I don't mention that I tossed and turned for a couple of hours before drifting off or that the bed was too soft. I'm appreciative of the accommodations, and I'll never state otherwise.

"Help yourself to some breakfast but make sure to pick up one of our famous apple turnovers. The fruit came from the farm." She winks, and her chipper attitude is *almost* contagious.

Finn has already started eating by the time I get in line. After I fill my plate and grab some fresh squeezed orange juice, I take the seat across from him. But I might as well be sitting alone.

I look at the eggs and bacon but decide to start with the pastries. The sweet cinnamon apples and homemade bread have my taste buds screaming. I can't help the small moan that escapes my throat.

Finn meets my eyes with a popped brow. "Those came from the bakery my mother and Aunt Paisley run."

"Wow, he speaks," I taunt, trying to shake myself out of the funk he put me in.

"Sometimes I do."

"Not in my experience." I take another bite.

He shoves a forkful of eggs into his mouth and then responds, "You talk enough for us both."

"You say that like it's a bad thing. Where I live, it's customary to make conversation and get to know people," I tell him as I eat the crispy bacon. It's exactly the way I like it. The smoky flavor of the meat combined with the perfectly cooked eggs has me contemplating getting seconds. "If every meal is like this, I don't think I'm ever leaving."

"Don't say that," he states, then when I glare at him, he quickly adds, "You'd never survive the winter months."

I'm not sure what he means by that, but I know it wasn't a compliment. I'm tempted to throw the rest of my turnover at him. But I'd never waste something so delicious. Instead, I laugh because that's all I *can* do. He still doesn't crack a smile.

After we finish eating, I thank Willa again and let her know the food was amazing. Finn leads me out toward the bakery. When we round the building and approach the entrance, I notice the full parking lot.

"What time does it open?" I'm shocked it's already so busy.

"Six on the dot. People start to line up around five so they can get the first round of pastries fresh out of the oven," he explains, opening the door. The bell above rings, and Finn weaves through the crowd.

I look at all the jams, jellies, and jarred fruits. I take a few pictures of the inside and then catch up to Finn. "So you said people wait outside every day?"

"Except for Sundays when the bakery is closed."

"Wow," I barely get out when an older woman with bright-red hair pulls me into a hug.

"And you must be Oakley," she sweetly says. "I'm Poppy, Finn's mom and Willa's daughter."

"She doesn't need a family tree," Finn interjects with disapproval.

"Zip it." She glares at him. "Anyway, it's so nice to meet you. Let me introduce you to my twin sister. *Paisley!*"

So much is going on around me that it's hard to pay attention to it all. Moments later, another woman who looks like Poppy comes out carrying a tray of individually wrapped cookies. They each have a cute logo sticker on them—apples in a barrel with their name: Bennett Orchard Farm.

"It's so nice to meet you. Mama has told us about you and your work. Has my nephew been treating you well?" Paisley glances at Finn.

"Well, actually—"

"I'm fulfilling my duties, as Grandma requested."

I glance at him right as Paisley reaches over and pinches his side.

"Hey!" he screeches, and I can't help but smirk at seeing his mom and aunt poke at him. It seems tougher for him to continue with the hard-ass act around his family.

"Be nice!" Poppy warns, wagging her finger at him like he's five. "If my son doesn't treat you like a queen, you let me know, and I'll take care of him."

I raise a brow and cross my arms. "Like a queen, huh? As in…kissing the ground I walk on and all that?"

"Not happening," he snaps, matching my stance. "Anyway, anything else you want to see here?"

"Sweetie, don't listen to him." Paisley turns to me, then continues, "You don't have to rush. Finn's always two steps ahead of everyone. It's okay to tell him to slow down and smell the roses."

"I don't like wasting time. It's called being *efficient*. Something that's necessary when it comes to running the farm and all the businesses attached to it."

"Loosen up. You're too serious." His mom laughs, then glances at me. "Have you figured out what you're painting yet?"

"No, I hope to have an idea after Finn shows me around today. Crossing my fingers, at least."

"Once you're in the orchards, inspiration will call, but don't let me keep you. Feel free to walk around the bakery and take as many pictures as you like. If you have any questions, let us know."

"Thank you," I say.

"Yeah, you all have work to do before the celebration," Finn adds as if he's the one in control.

Poppy and Paisley laugh at Finn's lack of humor.

His aunt clears her throat. "More help arrives tomorrow, so you don't need to worry or micromanage us. We've been baking since before you were born." She gives him a pointed look.

"Now take this woman on a proper tour without being a sourpuss the entire time."

I chuckle, and he groans at her bossing him around.

"I like them," I admit as Finn leads me around the bakery.

"Everyone does," he says, then introduces me to the other employees.

He explains the various items sold in the bakery, and I'm impressed by how much they do. Most of the desserts contain apples, but they also make other fruit treats.

Framed awards line the hallway that leads to another shopping area. Many are state- and national-level competitions. Vintage pictures of the store throughout the years are sprinkled along in different sizes. From what I can tell, the bakery and farm have barely changed since it opened for operation a hundred years ago. It's as if I've stepped into a time capsule.

When we say goodbye and leave, the sun hangs lazily in the sky. A cool breeze brushes against my skin, and I shiver, wishing I had brought a jacket and worn better shoes. If Finn notices, he doesn't say anything.

"So there's the bakery and the inn. What else is there to see?" I ask while Finn drives.

"We have a distillery for hard cider, a warehouse for the local wholesale fruit orders, and a lot of farmland." He turns onto the main road.

"Where are we heading now?"

"To the apple orchards."

Twenty minutes later, we're driving down a wide dirt road surrounded by trees on both sides. At the end, a large warehouse sits in a clearing with several parked cars outside.

Finn leads the way inside the building. I'm amazed by how large the facility is. It seems to go on forever.

"Most of the fruit is brought here to be processed after it's picked," he explains, nearly sprinting down the aisle.

"How many people work here?" I ask, speed-walking to catch up with him.

"A lot."

His constant vagueness is wearing me down. One minute, he's hot as fire, and the next, he's cold as ice. I don't know how to read him or why he's so bothered by me being here.

"This is Oakley. The painter," he says, introducing me to an older gentleman.

"Hi." I offer my hand, and he takes it with kindness in his eyes.

"I'm Daniel, the general manager. If you have any questions, please ask. We love talking about our process, don't we, Finn?"

Finn answers with a quick nod before we make our way around the perimeter of the packaging area.

"If you keep moving this fast, you'll give me shin splints," I say.

"Keep up, City Girl. There's no time to waste."

I laugh at his poor attempt to annoy me. "I'm *not* a city girl."

"No?" He flashes a shit-eating smirk, then glances down at my sandals. "Could've fooled me."

As soon as I open my mouth to tell him I was born and raised in small-town Nebraska, he talks over me. "Anything else you wanna see here?"

I refuse to let him dampen my shine, but before I can answer, he heads toward the exit. This man is testing my patience, and by the end of this job, I might not have a sliver left.

I wave goodbye to Daniel and offer a thank-you before stepping outside. Once I'm in the truck, I roll down the window and take photos of the passing orchard as the midmorning sunlight splashes through the trees.

Finn takes me to another area of the farm, and after he parks, we get out. It's quiet other than the leaves crunching under my feet. Finn doesn't say much, and for once, I'm happy with his silence.

Closing my eyes, I listen to the wind blow through the branches and realize I haven't experienced quietness like this since moving to California. Then I look down the long rows of trees that go as far as the eye can see.

Finn looks at his watch, and before he can ask me if I'm done, I speak up.

"I'm not ready to leave yet." I keep my tone light because I was taught to treat people the way I'd like to be treated, even if he's been grating on my nerves since the moment we met.

As I take in the fresh air and pretty colors, I realize it's the first time I've been excited to paint since I arrived.

Another few minutes pass, and he lets out a long sigh.

"Ten more minutes, please," I say, hating how he pulls me from my focus. Once his patience is paper thin, I lead the way to the truck. A part of me finds joy in seeing him so worked up.

"Are you always like this?" I ask, getting settled in my seat.

"Yep. Better get used to it."

I laugh. "No, thank you. I won't be here that long anyway, and then it'll be nothing more than a memory. So try to look on the bright side since you can't change it. That's what I'm doing, at least."

He ignores me, but I shrug it off, then check the time. I'm shocked to see it's almost noon. Before returning to the inn, Finn veers onto a gravel road that leads to a large red house with a dark brick chimney. The grass is bright green, and the sky's clouds reflect off the pond across the driveway. Several large barn-like structures surround the compound.

Finn gets out and leans against the hood of the truck.

"My grandparents live there." He points at the red ranch house. "My mom and dad live in the refurbished old barn behind it, and my aunt's family lives in the other one. These are the oldest structures on the property. Before I was born, the historic structures were remodeled into homes because my grandma wanted her daughters to stay close."

"Wow, I want to see the inside," I admit.

Finn glances at me. "I'm sure you'll be invited to dinner at least once before you leave."

My lips turn up into a smile because I hope he's right.

I can't take enough pictures as I breathe in the fresh air. When I glance over at Finn, I notice his demeanor has changed. It might be the first time I've seen him relax since I got here. He seems lost in his thoughts with his arms crossed over his chest as he gazes into the hill of surrounding trees. I snap a quick photo of him, then send it to my sister. She'll appreciate that when she's able to check her phone at work.

I could stay here all day and stare at the picket fence, surrounded by the red-, orange-, and brown-colored trees and structures.

His eyes trail over and meet mine.

"It's beautiful here," I whisper, the wind capturing my words.

"My great-great-grandparents started everything right here. I'm the fifth generation working this land. These buildings were constructed around the same time the first apple harvest was picked. The smaller barn was first, and they lived there while they finished the main house. Most of the wood you see is, well, a hundred years old."

"Incredible." I'm at a loss for words because I don't think I've ever been this close to something so historic. If I could stay here all day, I would.

"Can I get closer?"

"Sure, feel free to walk around," he tells me.

I amble past the pond and walk down the small driveway that ends at the base of the rolling hills. I climb halfway up and turn to take in the view. The different hues and contrasts have my creativity nearly bursting at the seams.

When my stomach growls, I know it's time to go, even though

I don't want to. I take a lot of pictures. However, this scene will be imprinted in my memory for the rest of my life because it's unique in a way I can't describe. A sense of calm washes over me, and I wish I could stay here forever and take it in.

I return to the truck and take a few more photos before joining Finn inside.

He watches me as I hurry to open my sketchbook.

"I have actual work to do after we eat," he says as I focus on my pencil and paper.

After I outline the primary lines, I reply, "Great. Let's go."

He shakes his head. "You'll get in my way."

I narrow my eyes. "I'm supposed to be learning about the orchard and farm. So right now, you're wasting *my* time."

He sucks in a deep breath and bites down on his lip as if he's holding back. "Fine."

That was too easy.

While we quickly eat lunch at the inn, I can't stop drawing. Usually, I'd give my attention to my company, but Finn is incapable of having a conversation, so I don't even feel guilty about it. When I'm in the zone, I tend to get lost in my work. It's obvious he doesn't care anyway.

"You don't need to look at the pictures you took?" he asks as I perfectly line up the main house and pond.

"I have a photographic memory. Beautiful scenes are imprinted in my mind, and I can draw or paint from memory. The pictures were for keepsakes and to show my sister."

"So is sketching a part of your painting process?" he asks around a mouthful.

I give him a smile—appreciating that he's intrigued—and swipe loose strands of blond hair from my face. "Yeah, kinda. I like to sketch the scene on a smaller scale first, then sleep on my ideas before transferring it to the canvas. It's easier for me to visualize the final product this way. Then when I have actual photos, I use them to color match because I want them to be as vivid as they are in real life."

His gaze lingers on the pages and meets mine before bringing his attention to his food. I can tell he's impressed, even if he tries to act like he isn't.

"We should probably get going," he tells me when I take the last bite of my club sandwich.

"As always," I singsong, then stand and put up my dishes.

We make our way to one of the maintenance barns a few miles past the cottage. Finn pretends I don't exist as he moves inside and grabs different tools.

"What are you doing?" I ask as he lifts the hood of the tractor.

"Oil change. We'll use it for the tours next weekend." He gets to work, and instead of watching him, I stand at the entryway and stare at the fields. That is until I hear a thud followed by Finn cursing under his breath.

The oil pan is tipped over, and oil spreads across the concrete and his boots. He grabs a towel, but before he throws it on top of the mess, I stop him.

"You should put sand on it instead." I point at the fabric he's gripping. "Not that."

"Sand?" He gives me an incredulous look.

"Yeah. It absorbs the liquid and makes it easier to clean. Can also use kitty litter, but I doubt you have any of that."

He grabs a shovel leaning against the wall, then pushes it toward me. Wearing a cocky smirk, he says, "Be my guest, then."

I take it from him, walk outside, and dig into the ground. When I return, I sprinkle half of the sand on his boots and the rest on the oil. "Now leave it for a couple of hours, then sweep."

I swear I see a sly smile touch his lips for a moment before he turns away from me.

"Are you always a smart-ass know-it-all?" he asks.

"Yep. Better get used to it." I throw out the same words he said to me earlier and he chuckles under his breath.

After he finishes, Finn grabs a set of keys from the wall and cranks the tractor. Thirty minutes pass as he tinkers with different items, and I can't stop thinking about getting my paints out.

"You can take me to the cottage now," I tell him, ready to get started.

"This too boring for you?" he quips. "Not as exciting as city life, huh?"

"You're not the only person who has work to do before next weekend," I remind him. "I doubt I'll find a way to add this into the painting."

He snorts and shrugs. "Fair enough."

Finn drives me to the cottage, and before I get out, he speaks. "I'll be back in time to take you to dinner."

"What if I need something in the meantime or to get a hold of you?"

"I'm sure I can get you a farm truck. That's if a city girl like yourself can drive a stick?"

I groan, hating that I can't prove him wrong *again*.

"To be fair, there aren't a lot of big farm trucks in the town I live in."

"I bet not," he muses. "You can call or text me if it's an emergency."

I open my phone, and he gives me his number. I program his contact as Mr. Big Grumpy Jerk, then shoot him a text. When his cell vibrates in his pocket, he narrows his eyes at me.

"Just making sure you didn't give me a fake number."

He scoffs. "I should've thought of that."

CHAPTER FOUR

FINN

DAY 3

OAKLEY WILL NEVER UNDERSTAND our culture or how passionate we are about the farm. Sure, it's beautiful to look at, but she'll leave and forget it ever existed like all the other tourists do. The orchard remains a snapshot in their minds, a memory of something they did for fun one time.

But it's much more than that to me. This is my life. My passion. My family's legacy. It's much more than a bunch of apple trees, and I take how it's run seriously.

Last night when I picked her up for dinner, I wasn't in the mood to shoot the shit. I had to force a full day of work into an afternoon because of her. To say I'm exhausted is an understatement, and this week will progressively worsen.

This morning, I woke up still annoyed that I had to chauffeur her around. When I arrive at the cottage, I honk twice instead of getting out. After ten minutes pass, I lay on the horn. As soon as I unbuckle, the front door swings open, and she strolls out at such a slow pace that I nearly bite my tongue off.

Oakley hops inside, wearing her signature smile. She smells so damn good that it's nearly intoxicating, and I hate it.

"Don't make me wait like that ever again. Next time you do, I'm driving away, and you can figure it out on your own."

"Try me," she warns. "I dare you. I know your sweet momma and aunt wouldn't allow it."

I roll my eyes at her petty threat. "You'd have to walk five miles to get to them first."

She groans as I put the truck in drive and make our way to the west side of the property. We spend most of the day driving around before stopping for lunch. It's nonstop between us, and all day we're at each other's throats about how fast I move and how slow she walks. Every punch I throw, she swings right back. One thing is for certain—Oakley is on her A game today and isn't taking my shit.

"It's time to go," I bark when we've spent too much time staring at an open field. My grandmother will be serving dinner soon, and I want to make sure we arrive at a decent time so I can get home and shower before bed.

"We'll go when I'm ready." Oakley takes more pictures.

"You're ready." I settle behind the steering wheel, then honk. She nearly jumps out of her skin, but then flips me off. I roll down the window. "Get in, or I'm leaving ya here."

After she shoves her phone into her pocket, Oakley makes her way toward me.

"Was that a threat?" She clenches her jaw.

"It's about to be a *promise*." I rev the engine before shifting into drive. As soon as I step on the gas, Oakley jogs after me, and after a minute of slowly cruising and her unable to catch up, I come to a hard stop. The truck slides on the gravel, kicking up dust.

"What the hell? You're so rude!" She jumps in and slams the door while trying to catch her breath.

"I don't have time for you to take a hundred pictures of the same thing. It's exhausting, and you're wasting my time."

"I'm trying to work!" she exclaims. "Don't question my process! You've purposely been an asshole all day. It's like you get off on interrupting my flow."

We continue arguing all the way to the inn.

After parking, we get out, and she follows me. "You're always rushing around, for what? Have you ever heard of living in the moment? I'm sure your mother taught you manners. There's no reason for you to keep acting like a douchebag."

I turn around and face her. "It's not my fault you can't keep up, City Girl." It only takes a few strides before I'm in front of her. "Respect my time and what I'm sacrificing to drive you around as you take pictures and play with your sketchbook. I *never* volunteered to be your tour guide."

"No kidding because a real tour guide would give a shit about my experience. It's clear that you don't, and you're only worried about all the little tasks you have to do. If this painting isn't finished and perfect…" She clears her throat, removing the little space between us, and I can feel her hot breath on my face. "I don't understand what your fucking problem is."

"Sweetheart, *you're* my problem," I murmur.

Her eye twitches as she glowers at me. She lifts her finger and digs it into my chest. "You're forty acting like a teenager with your mood swings. If only your grandma and mother knew how much of an asshole you are, they would've never stuck me with you."

That makes me chuckle. "I'm not forty, but please be my guest. They're aware of how I operate."

"Old enough to know how to treat people. It's a week's worth of your time. I bet you can spare that much for something your family will treasure for years."

"Then learn to keep up with my schedule, and we won't have an issue."

"Not everyone works at that speed. Have some consideration for others," she snaps.

"I lost my ability to give a shit a long time ago, so don't hold your breath, Little Miss Sunshine."

Oakley shakes her head as she walks past me toward the inn, and it's clear this conversation is over. As soon as I catch up and walk ahead of her, I freeze in place, and Oakley nearly crashes into me.

"What the—"

"Stay put," I tell her, then take a few steps toward my ex-girlfriend.

"Finn," Aspen purrs, her ruby-red lips turning up into a smile as she closes the gap between us.

"What are you doing here?" She's the last person I expected to see. It's been a year.

"Aunt Paisley practically *begged* me to help the bakery for the centennial celebration. You know how I can't tell that woman no." Her sugary-sweet voice makes me cringe.

"She's not *your* aunt," I remind her, crossing my arms. Aspen's the one who left without a single backward glance. She doesn't get to claim my family as hers.

She bellows out that fake laugh I hate. "I grew up here with you, so she will always be Aunt Paisley. Plus, I wouldn't miss this monumental milestone. One hundred years is a big deal!"

Aspen showing up like nothing happened between us—like we're old friends and she's still a part of my family—has me ready to explode. She has no business being here. I'm already dealing with enough. This is the last thing I need right now.

Aspen fiddles with her bangs, and that's when I notice the huge engagement diamond ring on her finger. It's impossible to miss, but I know she wanted me to notice it.

For years, Aspen was adamant that we needed to wait and there was no rush to get married. She kept saying she wasn't ready. But that was all a lie. She didn't want to marry *me*.

31

"Where are you staying?" I bluntly ask as Oakley joins and stands next to me. Before responding, she gives Oakley a dirty look, which pisses me off. I might give her a hard time, but no one else is allowed to, *especially* not Aspen.

"The cottage." Aspen's so confident in her answer that it's almost comical. Who the hell gave her permission for that?

Oakley speaks up, standing taller. "I'm already staying there."

Aspen narrows her eyes and gives Oakley a look of disgust. "And who are you exactly?"

I blurt out the words before I can stop myself.

"Oakley Benson. She's the painter my grandma hired. She's also my *girlfriend*."

I don't know why those words come out of my mouth, but I say them with my full chest. Before Oakley can react, I interlock my fingers with hers. I'm relieved when she moves closer to me and smiles. Oakley goes on her tiptoes and places a kiss on my cheek, adding the perfect touch to this lie.

I see something flicker behind Aspen's eyes—anger, jealousy, disbelief that I moved on from her.

"*Oh my God!* You're such a *cute* couple. How long have you been together?" Aspen's squeaky voice can nearly be heard across the farm.

"Um…it's recent," Oakley says.

"Like a month," I interject because I know Aspen's already mining for information. It's how she manipulates people into thinking she cares.

"If you're dating, why can't she sleep at your place?" Aspen asks, and I wish I had thought of that before I blurted out those words.

"Not that it's your business, but we're taking things slow. You'll need to find somewhere else to stay," I say firmly.

Her nose scrunches, and she pouts as if she's not used to being told no. "You know the inn is fully booked for the celebration. And all the hotels in Maplewood Falls are already booking with out-of-towners for the fall festival."

"Did you look outside of the area?"

She scowls. "Of course I didn't. I came here as a favor for your family and didn't worry about accommodations because—"

"Because you *assumed* you'd have a place to stay. Not our problem. You can always sleep in your Mercedes."

Aspen scowls, shaking her head furiously. "Absolutely not. How dare you even suggest that after everything we've been through?"

"The past doesn't matter anymore," I snap.

Before Aspen can argue, Oakley clears her throat. "If you have nowhere else to go, you can have the cottage. I'll stay at Finn's. That okay, *baby?*"

Oakley wears a cute little smirk, and I shoot daggers at her, wondering what the hell she's doing. This wasn't a part of the plan, but then I remember there was no plan. Still, she doesn't have to be so nice. Aspen doesn't deserve the courtesy.

"Thank you." Aspen beams, satisfied to have gotten her way. "Now that's settled, I guess we'll see each other around. Oh, do either of you have the keys to the cottage? I'd like to drop off my luggage before going to the bakery to get started."

"I'm not handing them over until I pack my *overly generous* girlfriend's things."

Oakley smiles wide. "Gah, you're the best. Isn't he the *sweetest?*"

"Yeah, he is. Finn was always so thoughtful." Aspen's gaze lingers on me, and it takes every ounce of control I have not to tell her to fuck off.

"He is." Oakley turns to me. "The best *boyfriend* I could've ever asked for. It's like one day, I woke up, and boom, we're dating." Oakley's tone says it all—she's pissed.

Aspen doesn't seem to notice the tension between Oakley and me, so I'm convinced she buys it.

"I'll meet you at the cottage, then," Aspen tells me before walking to her car. Once she drives away, I release Oakley's hand like it's burned my skin.

"What the hell were you thinking?" She scowls, crossing her arms. "What're we going to do now?"

"There is no *we*. You're going into the inn to eat dinner while I deal with Satan."

"You don't want me to join you?"

"No, you haven't eaten since lunch. Plus, you'll have a better time listening to my grandmother talk about the birds she saw in the backyard this afternoon than having Aspen grill you about our relationship. And trust me, she will."

She's nothing if not predictable.

Oakley pulls the cottage keys from her pocket and places them in my palm. "Be careful with my shit and pack it with care. Also, you're *welcome* for going along with your idiotic idea, and you now owe me big time."

I shake my head, cursing under my breath as Oakley walks inside.

When I arrive at the cottage, Aspen is lifting her suitcase from the trunk. I pass her, unlock the door, and look at all the shit Oakley has lying around. A small pile of clothes is on the bathroom floor, and her paint supplies are everywhere. I try to hurry as I put everything in the empty boxes, but I do my best to be careful with her art stuff. Aspen stares at me, but I try to ignore her.

"All this is hers?" she questions when she can't take my silence any longer. Aspen looks disgusted as she glances at the easel, paintbrushes, paints, drapes, and luggage.

"Yeah," I say, lifting a few boxes to load them.

When I return, Aspen sits on the edge of the bed and watches me. I refuse to make eye contact with her, but I can tell her mind is running wild.

"How have you been, Finn?"

"Good." I fold the easel and stack the paint bottles in a box.

"Just *good*?"

I meet her eyes. "*Amazing*. For the first time in my life, I'm truly happy."

The lies roll off my tongue like water. The truth is, I'm miserable, but I've learned how to be alone.

A small smile plays on her lips, and she glances down at her ring that reflects sunlight. "I've been amazing too. Got engaged a few months ago."

"Congrats." I grab more of Oakley's stuff and head outside because I need air. Aspen's confession means she said *yes* to someone within months of dating them.

I stall outside for five minutes, hoping I can get the rest of Oakley's things quickly loaded so I can get the fuck out of here.

When I return, Aspen strips the sheets off the bed and throws them in a pile on the floor. She struts to the small linen closet and grabs fresh ones.

"In case you christened the bed." She giggles, but I don't crack a smile.

Aspen continues talking and brings up old memories between us. It's torture.

The next time I see my aunt Paisley, I'm going to give her a not-so-nice thank-you for this. She or my mother could've at least warned me that the devil would be arriving. While good help is hard to come by on such short notice, they must've been desperate to ask Aspen. Regardless, blindsiding me was uncalled for.

"Remember that one time we made love on that hiking trail?" she asks.

"What are you doing?" I turn toward her.

"Reminiscing. We had some good times."

"Do us both a favor and don't."

She meets me with hooded eyes as I lift the last two boxes, then follows me to the door. "Hopefully, we can hang out before I leave. I'll be here through the weekend."

I don't respond. Just because she's here doesn't mean I have to be around her.

Before going to the inn, I stop by the bakery. They're already closed for the day because it's well after five, but I know they're playing catch-up. My aunt spots me as soon as I enter and tries to escape to the kitchen.

"Nope!" I pick up my pace, following her. "Don't you dare."

My mom carries a tray of peanut brittle and smiles when she sees me.

"Why didn't you tell me Aspen was the extra help coming?" I glower.

Aunt Paisley nervously laughs. "I'm sorry. I was going to tell you but never found the opportunity. You know how busy we've been—"

"I do, but I was caught off guard by her showing up."

"You didn't tell him?" Mom asks with her brow furrowed.

She shrugs. "I forgot. I'm sorry, Finn."

I huff but am unable to stay mad at her, especially when I know they're swamped. "Nothing can be done about it now. I came to tell you both that Aspen thinks the painter and I are dating, so go along with it. Aspen also assumed she was staying at the cottage, so I had to move every single box of Oakley's out of there because Aspen had nowhere else to go."

My aunt slaps her palm against her forehead. "I totally forgot to tell her she needed to find a place to stay. That's my fault. I can text her and explain what happened, then offer our guest room."

"No, what's done is done, but let me make it *very* clear that Aspen and I are over. I don't care how much you two like her.

36

She's engaged. I hope this wasn't some sort of sick matchmaking setup to try to get us back together."

"It wasn't, I swear. And we knew she was engaged. Her fiancé is driving here next weekend," Paisley explains. "But why does she think you and Oakley are dating?"

"It's a long story, but don't out us, please. I don't want her in my business. I don't want her knowing *anything* about my life. If she mentions me, shift the conversation to something else. She was the last person on the planet I wanted to see this week. I'm already stressed without having to deal with her."

"That's quite the predicament you've got yourself in, Finn," my mother scolds. "We won't lie for you, but we won't offer any info. If she brings it up, we'll tell her it's none of her business." Mom glares at her sister, who nods, and I imagine she'll have a few choice things to say when I leave.

"Secret's safe with us," Paisley promises.

"Thank you. Now I have to get Oakley from the inn and bring her to my house. Because of Aspen staying at the cottage, I will have no alone time in my own home."

Mom grins. "At least Oakley's a nice girl. She seems very sweet and easy to talk to."

I nearly choke on my tongue.

"You both owe me big." I check my watch, then head toward the door.

I already know I'm in over my head and am now stuck living with Oakley until she leaves. This has turned into a damn mess, and I'm not sure I'll be able to clean it up.

CHAPTER FIVE
OAKLEY

THE MOMENT I take a huge bite of an apple scone, the door swings open, and Finn walks in wearing his signature scowl. Crumbs fall on my lap, and I quickly dust them off. As he heads toward me with his sleeves rolled to his forearms, I study him. Too bad he has a shitty attitude because he checks all the other boxes—tall, muscular, and tan, with a perfect smile he hardly shows.

The way his ex looked at him piqued my curiosity, but it's not like he'll share with me what happened. A part of me feels bad that he had to load my things again, but he chose this when he picked me as his fake girlfriend.

"Did you eat dinner?" he asks.

"Not yet. Started with the pastries." I smirk without admitting that I waited for him.

"Let's grab some food, then we can head to my place and get you settled."

"Okay." I follow him to the kitchen, where his grandma serves each guest. She quickly makes us bowls of beef stew with a side of cornbread. We eat in silence as I scroll through all the photos I've taken over the past couple of days.

The stew is delicious, and I'm appreciative of the hearty meal. I worked up an appetite arguing with Finn all day. He's more tense than usual, and it's no secret why.

When we're finished, he takes our dishes to the kitchen. I stand, taking another scone with me to eat in the truck.

On our way there, he maintains a white-knuckle grip on the steering wheel. Frustration rolls off him in waves as we pull up to his house. He kills the engine, then turns to me.

"Why did you have to let Aspen have her way? You should've stood your ground, and she would've had to go somewhere else."

My jaw drops. "Are you kidding me? Don't forget that you randomly volunteered me to be your girlfriend for some reason. What you should be doing right now is *thanking me* for saving your grumpy, lying ass. I could've called you out and humiliated you, but I didn't. Maybe I should've because you've been nothing but rude to me since the moment we met. You're the last person to deserve my kindness."

He sucks in a deep breath and gets out of the truck, but I don't let him get away that easy.

"I was trying to help you because it was clear she was getting under your skin. Your reaction made it obvious that the breakup didn't go too well."

He doesn't acknowledge anything I've said as he unlocks the front door.

"Seriously? No response to that?" I ask, following him inside and looking around.

"What do you want me to say, Oakley?" He turns with a scowl.

"Forget it." I give up, knowing this conversation is going nowhere. He'll never admit I did him a solid or that he fucked up.

Finn goes to the truck and starts unloading my boxes.

I study the inside of the A-frame-structured home that looks like it was built a hundred years ago like everything else on the farm. There are many windows, and some overlook the patio area with a firepit and a view to die for.

Almost every flat surface is white except for the dark hardwood floors. He has a small kitchen, a tiny living room with a TV on the wall, a coffee table, and a small couch. My eyes trail up the set of stairs that leads to the loft. From what I can tell, it's his bedroom. The only room with a door is the bathroom. There isn't a lot of space, and the thought has me stressing out about where my painting supplies will fit.

"Great," I mumble, wondering if it's too late to tell Aspen I changed my mind.

After several trips, all of my things are in.

Finn glances around. "You have too much shit. Make sure it stays out of my way."

"Not sure if you've noticed, but I'm here to do a job, not kiss your ass."

I start unpacking, which aggravates me to do it all over again. I take my time setting up my paints and brushes. Finn watches me for ten minutes but eventually goes into the bathroom. A moment later, I hear the water running. Now that he's not micromanaging my every move, I decide to help myself to a tour since he was too rude to offer me one.

I sneak up the stairs to get a full view of his king-sized bed, which he didn't make before he left this morning. Dirty clothes are on the floor, and his nightstand has half-full glasses of water. I carefully make my way to the bottom floor and plop down on the couch. I push my hand into the cushions, and they're too firm. No way will I be able to sleep on cushions filled with cement, and I start to panic about what I'm going to do.

Without quality sleep, I can't speed paint. It takes too much out of me physically and mentally. I'm frustrated as hell as I lean back on the hard sofa. I close my eyes, trying to calm my racing heart.

When the bathroom door swings open, I turn and watch as Finn walks out wearing a towel and *only* a towel. I swallow hard, tracing the path the water droplets slide down his sculpted body. They fall down his inked biceps and chest, in the caverns of his chiseled abs, and continue down to that perfect V that points at his danger zone.

Heat rushes through me, and I swallow hard, then force my eyes away. I hate how my heart quickens, and I hope he doesn't notice. I move to my canvas leaning against the wall and place it on my easel.

"If you're going to stay here, you'll have to learn to keep your eyes to yourself and not ogle me."

"Fuck off. I wasn't ogling you." I was trying my best to erase that image that's been carbon copied into my brain. The last thing I need when I'm providing myself a little self-care is images of him in a towel.

"Then what would you call it?"

I roll my eyes. "Just confirming that you're *not* my type."

He gives me a smug look. "Right."

"I noticed there's only one bed."

"Great observation. The couch is yours, Sunshine. Good night."

"Whoa, I don't think so." I keep eye contact, but it's hard not to linger lower.

He shrugs, then takes the stairs.

I scoff. "I can't sleep on that brick!"

"You'll be fine," Finn says as I follow him up to his room. "I wouldn't come up here."

He moves toward his dresser and opens one of the drawers. Without warning, the towel falls to the floor into a crumpled heap. My eyes widen as I explore the muscles cascading down his back and ass. I lose my ability to speak and groan before storming downstairs without a plan.

My heart slams against my chest, but I try to breathe through it.

"Good night," he says, then I hear his faint chuckle, but I don't find any of this funny. At this point, I'm convinced he's trying to get a rise out of me. The lights upstairs flick off.

"I need a pillow and a blanket!" I shout.

A moment later, something flies from the loft and plops on the floor in front of the couch.

"Nice." I shake my head, scooping up the items and throwing them on the couch. If I could put a curse on him, I would.

"I think you're the one who's *Satan*," I shout, but he doesn't respond.

I go to my duffel bag and search for my phone charger, then plug it in so I can text-rant to my sister. I try to list everything that's happened in the past twelve hours, and my heart pounds as fast as my thoughts. Even my fingers struggle to keep up. Once I press send, I impatiently wait for her response because right now, I'm ready to quit the whole project and go home.

TIERNAN

OMG, that's a lot to take in. What can I do to help?

OAKLEY

Fly here and kick his ass, then make him go stay at his grandma's.

The thought has me chuckling because I can imagine Tiernan doing it in her assertive older sister tone.

TIERNAN

He can't be that bad.

OAKLEY

He is. Plus, nothing seems to be going my way, and I'm growing more frustrated. Maybe I should leave? Maybe I'm not cut out for this after all.

TIERNAN

You can't quit, sis. Don't let him get to you. Gotta play him at his own game, ya know? You're not intimidated by his good looks, are you?

I grind my teeth and playfully roll my eyes even though she can't see me.

OAKLEY

Ugh.

TIERNAN

Maybe that's HIS problem? He finds you attractive and doesn't like that he does.

OAKLEY

Very doubtful. I'm stressed about this bed situation. I can't sleep on this damn couch and have enough energy to paint all day tomorrow. It's not even long enough.

TIERNAN

How big is his bed?

OAKLEY

It's big-big. King size. Two adults could sleep comfortably without touching.

I imagine his warmth next to me and then swallow hard as I read Tiernan's next words.

TIERNAN

Then crawl in there with him. If he's asleep, he won't even realize it until morning.

OAKLEY

I don't know. He seems like the type to be an even bigger asshole in his sleep. He'd probably sleep-kick me.

TIERNAN

You need to show him that you won't back down when it comes to your job. Then remind him again that he chose this. He made his bed, and now he has to share it, HA!

I snort at her analogy.

OAKLEY

Maybe you're right.

I contemplate it.

TIERNAN

Well…Everett says you shouldn't do it. But I'm your sister, and I know what's best. Quality sleep is more important than pissing off this guy.

OAKLEY

I'll think it over and will update you if he kicks me to the hills.

TIERNAN

Great! Good night. Get some rest.

I open my sketchbook and glance over what I have, trying to fully visualize the scene. The fence and structures, the pond and blue skies—it's as vibrant in my memory as it is in real life. I quickly add more to the drawing, then decide to let it marinate until morning.

I happily text Tiernan and tell her I've finalized my idea.

TIERNAN

Did you go up there yet?

OAKLEY

No. I'm going now. Wish me luck ;)

TIERNAN

You've got this, sis. Be quiet like a mouse!

I flick off the kitchen light and stumble my way in the dark past the couch. Quietly, I listen for noise at the bottom of the stairs. I focus so hard that I swear I can hear him breathing from down here.

A shot of adrenaline rushes through me as I take the first step and then the second. Halfway up, one of the steps creaks so loud, I nearly jump out of my skin. I stop and listen for rustling but only silence lingers.

When I make it to the top of the loft, I freeze. Finn is under the comforter with his back toward me. It's now or never.

I tiptoe across the small space to his bed, hoping no more boards yell in the darkness, then carefully slide underneath the covers. My eyes feel heavy as I sink into the perfect mattress. Before I can think another thought or worry about what Finn will do, I drift asleep.

CHAPTER SIX

FINN

DAY 4

THE WARMTH of a soft body molded to my chest has me blinking my eyes open in confusion. I look down and see Oakley's hair sprawled around her face. My erection presses against the lower dip of her back. My body's obviously confused as hell. It's the only reason my arm is tightly wrapped around her waist, holding her like she's my lifeline.

My head finally catches up, and I push away from her.

"Oakley," I grind out, adjusting myself. "What the fuck are you doing in my bed?"

"What?" she mutters in a sleepy voice, barely moving. "It's too early for one of your tantrums."

"You can't sneak into my bed like this," I hiss, shifting to the edge of the bed.

"I told you I wasn't sleeping on that couch!" she bites out, stretching before she gets up.

"You're insufferable." I stand, grab a T-shirt from my dresser, then slide on some sweats.

"Okay, *Mr. Snuggled Me All Night Long*. I started on the

opposite side of the mattress and somehow got pulled into your arms, so that's on you."

Once I'm dressed, I turn and face her. "You better plant your ass on that couch where you belong. You're the one who told Aspen she could have the cottage, now you can deal with the consequences."

"Are you kidding me? This same conversation again?" she shouts. Oakley looks like she's ready to throw her fist in my face. "For the last time, I was trying to help your sorry ass! Something I'm seriously regretting!" She huffs and turns to walk away, then pivots and adds, "Should've let you make a fool of yourself and told her the truth. Maybe I'll tell her today and put myself out of my misery."

Before I can respond—and beg her not to do that very thing—a loud knock rattles on the door, startling us. Instead of dealing with Oakley, I flee downstairs and open the door.

"Aspen," I say, defeated that I'm once again facing my ex. "What are you doing here so early?"

Oakley walks up behind me, wrapping her arm around my waist and closing the gap between us. When I glance down, she smiles wide like we weren't at each other's throats two seconds ago.

She's in character, I remind myself.

"Good morning to you, too. I see you're still not a morning person. Anyway, I was hoping we could catch up and grab some coffee. I'd love to hear about how the farm's been doing."

Before I can tell her no fucking thank you, Oakley speaks up. "We'd love to! Neither of us got a lot of sleep last night, so we need our caffeine. Right, sweetums?"

Swallowing hard, I wish I could curse her out for not only volunteering us but also for giving me a ridiculous nickname. Instead, I cave and wrap an arm around her.

"Definitely." Then I meet Aspen's eyes that were on Oakley. "Meet you there in twenty?"

Aspen straightens her posture and forces the corners of her lips to tilt up. "Great. I'll save two seats."

Oakley leans into my side, and I hate how much I enjoy her closeness. She's so damn inviting, yet as soon as she opens her mouth, I want to shut her up with my tongue.

Waking up with a boner is one thing and not all that uncommon, but fantasizing about kissing Oakley is something I need to erase from my brain. As hard as it will be, I need to keep my distance when we aren't pretending to be a couple.

As soon as Aspen turns to leave, I shut the door and face Oakley. "What the hell were you thinking? I don't want to be around her, especially with *you*."

She winces as if I've slapped her across the face.

"Wait, no. That came out wrong. I—" I pause to gather my thoughts, scrubbing a hand through my messy hair. "I don't want her asking more questions or knowing anything about my life."

"Well, if we're going to fake it, we have to be believable. Dodging her could make her suspicious versus sticking to a story."

I cross my arms. "We don't have a *story*."

She shrugs as if she's not worried about it. "I'll make up something. Go along with it."

Yeah, sure. That sounds like a recipe for disaster.

"Go along with it?" I repeat, knowing that won't work.

"Stop worrying. Don't make it a big deal."

"Until the whole damn town finds out."

"If I can hate your guts and be your fake girlfriend at the same time, you can do the same. Act the opposite of how you are now—sweet, charming, and lovable." She flashes a snarky smile, and her quick insult almost has me bursting into laughter. Instead, I shake my head and climb the stairs to my room to get dressed.

After thirty minutes of nonstop touching Oakley and avoiding most of Aspen's personal questions over coffee, we escape the inn. With Oakley's hand in mine, we leave and head toward my truck.

"See, that wasn't so bad. She clearly wants to see you happy, so I don't know what you're so worried about."

I scoff, releasing her grip. "If that's true, she only wants to see me happy to relieve her guilt. She wanted a different life and kept trying to change me, but once she realized she couldn't, she broke it off. She made it clear I wasn't enough. So trust me, her wanting me to move on is for her own conscience," I tell her, then open the passenger door.

"Well, then it's her loss. The farm is beautiful. Who wouldn't want to live here?" She hops into the seat and buckles up.

I have the answer—my uptight, entitled ex-girlfriend who's now engaged—but I keep that to myself.

"I'd gain fifty pounds from the pastries alone, but hell, it'd be worth it. Which makes me wonder, how do you keep it off? You work out or lift weights or something?"

"Nope." I slam the door, then walk around the hood to the driver's side.

"Are you a runner?" she continues as I get in and crank the engine.

"I work on a farm, Oakley. An orchard. We're constantly on the go here, so any food I shove into my mouth gets burned off within hours."

"Wow. Lucky for you, then. I prefer meditating over exercising. But when you paint for a living and all through school, the majority of your time is spent standing or sitting on your ass."

"You could run?" I suggest, driving us to the hard cider operation building. It's prime apple harvest season, so their production is busy as hell. It's the worst time of year to visit. "Probably be good for someone who likes to talk shit so much. Would give your mouth a break."

She leans over and sucker punches me in the arm.

"The hell was that for?"

"Being a rude ass. I don't *run my mouth*. I speak the truth. There's a difference."

"Can you speak to yourself?"

As I glance over, I catch her rolling her eyes and crossing her arms. She clearly isn't used to someone going head-to-head with her, but hell, if this is the only foreplay I get for the rest of my life, I'd die a happy man.

And that thought should scare me.

As soon as I park, I tell her to stay put. She scowls, and before she can say anything, I hop out of the truck and go to her side. Then I open the door and hold out my hand.

She furrows her brow and glares at my palm as if it's covered in mold. "What are you doing?"

"We have a reputation to uphold," I remind her. "If people think we're dating, we need to keep up appearances everywhere we go. Never know who's watching, when my ex will randomly pop up, or who she's told." It wouldn't surprise me if she has people watching us, either.

"And you opening the door and helping me out is something you'd do as a boyfriend?"

"It is," I say firmly, then lower my voice and grind out between my teeth, "So slap on a smile and get your ass down."

Our hands stay tangled together as we enter, and I give her a brief tour while introducing her to some of the employees. Then

I talk about the process of making hard cider and how it's a big hit all year round.

"Where to now?" she asks when I lead her to my truck. We get inside and make our way across the property.

"Apple picking wagon tour. The next one is in ten minutes."

"How often do you have them?"

"This one runs twice a day during harvest season. During winter, people can buy tickets for horse-drawn sleigh rides."

"You're joking. Sleigh rides? In an orchard?"

"Yeah. They get to learn about the history and enjoy the farm covered in a blanket of white snow but without the apple picking. Then they'll stop for a warm treat and hot cocoa at the bakery."

"Wow. Sounds incredible but cold. How long does this one take? I need to get back to painting," she reminds me.

We turn toward the tour area. "It only takes forty-five minutes. You'll have plenty of time to play after."

She blows out a breath as if she's stopping herself from going off on me. This isn't a bag of Skittles for me, either, but it's important to my grandmother that she gets the full Bennett Orchard experience.

We arrive just in time, and when I walk up into the wagon, I find only one spot left.

"Shit," I mutter as Roy, the driver, announces everyone needs to be seated. The engine roars to life, and I know he's seconds from pulling onto the gravel road.

"You're gonna have to sit on my lap," I tell her.

"You can't be serious," she mutters with a glare so intense that I nearly freeze in place.

"Come on, *sweetie*," I hiss between my teeth, emphasizing the last word so she remembers we're in public.

As soon as I sit, I pat my lap, and she eventually uncrosses her arms to follow directions.

This is a bad fucking idea.

She shifts on my thighs until she's comfortable, which makes me *highly uncomfortable.*

Roy pops the tractor into gear. The wagon shakes as it's pulled across the gravel road and onto the grass. I hold Oakley so she doesn't go flying, but with each harsh movement, her ass grinds harder against my dick.

Roy goes through his typical tour script. The guests listen in awe, but I can only focus on one thing. *Her.*

"It's so pretty," she says, twisting her hips. "Do we get to pick any of the apples?"

"Yeah, he'll make a stop toward the end. You have to bear his monologue first, though," I say, keeping my voice low so no one overhears.

As soon as the wagon stops, I push Oakley off my lap. My dick can't take any more of her wiggling.

We're allotted ten minutes to browse and pick apples. I stand and watch Oakley, who's struggling to reach the one she wants.

"Need some help?" I muse, walking over to her.

"No." She jumps, reaching high above her head. "I just need—"

"To grow about six inches."

She scowls, then tries again. After her third sad attempt, I step closer and reach above her for it. She jumps again but falls against my chest. I instinctively wrap an arm around her waist and steady her.

Once I grab the apple, I hold it out for her. "Here."

She swallows hard as she takes it. "Thanks."

Being close is something we're supposed to do publicly, and while we haven't had to cross any boundaries, I'm not sure where her comfort level is when it comes to being physical. We never discussed it.

"You're welcome, babe," I say, then lean down and brush my lips over her cheek. She doesn't push away but instead melts into me, but I tell myself she's acting.

I release my hold on her, and as I walk around the tree, I feel her eyes following me. An older woman comes over and asks me to help her, and once I do, she thanks me with a wide grin.

"Your boyfriend is so sweet," she tells Oakley, who then glances at me as if she's in physical pain about having to say something nice about me.

Slowly turning toward the woman, Oakley swallows hard. "I couldn't agree more."

I chuckle under my breath and wait until she's alone before joining her. "That hurt to say, didn't it?"

"Trust me, there are worse things I could've said." She shoots me a sassy smirk, then we go to the wagon.

Once the tour is over, Roy drops us off at the field by the parking lot. With our fingers interlocked, we make our way to my truck, which is a short distance away.

I don't want to part ways with Oakley, but I don't want her to know that either, so I turn on my asshole act. "I have a lot of shit to do, so we're done for the day."

"Great. Drop me off at your house. I'm feeling inspired to paint now that my idea is fully sketched out."

"I'll be *more than* happy to drop you off." I shoot her a smile, but I'm pretty sure she sees right through me.

"Thanks for taking me on the orchard tour. Never been to one before, so it was fun and educational."

I snort. "Yeah, Roy has a good time with it." He's great at making the guests laugh at his corny farm jokes.

As soon as I pull my keys from my pocket, I spot Aspen chatting with someone. Her gaze quickly averts to mine.

"Shit," I mutter, stepping closer to Oakley even though we're already holding hands. "Aspen."

Oakley smiles in her direction and slowly speaks between gritted teeth, "Kiss me."

I blink hard but keep a straight face. "What?"

"She's watching," she says above a whisper. "Before you open my door, *kiss me.*"

She can't be fucking serious.

But I'm not about to argue. As soon as we're close to my truck, I press Oakley against the passenger door and cup her chin. Before either of us can change our minds, I lean in and slide my mouth over hers.

She tilts her head, and when she opens wider, I deepen the kiss. She brushes her tongue between my lips and though I'm tempted to give her more, I pull away before it's too late. My fingers dig into her hips as my cock pushes against the fabric of my jeans.

Oakley glances over to the side. "She's gone."

Quickly, I step back and cover my groin. "Thank God. I knew she'd randomly appear."

"Maybe she's still into you," she offers, and I bark out a laugh.

I open the door and motion for her to get inside. "Unlikely."

Once she's seated, I climb in and start the engine.

"Maybe she regrets ending it. I can't imagine why anyone would willingly go to where their ex lives to *help out his family,*" she says, using finger quotes.

I shrug, not wanting to think about it. Aspen and I dated for years, and it took months to get over her. Though I'm glad she ended it before I proposed, she still shattered my heart. After going through that, I vowed I'd never commit to another serious relationship. Although it was said in anger, I still doubt I'll ever trust a woman again.

"Even if that were true, I'd never give her a second chance after what she did," I tell her truthfully.

"Hmm...could be fun showing her what she's missing."

I furrow my brow. "And why would you want to do that?"

She shrugs with a smile. "You're not the only one who's

gotten hurt by an ex who said they wanted one thing but suddenly changed their mind and wanted something else."

"What's the story there?" I ask as we drive closer to my house.

"I'll save that for another day."

After I park, she hops out, but I stop her before she closes the door. "After work, I'm meeting up with a buddy. So I'll be back around ten."

"Oh. Alright. I'll probably be painting until then anyway."

I give her a nod, and she shuts the door. Once she's inside the house, I leave and head toward the bakery. My mom needs me to look at something, and I text Levi as soon as I arrive.

FINN

Wanna meet for a beer later?

We didn't have plans prior to me telling Oakley, but I needed a reason to stay away for a while. Between trying to keep my distance and pretending to be a couple, things are beginning to get confusing.

LEVI

Sure, 8?

FINN

I'll be there.

Maplewood Falls has only one bar, and unless it's a game night, it's quiet.

I greet my mom and aunt when I walk into the bakery while my grandma chats and rings up customers. Though she's normally at the inn, she stops in to help when it gets busy.

"How are things going with Oakley?" Grandma asks.

"Great."

I haven't told her about our fake relationship agreement, but

55

I'm sure the news will spread, and I'll have some explaining to do.

"Are you being a gentleman while showing her around?"

"Of course. Took her on an apple-picking tour earlier."

"Wonderful! I bet she enjoyed that."

Before I can respond, Aspen walks out from the back and comes toward me.

Fucking hell. Is she everywhere at once?

"Hey, Finn." She looks around. "Where's your girlfriend?"

"Painting," I quickly reply, moving away from my grandma before she asks questions. "I'm here to look at one of the ovens, then I'll be out of everyone's way."

"You have a girlfriend? Who?" my grandma blurts out.

Aspen crosses her arms. "You didn't tell her?"

"Like I said, it's recent," I grind out between my teeth, then turn to face my grandmother. "Yes, it's Oakley."

Her eyes widen. "Oh. When did—"

"Mom, I need you over here for a quick minute," Aunt Paisley blurts out, giving me an escape.

I mouth a quick, "Thank you," and head to the back. Luckily, Aspen doesn't follow and returns to restocking the shelves.

After a couple of hours of tinkering with the oven, it's eventually fixed, and I leave. I stop by the harvesting facility to check on something, then help Roy repair the other tractor. Double tours will be running during the celebration, so they have to be dependable.

At seven thirty, I head into town to meet with Levi. I arrive at the pub before him and start with a beer. When he shows up, he orders a whiskey and a basket of fries.

"You wanna talk about why we're drinking on a Monday night?" he taunts, knowing I save going out for the weekends. "Anything to do with your ex-girlfriend being here?"

"I needed some space and time away from home," I admit.

"From the new girl, huh? She driving ya crazy?"

Yes, but not in the way he's thinking.

"She snuck into my bed last night," I tell him, knowing what he'll say.

"Wow. So I guess it's safe to say you're over Aspen."

"She didn't like the couch," I clarify. "I woke up, and she was sleeping next to me."

"Bet that was a new experience for you."

"She's a pain in my ass. Like a little sister who won't leave me the hell alone."

He arches a brow. "You sure about that?"

"I don't know…" I sigh. "When Aspen showed up, I blurted out that Oakley was my girlfriend, so now we're pretending to be together."

"Wait…" He bursts out laughing. "You *what?*"

I down my beer, mentally slapping myself. "It was stupid, but then Oakley went along with it, and now she's staying at my house."

He smacks my shoulder. "You got yourself in a predicament, huh?"

"Yeah, and now my mom and aunt are smack dab in the middle of my lie."

"I don't know how in the hell you managed all this in four days." He laughs again.

I shrug, wishing I knew the answer. "She'll be gone in a week. Then hopefully, things will go back to normal."

"Is that what you want?"

I shoot him a look but don't respond. My stomach growls, so I order a pizza to go and another beer. Then I change the subject.

"Guess I'll see you Saturday," I say, smacking his shoulder.

"You know I wouldn't miss it. Plus, I need to meet this chick that has you all twisted." He waggles his brows. "See if she needs a fake baby daddy or something."

I grunt. "Shut the hell up."

After I leave some cash on the bar, I take my food and drive home.

I can't get Oakley out of my head, knowing she's at my house doing God knows what. Being in an enclosed space with her fucks with me.

When I walk inside, she's standing in the kitchen in front of her easel, facing away from me. Her blond hair is twisted up, exposing her pale neck. A smock wraps around her petite waist as she paints across the canvas.

She looks deep in thought while an audiobook plays from her phone, so I don't speak. Instead, I sit on the couch and eat my pizza and then plan to shower before going to bed.

I don't pay much attention to her book until I hear heavy breathing and panting.

"Count how many times I make you come."

"What?"

"Do it. Count. Now."

My brows shoot up as I listen to the extremely descriptive scene of a guy eating the girl's cunt while she begs for more.

"Fuck me. Please!"

A loud slap across my ass startles me until I'm crying out for more. *"Yes!"*

"Keep counting, sweetheart…"

My cock reacts as I envision Oakley bent over in front of me, taking all of me as she counts how many orgasms I give her.

Goddammit. *What's wrong with me?*

"Jesus, fuck. You listening to porn? That some kind of painting inspiration?"

My voice causes her to jump, then she spins around, wearing a mischievous smirk. "Stay a while. Maybe you'll learn a thing or two."

I scoff, grabbing the empty pizza box as I stand. "I don't need *lessons* from a romance novel."

She snorts, and it pisses me off.

After trashing the cardboard, I keep my gaze on her ass and head toward the shower.

I turn on the water and stand underneath the stream, hating how worked up I am by her. That stupid book and Oakley's comments have my dick rock hard. Gripping my shaft, I stroke it over and over. Visions swirl in my mind of Oakley kneeling in front of me with her mouth wide open as she waits for my cum, and I explode.

Groaning through my release, I throw my head back and tell myself it's the only time I'll jerk off to fantasies of her.

By the time I walk into the living room, Oakley and her audio porn are gone. I take a minute and admire her canvas, amazed by her progress so far.

When I head toward the stairs, I notice she's not on the couch.

I find her on the other side of my bed, snuggled under the covers with her blond hair sprawled out over the pillow.

"Oakley," I whisper, shaking her arm.

She doesn't move, and I'm too tired to argue, so I say fuck it and leave her be.

Once I put on my shorts, I climb into bed and stay as close to the edge as possible.

An hour later, when she rolls closer, I'm tempted to push her away but don't. My mind races as her sweet smell invades my space, and all I want to do is sleep.

Goddamn, this woman tests every ounce of willpower I have.

CHAPTER SEVEN
OAKLEY

DAY 5

THE STEEL ROD poking my lower back tells me it's morning before I even open my eyes. When I do, sunlight peers in through the skylight.

Finn's warm body presses against me, and there's no doubt he'll wake up pissed when he realizes our position. But I can't move without waking him since his strong arm is wrapped around my bare waist.

Deciding to taunt him, I wiggle my ass.

Perhaps it'll get him to release me so I can get up.

He doesn't move, but his dick does.

And it's more than just *morning wood*.

Arching my body, I push harder into him and rotate my hips. If that doesn't work, I'm declaring him dead.

His hand goes to my hip, and he squeezes *hard*. Then his mouth finds my ear. "You better stop that or *else*."

I'm tempted to ask him what *else* implies, but he slides out of bed before I can.

"Get dressed. We have a lot to do today," he demands.

I whip off the covers and slide to the edge of the mattress, realizing I'm in my lace pajamas. They barely cover my stomach and legs.

"Is there somewhere you can take me to get a wider view of the farm?" I ask, standing and fixing the bed covers. "I need it for my painting."

"Yeah." He sighs, grabbing clothes from his dresser before spinning around to face me. My eyes are drawn to the tent he's sporting, and as soon as he realizes, he covers his groin and turns.

I don't even bother holding in my laughter as I go downstairs to get ready. He may hate driving me everywhere, but his body likes me nice and close.

Neither of us speaks as we travel toward the inn. I take a few pictures with my phone, though I hope to get some better ones later.

After he opens my door, I'm reminded we're *on* as a couple. I take his hand, and we go inside.

"Shit," Finn mutters, brushing his free hand through his hair.

I glance over, assuming he's referring to Aspen, but it's a woman and a man coming toward us.

"Hey!" the girl greets.

"Morning. Didn't expect to see you guys here," Finn says.

"Came to visit Grams and have breakfast," the guy tells us.

"Who's this?" The woman smiles at me.

That's my cue.

I release Finn's hand and wrap my arm around his waist, pulling him closer.

"Hi, I'm Oakley." I hold out my other hand. "The girlfriend."

"*Girlfriend?*" The woman shakes it, then glances at Finn. "When did this happen?"

Finn scratches along his scruffy jawline. "She's the painter, and we're pretending until Aspen leaves."

The woman crosses her arms in amusement. "Oh, I can't wait

61

to hear how this happened." She laughs, then looks at me. "I'm Jessa, Finn's younger but *smarter* cousin. This is my brother, Sebastian."

"Nice to meet you both," I tell them. "I got roped into this."

Finn stiffens, and I release my hold on him. "It's a long story. Just run with it for now," he pleads.

"Alright, I'll play along. But only because I *never* liked Aspen," Jessa says.

"Saw the big shiny ring on her finger," Sebastian adds. "I can already guess how this happened."

I snicker, and Finn glares.

"It's not like that," he spits out.

Jessa's eyes widen. "Heads-up, she's coming in."

Finn quickly grabs me and pulls me against his side. Before I can even grasp what's happening, Jessa and Sebastian burst out laughing.

"Damn, you're way too easy."

I look over my shoulder and see an older woman and her husband entering.

Finn releases me and his arm drops. "You're gonna pay for that," he threatens Jessa.

She rolls her eyes with a snarky smirk. "If you get sick of Finn, let me know. Give me your cell, and I'll program my number."

I pull it from my pocket and hand it over. Once she's done, I send her a message, so she has mine too.

"Cool, thanks. See you two lovebirds later." She gives us a little finger wave, and we continue to the buffet.

"Don't hang out with her," Finn tells me once we're seated with our coffee and food.

"Why not? She seems cool. Sebastian too. Don't see the family resemblance, though. They have…what's it called…a *personality*?"

He shoots daggers at me as I grin.

"I assume they work on the farm too?" I ask, trying to make conversation as we eat.

"Yes, they do. They're my aunt Paisley's kids. Jessa handles most of the PR, marketing, and social media stuff for the orchard. Sebastian deals with the wholesalers and distributors we sell the fruit to."

"Sounds like you got stuck with the dirty jobs."

"I prefer it. I'd never want to work in an office or be forced to deal with strangers on the phone."

"You don't like talking to people? I'm shocked," I taunt.

"You love getting on my nerves, don't you?" He stabs his sausage link and pops it into his mouth.

"You're the one walking around with a stick up your ass. Should pull it out so it's not so easy to rile you up."

"I'm tempted to let Jessa and Sebastian deal with you for the rest of the week."

"You're lying. I know you love talking about the farm and taking me around. Plus, I doubt Jessa or Sebastian would be as good a snuggle partner as you." I grin, then take a sip of my coffee.

"You're the one who scoots to my side of the bed. Maybe if you slept on the couch, like you're supposed to, it wouldn't be an issue."

"Oh, *sorry*. Should we make a pillow wall so there are no more"—I lower my eyes to insinuate his morning wood—"*issues*?" I muse, noticing the blood vessel on the side of his neck is about to burst.

He scrubs a hand over his cheek, fuming silently as his jaw ticks. "Let's go."

Finn stands, taking his half-filled plate, and I quickly follow, setting our dishes in the tub.

As we go to his truck, he doesn't take my hand or open my door. I don't bother to ask where we're going next, so I silently look out the window as he drives.

He turns down a road I haven't seen yet, and I take more pictures. The colorful leaves are breathtaking, and I can't believe I'm here at the perfect time of year to witness their beauty.

"Wow…it's gorgeous," I say as he throws the truck into 4-wheel drive, and we climb higher up the hill.

"It's where I planned to propose," he says quietly, almost as if he hadn't wanted me to hear. I don't bother responding, but he continues anyway. "I even looked at rings."

"How long were you together?" I ask.

"Over five years."

"Was she your first long-term girlfriend?"

"No, I dated someone in high school, and we stayed together a few years while she went to college. Long distance didn't work out."

"So no disrespect, but if you've had previous relationships before, why did this last one make you so jaded?" I ask, turning to look at him.

He keeps his eyes on the road. "She was the first person I ever imagined a future with. I thought we wanted the same things."

"Here's a hard truth for you." I clear my throat, hoping he won't reach across the truck and strangle me. "She wanted those things. Clearly, she got engaged not long after you broke up. But not with you."

His jaw clenches as if he's holding back a scream, but I quickly add, "And I know that's harsh, but isn't it better to know before you proposed? Better to find out before you invested not only your heart but also your money into something she wouldn't have given her whole self to?"

"You talk like you've experienced a lot of breakups. How's that possible at your age?" he asks with sincerity.

"Just because I'm young doesn't mean I'm stupid. In fact, I was at the top of my classes from elementary through grad school. That's not to brag. It's a fact. Creatively brilliant but not always people smart. Did you know that was a thing? Well, anyway, I don't have to personally experience heartbreak to sympathize with how it must've felt for you." I breathe out slowly. "And FYI, I've had some relationships end badly. Not *close to settling down* type of breakups, but they still hurt."

"What kind of guy would break up with you?" he asks, then winces as if he hadn't meant to say that aloud. "Never mind."

"Oh, come on, we're fake dating. We should be able to talk about previous *real* relationships."

He cracks the tiniest of smiles. "Fine. Tell me what scrawny idiots you used to date."

I burst out laughing at his assumption. "One was an MMA fighter, six-two, and over two hundred pounds of muscle."

"So why'd you break up? He suck at fighting?" He smirks.

"Ha! Nah, we didn't have much in common outside of sex."

He swallows hard. I knew that'd get a reaction out of him. We're silent for a few awkward seconds.

Finn clears his throat and points. "Look."

I follow his finger and gasp at the view. We're at the summit of the hill. I can see the orchard farm, Finn's house, and even the inn, which is miles away.

As soon as he parks, I jump out and rush to take it in.

"Careful!" he shouts as I move toward the steep edge. "There are no barriers out here."

"It's…I don't even have words. It's beautiful. I'm adding this into my painting somehow."

I snap photos from every angle, wanting different perspectives of the trees that overlook the farm.

"Oakley, I'm serious. Be careful."

"If you're so worried, why don't you come closer and make sure I don't fall?" I inch toward the edge.

"Dammit, woman," he mutters, and I quickly feel him at my back.

I pretend to take another step forward, and he grabs my waist, pulling me against him.

"Look at you being all heroic and trying to save me. Proof that you care." I close my eyes when the cool breeze brushes against my cheeks, and I breathe in the fresh air.

He snorts. "The last thing I need is people thinking I murdered my new girlfriend."

"Just admit you'll miss me when I leave."

"Miss what? Your loud mouth? You hogging my bed? Chauffeuring your ass everywhere?"

I shrug as if he didn't hurt my feelings. "I think you'll miss *much* more than you're willing to admit. Don't think I didn't hear you in the shower last night."

His body stills, and I know I've got him. Though I'm bluffing, his reaction confirms my suspicions. After he listened to some of my naughty audiobook, Finn rushed to the bathroom. Now I have no doubts he was as turned on as me.

"Did you get enough pics? I need to get back to work." He releases me and walks toward the truck.

I take a few more, and once I'm satisfied, I meet him inside.

"I'm feeling super inspired now and am ready to get some painting done," I admit as he drives us.

"Great, I'll get to work in peace today." His fingers grip the steering wheel so tight his knuckles turn white. It's hard to believe this is the same man who opened up about his ex twenty minutes ago.

"I'll be back later. Text me if you need anything," he says, parking in front of his house. He's yet to look at me during the ride here, so I don't poke the bear.

"Will do, thanks."

For several hours, I get lost in my work. The summit and gorgeous sky inspired me to tweak my painting, and now it'll be even more perfect.

I've successfully captured the hill of trees above Finn's

grandparents' red ranch house. Mixing the dark and light colors for the two large barns wasn't easy, but it's nearly an exact match to the pictures I took. Though I won't have enough space to incorporate the large pond, I've decided to add some of it at the bottom.

I want this painting to fully represent the family behind the farm and where it started.

It's kind of sweet how they live so close to one another and work together every day.

I wish I had that family dynamic.

With my sister being sixteen years older, we weren't close until I was a teenager. Even then, she was married to her ex and living her own life. It was mostly my mom, dad, and me until I moved to California for college.

Then I was on my own.

Needing a shower, I decide to take a break and relax under the hot stream. I'm impatiently waiting for Tiernan to check in since her and Everett's surrogate is supposed to announce the gender of the baby.

Finding out I was going to be an aunt was an exciting time. My sister has wanted kids for years, though once she left her abusive ex, I wasn't sure she still did. But once things got serious with Everett, starting a family was all she thought about. He's her perfect half, and I couldn't have asked for a better man for her. Even if he's closer to my age.

Their romance sounds like one of the books I'd listen to while painting a romantic setting. I already plan to paint something for the baby's nursery as soon as they settle on a name.

Once I've shaved and exfoliated every inch of my body, I wrap a towel around myself and head upstairs to get dressed. I look at the bed and wonder if sleeping next to Finn is as bad as he makes it sound. When my head hits the pillow, I'm dead to the world for hours. Where my body rolls to is not always something I can help. He's the one who curls his arms and wraps his legs around me.

If he weren't such a damn grumpy asshole ninety-five percent of the time, we could explore the undeniable attraction lingering between us. Still, he'd rather act like I'm the biggest inconvenience of his life.

For someone in his early thirties—not *that* much older than me—he sure likes to make me feel like a little kid who gets on his nerves.

When my phone rings and I see Tiernan's name, I quickly answer the FaceTime call.

"Hey!" I smile, and my mood immediately shifts to excitement. "Do we have the news?"

"Let me tell her," Everett blurts out before Tiernan can respond, then adds, "You told Payton!"

Payton is Everett's sister-in-law who lives in New York with his brother, Theo.

"But Oakley's my sister! I wanna tell her."

"How come I didn't get to tell my brother then?" Everett counters, and my patience wavers as they bicker back and forth.

"Oh my God!" I snap. "Will one of you freaking tell me? Is it a taco or a frank and beans?"

"Ew! Don't be inappropriate about your niece."

Everett gasps loudly. "You little cheater!"

Tiernan giggles, and Everett tries to tackle her, but she quickly pushes him away.

"Yay, it's a girl! Now let's discuss my niece's name."

"You're not picking it," Everett blurts out.

"Oh, come on. I'm not having kids for like thirty years. Let me choose."

"Then get a puppy, and you can name it whatever you want," Everett says firmly, and I frown.

"You owe me, *brother-in-law*," I remind him, emphasizing every word.

"How so?"

"If it weren't for me, you would've never asked my sister to marry you that day. You probably wouldn't even be engaged right now."

"Nah, that's not true," Everett argues, but I know it is.

"It's kinda true," Tiernan interjects. "I mean, we would've gotten engaged eventually, I'm sure."

Everett sighs. "Fine, I will agree to this on *one* condition."

I'm immediately giddy. "Okay, what is it?"

Just then, the front door opens and slams shut. I look to the lower level and see Finn wearing an angry expression.

Of fucking course. It'd probably kill him to be in a good mood.

"Great, he's back," I mumble with a groan.

"Uh, who?" Everett asks.

"Finn," I tell them. "The innkeeper's grandson whose only life goal is to make mine miserable."

"The one you're staying with while you're there?" Tiernan smirks. We talked about this job for weeks before I flew here. I hadn't realized I'd have a babysitter the entire time, though.

"Yep." I grind out between my teeth, then move closer to the screen and whisper, "Please come rescue me."

They snicker, and I glower at their amusement.

"Oh my God." I roll my eyes as I watch Finn. "He tossed his boots in the middle of the living room, then flung his shirt on the couch. Oh, now he's digging through the fridge like a strung-out raccoon. Christ, they're raising barbarians out here!" I scowl, watching him trash the downstairs area. My painting supplies are on the table, and my canvas is still on the easel, and I almost yell at him to be careful as he storms past it. The last thing I need is his negative aura rubbing off on my masterpiece.

Now they're both laughing hysterically at my expense.

"Just…give him a chance," Tiernan says. "They're culturally different up there."

I furrow my brow at her attempt to excuse his asshole ways.

"It's not that he's a slob, but he's also a jerk and all-around rude host. He brought a pizza in last night and ate the entire thing! Didn't even offer me *one* slice."

"Did you ask for one?" Everett asks.

"No, but I shouldn't have to. It's called manners. Clearly, something he doesn't have."

He should've known I hadn't had dinner since I had no way to get to the inn to eat. I'd expected him to at least text and ask if I wanted anything, but he didn't. When he came home, I smelled pizza and anticipated him offering me some.

He's either greedy or selfish. I haven't figured out which yet.

"I'm gonna take a bath. Maybe you should too. Try to relax," Tiernan suggests.

I scowl at the thought. "I'm not soaking in that tub. It probably hasn't been cleaned since the day it was built, which was a hundred years ago. How could anyone forget?"

"Then take a walk to blow off some steam," Everett chimes in.

I exhale slowly. "Shoving my fist in his mouth would help with that."

"Okay, well, don't do that. This is a great job opportunity, so don't mess it up because you want to bang the asshole who won't give you the time of day," my sister taunts.

My jaw drops. "That is *so* not true. He'd probably give me rabies."

"*Oakley Jane*! Be nice."

I roll my eyes. "Fine."

"Bye, sis," Everett singsongs.

"Wait, don't think I forgot about our agreement! Bluebell Rayne has an adorable ring to it, don't ya think?" I blurt out quickly.

"Oh hell no. We're not naming our child after a flower," Everett responds, then looks at Tiernan for backup, but when she ignores him, he continues, "Babe?"

"I'll have you know Ginger Halliwell named her baby Bluebell Madonna."

"Who?" He scrunches his nose.

I roll my eyes at his lack of knowledge about the Spice Girls.

She turns toward him. "I kinda like it. It's unique and beautiful."

"Yes! I win!" I cheer.

"We'll talk later." Tiernan quickly tells me goodbye and ends the call.

I smirk, knowing she'll wear Everett down until we both get our way.

Once I'm dressed, I throw my wet hair into a messy bun, then make my way downstairs.

"What's your deal?" I pick up his shirt and boots before dropping them on the coffee table with a thud. "Can you at least try to clean up after yourself while I'm here?"

He chugs his beer and glares at me over the rim.

I scoff. "What's up your ass?"

"This is *my* house," he growls. "But if we're offering suggestions, stay out of my bed for once."

I place a hand on my hip. "Pretty sure you liked me being in your bed this morning."

He slams his beer bottle on the table, then stands and walks to the bathroom.

Jesus Christ. Someone must have pissed in his Cheerios because he's being more of an asshole than usual.

Moments later, I hear the water running and let out a long sigh.

Hopefully, he gets over his problem by the time he's finished showering because I refuse to take his infant attitude.

CHAPTER EIGHT
FINN

DAY 6

YESTERDAY AFTER MY SHOWER, Oakley curled up on the couch with a book, and we didn't speak for the rest of the evening. When she thought I fell asleep, she slid under the blankets and stayed on her side of the mattress all night.

As I stretch, I'm a little disappointed to see the spot next to me is empty, and the sheets are cool to the touch. It almost pains me to admit that I miss waking to the feeling of her ass rubbing against me—even if she did it to rile me up.

That was a part of our little game.

She knows my body will respond to her, even when I try like hell not to. Oakley's gorgeous and witty, smart and sassy, but she's too damn young.

And she's leaving in less than a week.

Which is why I pushed her away after being too vulnerable yesterday. Talking about my past is one thing, but discussing my relationship with Aspen and how it broke me is something I never should've mentioned to her. There's no point in getting close.

Opening up to her only opens my heart to break again.

I should've blown off some steam before I came home because I was still annoyed at myself. Seeing her on my bed, surrounded by my things, pissed me off. She fits in so damn well, even if she's constantly pushing my damn buttons. And yesterday, she hit the nail on the head—I *will* miss her.

Not to mention, my family already loves her.

Hell, we're already acting like a couple in public, and by this weekend, the entire town will believe we're together.

But that's all it can be—*pretend.*

Regardless, I should still apologize for how I acted. Oakley's here to do a job for my grandmother, and I'm making it harder for her. I love my family and don't want to let them down by upsetting their guest. If she were to quit, it'd be my fault.

Reluctantly, I pull on some sweats and a hoodie, grab my phone, then search for her. It's barely six, so I know she hasn't gone far. From what I've learned about her, Oakley isn't an early-morning person. But that could also be the time difference.

I notice her easel and painting supplies are gone when I get downstairs.

What the hell?

Did she take my truck and bail? *Would she do that?*

If I were stuck with some asshole, I'd have already left. Wouldn't even blame her for it.

Slipping on my shoes, I open the front door and am greeted by her silhouette on the front porch. Oakley stands with a brush in her hand in front of the easel holding a canvas, but it's not the one she's been working on. It's something new.

With her back toward me, I drink her in as she paints the sunrise as it appears over the horizon.

"Oakley," I say softly, not wanting to startle her. "You're up early." Standing next to her, I admire how damn gorgeous she looks. Messy bedhead and all.

"The sunrise inspired me, and I wanted to take full

advantage while I'm here," she says without meeting my eyes. I watch as she meticulously blends the bright colors and wisps of clouds.

"It's stunning," I tell her truthfully, staring at how effortlessly she makes it look. "You're good."

She snickers, and a pink hue covers her cheeks. "Thanks. Guess that means your family is getting their money's worth."

"They wouldn't have sought you out if they weren't impressed by your portfolio. Considering you were at the top of your class, I shouldn't be surprised by how badly my grandma wanted to hire you."

"Wow, guess you *were* listening." She smirks, keeping her focus on the canvas.

"Kinda hard not to when you talk so much."

That gets her attention. "You have something against making small talk?"

I shrug. "Depends."

She rolls her eyes. "Typical answer for someone who deflects anytime something serious comes up."

"That's not true. I listen to *everything* you say," I admit. "Even if it seems like I'm not."

My heart hammers in my chest as I wait for her response. My body aches to touch her, to pull her close, and carry her into my bed.

Only God knows why.

We're opposite in every way, so she shouldn't *always* be on my goddamn mind.

"So what got you into painting in the first place?" I ask when the silence lingers too long.

"Growing up as a gifted child, I constantly needed stimulation for my brain. I'd get into trouble if I wasn't drawing, writing, reading, or doing something creative. One day, I got a painting set, and it became my new obsession. It challenged me. I started with landscapes, which have always been my favorites. When I was in middle school, my art dominated college-level painting contests and won scholarships."

"Wow, so you're self-taught?" I ask.

"At first, it all came naturally. I taught myself the basics and practiced a lot. Painting helped calm my brain because I could hyper focus on something productive, which kept me out of trouble in school. Once my teachers learned I was painting, they let me do more creative extracurriculars. Instead of being labeled the weird smart kid, I was the weird artsy kid. I preferred that stereotype over the first one. It gave me more opportunities to make friends. Still, most couldn't relate to me. I didn't meet people who were at my level until college." She pauses and flashes a cheeky grin. "Well, *almost* my level."

I smile at how proud and confident she is. I don't know much about any of this, but she makes painting look easy.

"When I'm done with this, you can keep it if you want," she says, glancing at me. "No pressure, of course. Otherwise, I'm sure your grandmother wouldn't mind an extra piece."

"She'd love it," I agree. "But I'd be honored to have it, too."

I move to get a better view of the piece. Though this canvas is smaller than the one for the commemoration, it's already nearly complete.

"I'll need something to remind me of the sassy pain in the ass who keeps sneaking into my bed," I add.

She snorts, then steps back until her ass nearly presses against me. I grip her hip, tempted to spin her around and do something I shouldn't. Since that first time we kissed, I've thought about doing it again.

Oakley turns and meets my eyes. "You call me that, but I think you'll secretly miss my company. I bet it gets lonely out here."

She's right, but I'm not about to admit that to her.

I'm also not ready to admit how much I want her right now.

75

"Oakley." I lower my voice as our mouths pull toward each other.

Right before I do something stupid, my phone rings in my pocket.

"Shit," I mutter, taking a few steps back when I realize how close we were. "It's probably my uncle Jack."

I quickly silence it. "I better return his call and get ready to go meet him. He needs an extra hand in the orchard. Gonna be getting dirty today."

"Oh yeah? Maybe I should come watch. Sounds entertaining." She smirks, then returns her attention to the canvas.

I walk to the door but stop before I go inside. "I gotta help set up for Saturday after I help my uncle, but I'll pick you up for lunch. Text me if you need anything before then."

"Will do," she says without a second glance.

Maybe I'm broken, or maybe she's growing on me, but I look forward to eating meals with her, even if it slows me down.

"So I gotta tell you something," Oakley says. She's sitting across from me at the inn as we eat lunch. I'm filthy, and my shirt has grass stains, but I can't go home and shower. After this, I'll be heading out again.

I drop my fork and flash her a deadpan expression. "I don't like the sound of that."

"Aspen stopped by your house shortly after you left and asked if we'd join her and her fiancé for dinner."

"Please tell me you didn't—"

"I had no choice! If I came up with an excuse, it'd be fishy."

"*Hell no.* I'm not going on some weird double date with my ex," I say firmly.

"Well, suck it up, buttercup. I already agreed and told her we'd be happy to join them. If we bail now, it'll be too suspicious. She was already looking at me weird."

"Tell her I couldn't break away from work on time. She knows I'm busy preparing for Saturday."

"Oh, come on, it won't be that bad. Pretend you like me, and I'll do the same, and she'll be none the wiser." She shrugs.

"Yeah, that's easier said than done," I mumble.

"Trust me, it's no picnic for me, either, especially considering your mood swings. But I'm already in too deep to confess the truth, and I don't want to look like a fool."

I hadn't considered how this would affect Oakley, and now I feel guilty as hell.

"Fine," I grind out. "One hour max and then we get the fuck out."

"Works for me. The less I have to listen to her squeaky voice, the better."

That makes me snort. "She wasn't always so damn annoying."

She gives me a *doubt it* look. "You were probably too blinded by love to see it."

Probably true.

Before we leave, I say hello and goodbye to my grandparents. They chat with the guests while they check in. Thanks to Aspen's loud mouth, my grandma thinks Oakley's my girlfriend, so now we have to play the part when she's around too.

"You two make the sweetest couple," she gushes. "Are you planning to date long distance, or are you moving here?" She directs her question at Oakley, and again, I feel awful that she's put on the spot, so I quickly chime in.

"We're still figuring things out, Grandma. Nothing's set in stone." I wrap my arm around Oakley, pulling her into my side. She snakes her arm behind me and pinches my waist.

"I'll be visiting often," Oakley tells her.

"That's great to hear." My grandma smiles.

After we escape the inn, we unglue ourselves on the way to my truck.

"I finished that painting," she tells me once we're buckled.

"Yeah? I'll have to find a place to hang it. There's a nice empty wall above the toilet."

She punches my bicep as I drive us out of the parking lot. "You better not. I don't want you thinking of me when you're taking a piss."

I chuckle at how easy it is to push her buttons.

Once we're at my house, I get out and walk inside with her.

"Wow…" My brows shoot up when I see the finished painting. "It's…*breathtaking*."

I glance at her wide smile, admiring the other beautiful thing in my house.

"I'm glad you like it. I'll find a place to hang it because I don't trust you."

Chuckling, I shrug. "Go ahead." As long as it's not in my bedroom because that will haunt me long after she's gone.

I wash my hands in the sink, then as I dry them, I turn toward her. "Oakley." I grab her attention. "I'm sorry for last night. I shouldn't have acted how I did or treated you that way."

She lowers her eyes as if she hadn't expected me to apologize, but I can admit when I'm wrong. Even to her.

"Thanks. Sorry for getting on you for being a slob. I was talking to my sister and complaining about how you didn't offer me any pizza, and my frustration snapped when you came in."

She meets my gaze, and I frown. "You mean when you were painting and listening to your porno book?"

She shoots me a glare. "I'd been working for hours and was starving."

I scrub a hand over my scruffy jawline, feeling like shit for not asking if she was hungry. "I figured you'd help yourself to the food in my fridge like you do with everything else around here."

"Or you were worked up from all the panting and moaning." She smirks.

I shake my head, not jumping into another battle with her. "I'll be back in a few, then I'll shower and get ready for the worst date of my life."

She gasps. "I take offense to that! I'm a great date, thank you *very* much. Even when I end up with assholes like you."

Oakley flashes a cheeky grin.

"It's not a *real* date," I remind her. "It doesn't count."

"Yes, it is! Aspen thinks it is anyway, so we have to treat it as such."

"Well, if that's the case, prepare to put out afterward. I like eating my dessert in bed."

Her jaw drops, and I chuckle. I've left her speechless—*for once*.

After I leave, I drive to the bakery and meet up with my mom, who gives me a to-do list. With the celebration in only two days, we still have a lot of things left to get done.

"How's Oakley?" she asks.

"Fine."

"I can't wait to see her painting."

"It's coming together nicely."

"And?"

I face my nosy mother. "And what?"

"How are you two getting along?"

I shrug, not wanting to share any details. "Alright, I guess."

She comes closer, lowering her voice. "Aspen's been asking personal questions about her nonstop. I think she's jealous."

Rolling my eyes, I scoff. "Doubtful."

"She told me you're going on a double dinner date tonight?"

"She asked Oakley, who agreed. I wouldn't have."

"Well, I'm sure you'll have a lovely time."

By the time I get home, I'm ready to crash and cancel our plans. However, as soon as I see Oakley coming down the stairs, I change my mind. I also completely forget how to breathe.

"Wow..." I admire every inch of her curvy body.

"Too much?" she asks self-consciously, smoothing her palms down the sides of her dress. "Jessa let me borrow it."

"No, I think it looks great. Surprised my cousin had something like that in her closet. Honestly, I don't think I've ever seen her wear a dress."

She giggles. "Yeah, she said she's only worn it once and never plans to again."

"Fits you perfectly," I tell her. "I'll go shower and be ready in a half hour."

Once I'm dressed in black slacks and a button-up, I meet Oakley downstairs. She's sitting on the couch, scrolling on her phone. When she lifts her head, she quickly lowers her gaze down my body.

"You clean up nice, Country Boy. But you're missing something."

I look down at myself, mentally checking off all the boxes—shoes, pants, shirt. Brushed my hair and teeth.

"What are you talking about?"

She gets to her feet, then points at the couch. "Sit."

I look at my watch, seeing that we don't have much time, but I'm curious, so I obey.

She takes me by surprise and straddles my legs after I sit. When she moves against my groin, I instinctively grip her hips.

"What are you doing?"

She leans in with a devilish grin. "Giving your ex something to look at." Her amused tone is almost frightening, and when her mouth latches onto my neck, I nearly jump out of my skin.

"Oakley." I squeeze her hips harder as she rocks against me. My traitorous cock responds, begging for more. "I don't think this is necessary."

She continues sucking, no doubt giving me a hickey. On top of Aspen seeing it, so will my entire family.

"*Fuck*, Oakley…" I hate that my voice comes out strained and desperate, but her moans and hot breath test every ounce of willpower I have left.

Finally, she pulls back and smiles in satisfaction. "That should do it. Will be nice and dark by the time we get there."

She's proud of herself as she wiggles off my lap and adjusts her dress. "Ready?"

I've never been more uncomfortable in my entire life.

Aspen hasn't stopped talking since the moment we sat down. Oakley's trying her best to be polite and engage in conversation, but I'd rather drive a fork through my skull.

"The moment Austin and I met, we immediately bonded over having city names," Aspen says, barely taking a breath to eat. "Basically love at first sight."

"Aspen and Austin, that does have a ring to it." Oakley pretends to gush right along with Aspen like they're friends.

Every detail Aspen shares about meeting and falling madly in love with Austin makes me want to vomit. I couldn't give two shits about how they met or anything that happened after we broke up. The more she talks about herself, the more I notice how self-absorbed and insufferable she is. I can't believe I put up with someone I had nothing in common with for so long. As I sit here, I can't think of one likable quality that made me want a future with her.

I'm fidgety as hell as I try to keep my composure. It isn't until Oakley leans over and squeezes my knee that I realize my leg is shaking.

Remembering I'm supposed to act like her boyfriend, I wrap an arm around her and pull her close. "We know a thing or two about love at first sight, don't we?" I blurt out, my gaze lingering on her lips.

"How'd you two meet?" Austin asks as Aspen narrows her eyes on my neck. Confirmation that the hickey is dark and noticeable.

Before I can come up with something, Oakley's already sharing our story as if it's one hundred percent true.

"About a month ago, I visited the farm for an in-person interview. Finn was my ride from the airport. He introduced me to his family and gave me a tour of the orchard. We connected, and it was almost like we'd known each other our entire lives. When it was time for me to leave, we exchanged numbers and talked every day. We took the time to get to know each other over text and FaceTime and decided we'd figure out if doing long distance was worth it when I returned for the celebration."

"Safe to say it was an *easy* decision," I quickly add, unable to look away from her.

"Couldn't agree more," she muses.

Though sprinkles of truth line her fabricated story, it sounds legit.

Without thinking, I lean in and press my mouth to hers. She stiffens briefly before opening wider and letting my tongue slide across her lips. When we pull apart, I meet her heated gaze, then we continue eating and chatting. But after that, I hardly pay attention to what anyone says. My body's aching to touch or kiss her again, but it's a bad fucking idea.

Thankfully, the rest of the date seems to pass in a blink.

"See, that wasn't so bad." Oakley gloats as we hop in the truck. "I think she bought it too. You even did a good job pretending to like me. I'd say you're almost at pro level because I almost believed it myself."

I'm tempted as hell to admit I don't have to pretend anymore. I *do* like her, and that's the fucking problem.

But what's the point when she lives across the country, is much younger, and is too talented to be stuck here with a guy like me?

CHAPTER NINE

OAKLEY

As soon as we walk into Finn's house, I'm ready to collapse. But since we took dessert to go, I decide to eat it before passing out.

Although the initial introductions to Aspen's fiancé were awkward, the rest of the dinner wasn't so bad. Once Finn settled his nerves and he remembered our mission, things went smoothly. Aspen may annoy the hell out of me with her passive-aggressive politeness, but I don't think she means any harm.

Or maybe she's good at acting like she doesn't.

Either way, we survived her drilling us with questions, and I'm glad to be at Finn's.

"I'm gonna change, then crash. Gotta be up at the ass crack of dawn again," he says.

"Okay, I'm gonna try some of that Boston cream pie."

"It's to die for," he tells me.

"I bet it is. If you hear me having a foodgasm down here, mind your own business."

He makes a choking sound as he climbs the stairs, and I snicker at how easy it is to get a reaction out of him.

"Good night, fake boyfriend," I singsong.

"Night, Miss Pain in my Ass."

I smirk, knowing how much he adores my ass. I've caught him checking it out several times this past week. So while he pretends I'm a nuisance in his life, I know damn well he'll miss me when I'm gone. If he thought of me like his annoying little sister, I wouldn't wake up with his erection poking my back every morning.

Once the lights are off upstairs, I quietly go up there and grab some comfy clothes from my suitcase. Finn's passed out, and though I'm tired, I decide to watch some TV while I eat.

Oh my God.

My eyes twitch after swallowing the first bite of pie.

"Fuck. I need a cold shower after that one," I muse, then curl up on the couch and flick through the channels. There aren't many options, so I settle for *I Love Lucy*.

My eyes grow heavy, but the food baby in my stomach makes me too tired to walk, so I surrender to his uncomfortable couch.

I don't know how long I'm in dreamland before I'm being lifted. His hard, bare chest presses against my body, and I instinctively wrap my arms around him so I don't fall.

"What are you doing?" I mutter as he carries me upstairs.

"Shut up and go to sleep," he says, laying me down.

I flash a lazy smile. "I knew you liked me in your bed."

He scoffs, pulling the blankets around me. "I didn't wanna hear your whining tomorrow about a stiff neck."

"Mm-hmm, I'm sure that's it." I roll onto my side and get comfortable. "If you wanted to spoon me, you could've asked."

"You're making me regret this," he murmurs, sliding in next to me.

Suppressing my laughter, I wiggle closer to the middle because I know it won't be long until his body wraps around mine.

I fall asleep quickly, but sometime later, I wake up with his palm pressed against my stomach, right above my panties. My back is plastered to his chest, and if anyone were to walk in, they'd assume we were a real couple.

By his cock jerking behind me, I know he's also awake. Or maybe he never fell back asleep.

"Touch me," I whisper, then add, "*Lower.*"

"Oakley…" He hisses my name like it's painful to say. "Don't tempt me more than you already do."

"What's stopping you?"

He swallows hard, his lips faintly brushing my ear. "Go. To. Sleep." He harshly emphasizes each word. "*Please,*" he adds, softer this time.

When I realize he's struggling with his feelings, I drop it.

DAY 7

He's already left for work by the time I wake up. After being here officially for a week, I'm finishing my first commissioned painting today. I feel proud and accomplished.

It still needs eight hours to dry before being presented at the centennial in two days.

Finn picks me up for brunch. Neither of us mentions last night, and we barely speak until we run into Aspen at the inn.

"Hey! How's the happy couple?" She beams, glancing at me before her gaze lands on Finn.

"We're great!" I answer even though she's ignoring me.

"It was so wonderful dining with you two last night," she says, meeting my eyes. "Austin and I had a *fantastic* time."

Finn's jaw clenches as if he can't stand hearing her voice, and I'm starting to feel the same.

"Could I have a quick private moment with Finn?" Aspen asks me with a phony smile plastered on her face.

I awkwardly nod, then grab Finn's face and smack my lips to

his. His brown eyes widen, and I flash him a wink. "I'll be over at the buffet."

"Okay, save me a spot."

"Will do, baby," I singsong, then walk away.

When I grab a plate, I glance over my shoulder and see Aspen nearly glued to Finn as she talks his ear off. Seeing them so close nearly has me dry heaving. She never deserved a man like Finn, and now she's here, flashing her engagement ring and new man in his space.

"I *never* liked her," a voice next to me says. I'm relieved when I see Jessa. She's leaning against the buffet as I scoop diced sweet potatoes onto my plate. "You're way better for him."

"We aren't a couple," I remind her, keeping my voice low so no one else overhears.

She flashes a mischievous smirk. "Maybe you should be."

I snort, piling some fruit next to my potatoes. "He can hardly stand *pretending*."

"Finn doesn't show emotion well, but I see the way he looks at you. He's fighting every urge he has. I can tell," she says confidently. "He never looked at Aspen the way I've caught him staring at you."

Pfft. "I find that hard to believe," I tell her. "We're at each other's throats more often than not."

Not to mention, I asked him to touch me and was denied.

She waggles her brows. "Sounds like foreplay to me."

Finn breaks free of Aspen, fills a plate, and joins me at the table. I'm tempted to ask what she wanted, but it's not my business. If he wanted me to know, he'd tell me.

"What did the Wicked Witch of the West want?" Jessa asks, sitting across from us. Apparently, she has no problem asking, and I'm thankful.

The corner of her lips condescendingly tilts up, and I shove food in my mouth so I don't laugh. Instead, I glance at Finn, who shoots her a glare.

"What? She's evil." Jessa shrugs, stealing a piece of bacon from Finn's plate.

"Don't you have to go take a selfie or something?" he barks.

She chews loudly to annoy him, I'm sure. "As a matter of fact, I do need to take some photos for our social media accounts today. We're in peak season after all!" She beams, not at all offended by his question, which I find hilarious. Jessa seems easygoing and gives it as much as she takes it.

"You two always bicker like this?" I ask.

"Oh, this is nothing. Should've seen us when we were kids, constantly getting into trouble with my brother and ratting each other out. Though it'd ended with all three of us getting scolded." Jessa chuckles, then looks at Finn. "Remember when you and Sebastian pushed the trampoline against the barn, then dared me to jump off the roof?"

My eyes widen in horror. "That sounds so dangerous."

"Oh yeah, I broke my arm," she says casually. "The boys were grounded for a month."

"It's not my fault you don't know how to land properly." Finn shrugs. "Sebastian and I did it dozens of times without getting hurt. You're being dramatic."

"I was *seven!*" Jessa defends, and I burst out laughing. "You were a little instigator, calling me a baby and making me feel like I had to keep up with you two."

"That's mean," I admit. "How old were you?"

"He's six years older than me, so he would've been thirteen. My brother was only nine but did whatever this little asshole said." She nods toward Finn.

"I bet you have tons of stories from growing up here," I say, genuinely curious.

"Dozens. Too bad you aren't staying longer. We could hang out with some hard cider, and I could tell you all about it."

"We might need to make that happen…" I glance at Finn, who's shaking his head.

Finn and I finish eating, and Jessa excuses herself. Aspen's long gone, and then it's the two of us.

"Ready? I gotta get to work, and I assume you do too."

As soon as Finn delivers me to his house, I dive into my painting.

I blast some instrumental music and hyper focus on finalizing the piece. Once I'm happy with all the final touches, I set it aside to dry and immediately begin another. I want to paint the inn because the architecture intrigues me. Since Finn is keeping the sunrise I painted this morning, I'll give this one to his grandmother as an extra thank-you.

After several hours, I'm covered in paint and sweat. While the main canvas dried, I decided to add some extra colors to the leaves, then return to the inn painting. I add the apple orchard behind it and as many details as possible. I'm pleased with it and can't wait to present it to her.

Deciding to take a shower, I strip off my clothes and turn on some calming spa music. I have no idea when Finn will return, so I take my time exfoliating, shaving, and relaxing under the hot stream. The window fogs up, but when I wipe it with my hand, I can see the beautiful line of trees behind his house.

My heart jumps into my throat when the bathroom door bursts open. Next, Finn barrels in through the shower curtain and then closes it behind him, maneuvering himself under the water.

"What the fuck are you doing?" I quickly cover my chest as I lower my eyes down his sculpted body, admiring every inch of his hard muscles and the tattoos on his arms.

"You've been in here for almost an hour, and I had no more patience. Other people need to shower, too." He lowers his head, then scrubs his hands through his hair.

"And nicely asking me to hurry up wasn't an option?"

"You've used enough of the hot water."

"Like I said, you could've knocked and let me know you

were waiting. I had no clue you were home." My anger brews as I watch him lather soap and wash across his broad chest.

"Well, now you do, and you can help yourself out of my bathroom."

Is he fucking kidding me right now?

I drop my arms, no longer feeling the need to cover myself. "What's your damn problem? Why are you hot and cold with me? Why do you treat me like a nuisance one second and then carry me into your bed the next? You hold me all night and then tell me I'm a pain in the ass by morning. I'm so tired of your games!"

"This isn't a game," he snaps and meets my eyes. They're dark and hooded, like he's ready for a fight.

He steps toward me until my back presses against the shower wall. With his palms on either side of my head, Finn cages me in. "I didn't want you sleeping on the couch because I know it's uncomfortable, and I *like* having you sleep next to me. Even if you're a pain in my ass, I crave your warmth and being close to you. And for whatever fucking reason, I can't get you out of my goddamn head. You've embedded yourself under my skin, and now I think about kissing you every time I'm around you. Not only for the sake of keeping up appearances but because I need to taste you."

My breath hitches as his lips brush mine, and he whispers softly, "And even though I shouldn't, I'm losing the willpower to keep my distance."

His erection jabs into my lower stomach, but when he palms his shaft and strokes himself, it pushes against my clit.

"Tell me to walk away, Oakley."

I can hear the strain in his voice, but I can't do it.

"Or you could give in to what we both want and need," I suggest, moaning when the tip of his cock rubs over my clit again.

His other hand cups my breast and plays with my nipple. "Fuck."

I'm not about to let him walk away now.

"Touch me," I beg.

"You're leaving soon," he states.

"Yeah, so maybe we should make the most of what time we have left. Whatever this is between us is undeniable, Finn."

I reach down and touch him, loving the way he reacts and knowing he can't deny the truth. When I look up into his eyes, he's staring at my lips.

"You're sure about this? Once you give me permission—"

Increasing my pace, I stroke him faster, giving him my answer.

"Fuck, Oakley."

Cupping my face is the only warning I get before he slams his mouth to mine.

CHAPTER TEN
FINN

SLIDING my tongue down Oakley's throat has been a week in the making, and I have no regrets at this point. There are a dozen reasons this is a bad idea, but none are strong enough to keep me away from her.

As she strokes my cock, I cup her face and slide my hand down to her plump backside.

"This fucking ass has been taunting me for days," I say hoarsely, giving it a slap.

Oakley's ragged breathing and whimpers tell me how badly she wants this. Every inch of her is dying for my touch.

"Turn around, Sunshine."

As soon as she does, I bring my hand between her thighs and slide my fingers between her wet slit. She spreads her legs wider as my body guards her from the water. I thumb her needy clit, then thrust two fingers inside her.

"You wanna come, *My Little PITA?*" I whisper in her ear. "I can tell how badly you need to."

"I know you didn't call me that while fingering me," she hisses between moans.

Chuckling, I drive in harder, twisting my wrist until I find her G-spot. She gasps.

"I thought you'd appreciate that little nickname," I taunt. "Has a nice ring to it, don't ya think?"

"Calling me a *pain in the ass* while giving me an orgasm confuses my brain," she admits.

"Then allow me to be crystal clear…" I bury myself in her neck, sucking between her throat and collarbone. "I've never wanted anyone as much as I want you. I shouldn't because I know the situation it'll leave us in, but consequences be damned. You've driven me crazy from the moment we met, and I know that'll continue until the day you leave."

"I can't tell if that's a compliment or not."

"You're the only woman who's ever had the power to get under my skin and make me lose all control. I need you next to me to fall asleep. I'm addicted to you, Oakley. No one's ever had that effect on me. You've made me dependent in a matter of days, City Girl. Hence why you're a true pain in my goddamn ass."

"And here I thought you couldn't stand me," she muses as her head falls against my chest. "Turns out, you're obsessed with me, Country Boy."

I wrap a hand around her throat, increasing my pace between her thighs. "Keep talking all that sass, and I'll find a way to shut you up."

"Prove it."

Giving her hair a tug, I release her body and turn her around. "Kneel and open wide."

I stroke my cock as she obeys. A devious smirk forms on her lips before she makes a perfect O with her mouth.

"My girl likes being told what to do," I say as she teases my dick with her tongue. She opens wider, hollowing her cheeks, and I sink in deeper. "Fuck, *yes*."

She strokes my shaft and sucks hard.

"Shit, Oakley. You do that so well." I brush my thumb along her jawline, gazing into her beautiful green eyes. I'm in complete disbelief that my fantasies have come true, and I won't waste the opportunity to worship every inch of her.

She chokes on my cock, rotating between sucking and stroking, and I'm so close to the edge that I have to tell her to slow down.

"I'm not coming in your mouth, baby." Grabbing her hand, I help her stand. Once she's steady, I cup her face and smash our mouths together. "Tell me you want this as badly as I do."

"I was just on my knees for you, Finn."

"That doesn't answer my question."

She pulls back, a devious smile on her face as she stares at me. "I want everything that time allows us to have. So yes, I want you…" Her hand wraps around my length, and I groan.

"Turn around and brace yourself."

As soon as she does, I line myself between her spread thighs and sink into heaven.

"Christ, you feel so perfect." As I thrust in and out, her pussy squeezes tighter with each movement.

Oakley gasps, pressing a flat palm to the wall. Between the sound of the water and my racing heart, the only noise that can be heard above them is our loud panting.

"Yes, right there," she murmurs as I wrap my other hand around her throat.

As our bodies rock and I thumb her clit, I kiss along her jawline.

"So goddamn good, Sunshine. Shit, I wanna go deeper but don't want us to fall on our asses."

"Grab my hips," she commands. When I do, she widens her legs and bends at the waist, exposing more of herself to me. She gracefully balances against the wall and my grip. "Don't let go, and we'll be fine."

Sliding back inside, I nearly roll my eyes to the back of my head as I sink so goddamn deep, I'm afraid I'm hurting her. "You okay?"

"Fuck…yes…don't stop. Keep doing that," she demands between harsh breaths.

Oakley's body shivers and shakes as I drive hard, seeking her G-spot. I hit it over and over, wrapping an arm around her waist, giving her clit equal attention.

"I'm so close," she murmurs.

"You take this cock so well. Come all over it."

And moments later, she squeezes me so goddamn hard, we fall off the edge together.

The water's cold by the time we clean and rinse off. I hand her a towel before drying off and wrapping one around my waist. Though I shouldn't, I can't stop thinking about how she fit herself into my life so quickly.

Fit might be an overstatement, considering the amount of arguing we've done, but I can visualize Oakley here, in my space forever, and that thought scares the shit out of me.

"Are you hungry?" I ask to break the silence.

"Yeah, I think I've worked up an appetite."

I chuckle at her smart-ass comment and lead her to the kitchen. "How about pasta? I have fettuccini alfredo with some chicken. It's my favorite."

"You can cook?" she asks as if that thought never crossed her mind.

BROOKE FOX

I look over my shoulder before closing the fridge. "Of course I can cook. Can't you?"

"Um…it depends what you'd consider *cooking*. I'm surprised you can because you seem like a frozen dinner kind of guy."

I hit her with a deadpan stare, unsure of what the hell that means. "I'm thirty-four and live in the middle of nowhere. Frozen dinners wouldn't be enough for my appetite."

Her eyes widen. "*Thirty-four*? Damn. You *are* old."

"Excuse me?" I strut toward her. "You sound like I should be getting the senior citizen discount at the diner. Can you even legally buy alcohol?"

She snorts, bracing herself against the counter as I stand between her parted legs.

"I've been buying booze for two years, thank you. And remember, you've chosen to act like a grumpy old man."

Her smug smile makes me grin.

"Always with that smart mouth." I grip her hips and close the gap between us, then bury my face in her neck. "I'm about to prove to you what an *old man* is capable of doing," I whisper against her ear. "Hope you can keep up, City Girl."

Without warning, I yank her towel knot and watch it fall to the floor. Then I grab under her thighs and lift her. She yelps while clinging to my shoulders, and I set her down on the counter.

"That's cold!" she hisses.

"You're not going to notice in about five seconds, sweetheart." I kiss down her throat, then capture one nipple between my teeth and gently suck. I palm her other breast, massaging and flicking her nipple with my thumb.

"Mmm…" Her head falls back with a moan as she grips the edge of the counter to steady herself. She's about to have to hold on for her life.

96

"Your tits are perfect," I tell her, tempted to leave my marks all over her skin. I slide my tongue between them, giving both attention.

"That feels good," she murmurs as her ragged breaths echo between us.

"Spread your legs for me so I can make you feel even better." I inch my way down her smooth skin.

Once she does, I step back and take in the view. Oakley on my kitchen counter with her thighs wide open, her bare pussy waiting for my tongue, is a sight to see. The need to taste her is nearly unbearable as my erection pokes against the towel, dying to get back inside her. But that can wait because I need to taste every inch of her first.

"You changing your mind or what, Country Boy?" She pops a brow as she impatiently waits.

"Are you rushing me?" I slide a finger down between her breasts and stop at her clit.

Her jaw drops. "Says the one who's always in a hurry!"

I smirk because she's not wrong. "My need for consistency and staying on schedule is about to pay off." Flashing her a wink, I lower to my knees.

As soon as I make my way to her center, Oakley gasps and tangles her fingers in my hair. She tastes like fresh soap and vanilla. I inhale her sweetness, hoping it'll be embedded in my mind long after she's gone.

"Holy shit, right there." She arches her hips toward me as I continue to devour her delicious cunt.

Her breathing grows heavy, and I know her impending release is about to shatter through her. Before she comes, I slide two fingers inside her tight pussy and twist in deep.

"God, yes!" She thrashes against me as I focus on the rhythm of my tongue. Her thighs tighten around my head as she rides my face. And as soon as her breathing stops, I know she's there.

Oakley screams through her orgasm, coating my fingers as she climbs to heaven, and I taste her sweet arousal.

When I lean back, I admire how breathtakingly gorgeous she is. Her glowy just-fucked skin and hooded eyes have me itching to get back inside her already.

"Well, I'm full now," I taunt, getting to my feet and brushing my lips to hers.

"You're funny," she deadpans, still struggling for air. "Now remove your towel."

I arch a brow in amusement, thrusting my hips toward her so she can feel how hard she makes me. I slowly do as she says.

"Just know, this is the only time I'll allow you to boss me around," I warn, grabbing my shaft and stroking it as she spreads wider.

"Keep telling yourself that." She licks her lips because she knows she's right. Considering she sneaks into my bed every night, and she knows I'm weak for her, I don't have a defense.

As she hangs onto the edge of the counter, I slowly slide inside her, bracing myself for how tight she is.

"Fuck, your cunt takes me so well," I murmur against her mouth as I grip her hip and thrust in deeper.

As I pound into her, her head falls to the side, and I suck her neck. She holds my arms as we brace ourselves for impact on this roller-coaster ride. Oakley's sweet moans give me a high I've never felt before, and I find myself craving it more and more.

"God, Oakley," I growl as she squeezes my dick so hard, I'm ready to spill inside her.

"It's so good…" She pants, clinging to me as I pinch her nipple.

I grab a handful of her ass, pushing her harder against me, and impale her with my cock. My balls tighten in warning, but I'm not finished with her yet.

"Give me another one, Sunshine. Come on my dick," I demand as our sweaty bodies smack together.

Reaching between us, I thumb her clit and coax her there with every thrust and flick.

Her breath hitches as she rides it out, and moments pass before I follow. I slam my mouth to hers, twisting my tongue in deep, and groan as I fill her up.

"Fuck. Now we're dirty again," I admit as we float down from our highs.

She chuckles. "Too bad we used all the hot water."

I smirk as I grab my towel off the floor and bring it between her legs. She watches intently as I clean her up, then myself.

"So we're doing this, right? You're not gonna wake up tomorrow morning and yell at me for being in your bed or scold me for taking up space in your house?"

I can see why she'd be wary after how I've acted, but things are different now. Instead of fighting my feelings, I'm going to let them out and not waste any more of our limited time together.

Helping her off the counter, I pull her into my arms. "I know this is only short-term, so I'm gonna make the most out of it. You'll still be a major pain in my ass, but at least I'll be able to fuck the attitude out of you instead."

"Wow, not sure if I should swoon or knee you in the nuts."

The corner of my mouth rises, and I place a soft kiss on her lips. "You still think I need to take lessons from your romance book?"

She rolls her eyes. "Better stop being so romantic, or I might fall for those one-liners."

I smack her ass, and she squeals. "Let's get dressed, and then I'll make us dinner."

CHAPTER ELEVEN
OAKLEY

DAY 8

MY EYES FLUTTER OPEN, and butterflies swarm through me as Finn holds my body against him. He spoons me, and I'm almost tempted to fall back asleep, but then his hardness presses into my back. He's hard, begging for me, and I know exactly what he needs.

Carefully, I slip away from his hold, then slide headfirst under the sheets. I take Finn out of his boxers and place my hot mouth around the tip. Slowly, I swirl my tongue, and when he moans my name, I grin in satisfaction.

Without rushing, I glide down farther, not able to take all of him at once, and nearly choke trying. When Finn pushes the covers down, I remove his boxers.

I steady my pace, loving his hearty groans as I tease my tongue down his thick vein.

"Jesus Christ, Oakley," he growls, fisting my hair.

Before I can finish him off, he's pulling me up next to him.

"Good morning," I say as he moves my panties aside and rubs between my folds.

"It's about to be," he mutters, pushing one digit inside me. "Mm. So wet already."

When I release an eager moan, he thrusts in another.

After thoroughly finger fucking me, he sucks them between his lips. "You taste sweet, like my favorite kind of apple. But I need more. Back that ass up on my face, Sunshine."

I can't deny wanting to do that very thing.

I toss my leg over him, then straddle his head, settling on his warm mouth before taking his cock back into my mouth. His scruff tickles but also creates the perfect amount of friction as we sixty-nine.

He grabs a handful of my ass and pushes me down onto him, forcing my clit against his strong tongue. I grind against him, loving how sensitive he's making my clit. He laps me up and tongue fucks my pussy, and when he smacks my ass, I'm ready to explode.

I nearly choke on his cock, hoping he feels as good as I do. His groans as he thrusts to the back of my throat tell me he is.

"Don't let me come yet," I beg as he devours me like his last meal, the pressure feeling so fucking good I might collapse. I want to savor the high and enjoy it a little longer.

"So you like to be teased?" he mumbles against my bare pussy as I grind against his face.

"Yes, please."

He slows to an almost painful pace, and I allow him to fully take control of me as I dangle by a string.

I stroke and suck, and when his muscles tense, I know he's fighting the same war as me. Finn gives my greedy pussy his fingers, and my thighs shake. One more lick and it's over.

Within a few seconds, we're losing ourselves together. I capture every bit of his hot come, not wanting to waste a drop, then swallow him down.

I fall on the bed next to him, trying to breathe. He rolls onto his side and places his inked arm around me, kissing the softness of my neck. "I could get used to that."

"Agreed," I mutter when he slides his lips across mine, allowing me to taste myself. If we didn't have so much stuff to do today, I'd beg to stay in bed with him.

But it's another reminder that our time is coming to an end. Two days and that's it.

After we're dressed, Finn makes breakfast and a pot of coffee.

"Are you getting nervous?" he asks after he finishes cooking and plates our food. It's the event of the century to celebrate a century, and I can't believe it's already tomorrow.

I take a bite of scrambled eggs, and then answer, "A little, but I'm more excited for your family to see the painting."

"They're going to love and cherish it." Finn glances over at the finished painting still on the easel. While it won't be completely cured by tomorrow, it'll be dry enough to display.

"Every time I look at it, I'm amazed by the details you captured."

I smile proudly. "Thank you."

Once we finish eating, I decide to grab a sweater from my suitcase. The temperature has steadily dropped since I arrived, and I'm still not used to it. I thank past me for all the thick socks and boots I packed.

Finn grabs his coat and puts on a beanie. I give him a half smile, admiring how handsome he is. I file that snapshot of him in my memory.

"What?" he asks, allowing me to lead the way to the truck.

I shake my head. "Nothing at all."

"Tell me." He playfully chases after me. I'm too slow, and he easily catches me, then lifts me over his shoulder. I laugh as he hauls me to the truck like a caveman.

"You can't pick me up to get what you want!"

"Sure, I can. Now tell me." He smacks my ass.

"Okay, okay. I was thinking about how sexy you look in that hat."

Finn sets me down and cages me in against the door. I look up into his brown eyes, arching my hips toward him until I feel the erection pushing into his jeans. My heart hammers in my chest when he leans down and whispers in my ear, "Keep it up, and we won't make it out of the driveway."

I bite my bottom lip. "It's not my fault you find me irresistible."

He pulls away, placing his other palm on my cheek, offsetting the briskness of the cool weather.

"You're adorable," he tells me with a cute smile, then pulls away and opens the door for me.

I don't know what I expect or even want from him. What we're doing is purely physical, but this feels like it's growing into something more than either of us bargained for.

When we arrive at the inn, I'm pleasantly surprised by how quickly it's transformed from yesterday. Vehicles are parked along the driveway, and tons of employees are running around.

A few men carry random picnic tables as others set up hay bales for extra seating. Finn is all smiles as we walk hand in hand and look at the progress. I can see he's mentally checking things off his list. The man is meticulous when it comes to the farm, so none of it surprises me.

Time is running out, and it's all hands on deck as people rush around to finish everything that has to be done by tomorrow.

"There's the stage where the live band will play," he explains as it's being assembled.

"Oh wow." Of course I knew it would be big, but I didn't realize it would look like a mini carnival. There's a bouncy house for the kids and tons of booths set up for activities. Food trucks are parked around the perimeter too.

"This is incredible." I take it in as we walk across the crunchy leaves scattered on the ground.

"And it's all free for the public."

"*Really?*" I hadn't realized they weren't profiting from this.

"Yep. We're expecting the locals and tons of tourists. That field will be full of cars by daybreak. Speaking of, we need to set out the signs so no one gets lost."

"Sounds good." I follow him inside the packed inn. Finn keeps me close to him as we look for his grandma. When we find her, she glances down at our interlocked fingers, and I almost pull away but don't when I see her smile. She still doesn't know we're faking.

We're faking it, right?

"There you are! Was wondering when I'd see you. Have you two eaten yet?"

"Yes, we had breakfast already," Finn explains. "We were going to put out the signs starting at the main road. Is there anything pressing you need done after that?"

"Nah, we've pretty much gotten it all taken care of. You could check with your mother and see if the bakery needs anything."

Finn gives me a side-glance, and I know he doesn't want to step foot near it with Aspen lingering around. She seems to conveniently pop up at the exact wrong times.

"I'll call my ma and see if they're doing okay," Finn states, keeping his tone steady, but I notice his clenched jaw.

"Great. Everything is waiting for you in the shed. James reminded me this morning they were there. You know your grandpa won't let me forget a thing."

I chuckle because they have the cutest relationship. We say our goodbyes, and as soon as we're in the storage shed, I see a large stack of signs.

I try to lift half, but they're too heavy, so Finn carries most of them. He throws them in the back of the truck, and I do the same.

Once I'm inside and buckled, he turns on the heat.

"Thank you," I offer as a shiver runs through me.

He snorts. "Such a baby. I've worn shorts in colder weather."

"Of course you have." I snicker. "I mostly wear dresses or skirts with bikini tops."

"Wow, must get hot there."

"Yeah, but I love it. The earthquakes are unsettling, but the views and nightlife are incredible. There's always something to do. Poetry readings, open mic nights, wine and paint nights at local galleries—those are my favorites."

Finn nods, and his lips turn down. I hate that I can't read him.

We spend the next few hours placing signs every mile or so on the property. Tiernan texts me for an update, but I tell her I'll chat later after I'm done.

When we shove the last one into the ground, I turn to him. "How many people do you think will still get lost?"

He chuckles. "Handfuls. People don't read or pay attention."

"But they're neon orange." I glance down at the blinding bright color.

"A few distillery employees will be out here with flags, guiding people in the right direction."

"Smart. I guess it does take an army for an event this size?"

He nods.

"Is this the first time the farm has had a celebration this large?" We climb back in the truck and head toward his house.

"They had a seventy-fifth-anniversary one when I was nine. But now that social media is a thing, it'll be much bigger. Jessa's been posting about it nonstop."

"Wow, that's a good point. I don't know what life is like without having a mini computer in my pocket."

"Live out here for a few years, and you won't even care about the internet. It's one of the many advantages."

I'm sure it is, but I can't relate. Not when I have to market myself as an artist, apply for commissions, and network.

When we go inside, I look at my painting again and lightly brush my fingers against the edges of the canvas.

"It's getting there," I say as Finn stands beside me. I watch him admire it as pride rushes through me. I figured he'd be my biggest critic, but I still wanted to impress him.

I was waiting for him to say the colors were wrong or the details were off, but I was so meticulous that it nearly looks like a photograph. The only thing that gives it away is the textures made by my brushstrokes.

"Oh, I almost forgot about this little guy," I tell him, grabbing the small 12x12 canvas I painted for his grandmother. I left it sitting on the kitchen counter after I finished it a few days ago.

Finn reaches out, and I hand him the small painting of the inn. "She's going to love this."

"I hope so," I say, heat rushing to my cheeks. With one look, I'm putty in his hands.

"When I met your grandma, I instantly adored her. She was so sweet and gushed about my work like I was someone important. I'd never had anyone know so much about my short career as a professional painter. In the grand scheme of artists, I'm obscure. I'm going to give it to her as a thank-you gift for giving me a chance on the project."

Finn meets me with soft eyes. "You know she's not gonna let you leave after this."

I chuckle, though it's covered in sadness. "Wonder where she'll hang it in her house."

Turning, I look at the sunrise painting I made for Finn hanging above the mantel. It was the perfect place for it.

"Somewhere so everyone who visits will see it, and she can brag about it."

I smile at the thought. "I hope she does. Maybe that way you won't forget about me."

Finn pulls me into his arms as a smile creeps across his lips.

"Oakley Benson. You're *unforgettable*. My family will talk about you nonstop to the point I'll have to beg them to stop."

I laugh at his attempt to compliment me. "And who said romance is dead?"

He brushes his nose along my cheek, feathering kisses as he moves down my jawline. "I'll miss you, Sunshine. Don't think I won't."

I hold on to those words like they're a promise. But I'm sure someone will come along and snag Finn up as soon as I'm gone. He's too much of a catch when he drops the grumpy man act.

After our moment comes and goes, Finn dials his mom to see if they need any help. When he ends the call, he sits next to me on the couch.

"They need me to grab more folding tables and chairs because Grandma doesn't think there'll be enough picnic tables."

"Do you want me to help?"

"Nah, I've got it. Plus, you've got a lot of packing to do." He looks around at my supplies, which are exactly where I've left them.

"You're right," I say, knowing I've been procrastinating. Putting everything back in their boxes means my stay here is nearly over. And I'm not sure I'm ready to say goodbye yet, a feeling I've never experienced.

I'm a free spirit at heart, and after I graduated with my master's, I promised myself I'd travel the world. Be a painting nomad, get a camper van, and hike the Appalachian Trail. But staying with Finn makes me appreciate the slower pace in the country.

Finn opens his mouth like he's going to say something but then closes it. After clearing his throat, he speaks up. "I'll see you in a couple of hours. However, I'm sure they'll find a million other tasks for me to do. I'll pick up dinner from the inn if I'm gone that long."

"Sounds great."

He grabs his keys off the counter, then leaves. As I look around his place, I laugh at how my stuff has completely taken over. I carefully open the empty boxes and can't find it in me to pack. Not yet. It seems too soon. Funny because a week ago, I was ready to quit.

Instead, I text my sister back.

OAKLEY

> Sorry! It's been wild. How are things going?

TIERNAN

> Not me wondering if you fell into a sex coma or if you were ignoring me all day.

OAKLEY

> We'll go with the sex coma.

I sigh, replaying everything that's happened between Finn and me.

TIERNAN

> Fill me in! The PG-13 version. I am your sister, after all.

I snort, hearing her big sister voice in my head.

OAKLEY

> Finn worships my body in all the right ways. Crawling in bed with him was the best idea you've ever had. So tell Everett to suck it.

TIERNAN

> Ha! I'll let him know.

OAKLEY

> I'm sad to leave even though I have so much shit to do at home.

TIERNAN

Aw. It's normal to feel that way when you've had a good time. You can always visit again. Make it a yearly tradition or something.

OAKLEY

I know. But it's more than that.

TIERNAN

Ready to admit that you've fallen for your crush?

OAKLEY

No.

This feels like much more than an infatuation or a *crush*, but I keep that to myself for now.

TIERNAN

I felt the same way when Everett and I first stayed at the beach house. But remember, everything works out the way it's supposed to. Have faith, little sis.

OAKLEY

I want the type of love you have.

TIERNAN

You'll find your Prince Charming. Maybe you already have.

I need to change the subject because it's making me sad. No reality would allow us to be together long-term. Not with three thousand miles between us.

OAKLEY

Enough about me. How's my niece doing?

TIERNAN

Amazing. She's been keeping us updated on every little thing, and it's feeling more real each day. Even did some baby shopping today.

OAKLEY

And you didn't send me pictures?

TIERNAN

I will! We were so tired after shopping that we took a nap when we got home.

OAKLEY

Sounds like you had a good time. I'm so excited to meet little Bluebell Rayne.

She sends me laughing emojis because we both know Everett is outnumbered on the baby's name.

TIERNAN

Me too.

I yawn and let Tiernan know I'm going to take a nap. Packing doesn't sound appealing, so I'll rush on Sunday to get it all done, as usual. At least then, my mind will stay busy after the excitement of the celebration wears off.

After we say our goodbyes, I go upstairs and crawl into Finn's bed that smells like him and sex. I wish I could inhale the sheets or bottle up the scent and take it home with me.

I try to drift off and the dread of getting on that plane in two days creeps over me. Falling for Finn wasn't something I planned or expected. Maybe it's my heart playing tricks on me, but it's never steered me wrong before, so why would this be an exception?

CHAPTER TWELVE

FINN

DAY 9

I WAKE before my alarm sounds. I should've known my internal clock wouldn't let me sleep in. The anticipation and excitement of today's celebration wouldn't allow it either.

I hear Oakley's soft breathing, but instead of waking her for a quickie, I decide to let her rest a little longer and go shower. We stayed up late last night and lost count of how many orgasms I gave her. Pretty sure we broke another record.

Oakley's a goddess between the sheets, and I love how she takes what she needs without apology. And damn, do I enjoy giving myself to her.

I undress and step under the hot stream, allowing the warmth to wake me. As I reach for the soap, the shower curtain peels back, and Oakley steps in. Immediately, I grin.

"Thought we could conserve water," she tells me, taking a step forward, allowing her breasts to press against my chest. She wraps her arms around my neck, and our lips gravitate toward one another. When we pull away, desire is written on her face.

"I need you," she admits, and those words have my heart

hammering. Oakley reaches down and strokes my cock, but it's already hard for her.

"Mm. Always ready for me," she says, lifting her thigh to give me better access. I latch onto her leg and slowly ease inside. She sighs when I fill her.

She holds on to me for dear life as I pump inside her. Her back presses against the wall as she moans through the pleasure.

"Fuck," I groan out as the orgasm quickly threatens to take over, but I don't come yet. Instead, I drop to my knees, the stream running down my back, and devour her pussy for breakfast.

I position her thigh over my shoulder, knowing exactly how she likes her cunt devoured. Her wet hair sticks against her forehead, and she pants as she leans her head back.

Oakley tugs my hair with one hand and her nipple with the other as she rides my face. She tenses. "Finn. Fuck. I'm so close."

And when she comes on my tongue, I don't stop. I urge her with my eyes to give me one more as I taste her sweetness. She likes this game and plays along, getting back into her rhythm.

Minutes later, she's losing herself again. I hold her tight as she almost falls, then I stand.

"That's my good girl," I praise, sliding my tongue into her mouth, allowing her to savor my new favorite flavor. Oakley looks at me with hooded eyes, then latches onto my cock with a tight grip. "Are you going to continue what you started?"

"Turn around, Sunshine."

Oakley spins and pops her ass, giving me access to her perfect pussy from behind. I grab onto her hips and slam inside her, my vision nearly blurring from how good she feels.

She presses her palms against the wall, creating more friction.

"God, yes," she whisper-hisses, and within minutes, she's falling over the ledge. "Keep going," she commands, reaching down and flicking her clit. Oakley's high sex drive and momentum might snap off my dick as I fill her with my cum.

We stand there, catching our breaths. After I pull out of her, she drops to her knees and licks the tip of my cock, then takes as much of me in her mouth until she gags.

"Shit," I hiss, the tip extra sensitive. "I've never had a woman do that before."

"No? Then you've been dating prudes. I love the way we taste mixed together."

I place my finger and thumb under her chin and force her to look up into my eyes. "You're so perfect."

There are too many unspoken words I wish I could say, but instead, I give her a quick kiss as she stands.

We take turns washing one another, and then I help with her hair.

"You're trying to spoil me." Her eyes roll to the back of her head as I massage her scalp. I'd spoil her every day for the rest of my life if she'd let me, and that thought alone is frightening. I shouldn't let those visions give me false hope.

Once we finish showering, Oakley bends over to dry her legs, giving me the perfect view of her gorgeous ass. Over her shoulder, she shoots me a smirk, knowing I'm staring.

"I like the way you look at me."

"And I like looking," I admit, wrapping my towel around my waist after I finish drying off. "You're beautiful."

"Well, I'm glad you think so, considering I'm your fake girlfriend and all."

"Do you think it's believable?" I ask after she wraps herself up and grabs the hair dryer.

"Yeah, our acting skills are fire." She meets my gaze in the reflection of the mirror. "No one doubts it, even those who know we're pretending."

Unspoken words swirl between us, and there's so much I wish I could say. The last thing I want is for things to be awkward between us before she leaves. So I push those thoughts away.

"I'm going to get dressed and check in with everyone, then we can head that way."

"Okay, gimme twenty to finish up."

"Make it fifteen." I wink, and she rolls her eyes.

After I put on my clothes, I call my grandmother and mom, and they confirm everything is in place and all we need to do is show up.

Next, I call Levi, and I brew a pot of coffee as we chat.

"I'm probably going to leave and start heading that way. Don't want to get stuck in traffic," he tells me.

"Perfect. Be on your *best* behavior today. You know Aspen's here," I warn.

"Ugh," he groans. My best friend was never a fan of her. "Fine. I'm more excited to meet your girlfriend anyway."

I chuckle as Oakley prances past me, accidentally-on-purpose dropping her towel with a giggle.

"Did you hear me?" Levi asks when I sound distracted.

"Uh, yeah."

He clears his throat. "Okay, well, I'll see you there."

"Great." I pour two cups of coffee to go and move farther into the living room so I can watch her get dressed.

"You're a mind reader," she says, looking at the one I made for her.

"Or you're predictable," I tease.

After she slips on her boots, we carefully load the canvas, easel, and cloth cover into the back of the truck. I can see her mind racing as we drive toward the inn. She quietly sips her coffee.

"You okay?" I ask, and she unbuckles and scoots closer to me, sitting in the middle. She's holding the small painting of the inn. I lift my arm and hold her as we continue down the gravel road.

"Nervous," she admits. "I don't know why. Sometimes self-doubt creeps in."

"Oakley Benson, you're the most confident person I know. You're the real deal, and don't you dare think otherwise."

This makes her smile wide, and I grab her hand, interlocking my fingers with hers.

We pass the neon orange signs we placed, and every few miles, an employee waves people forward. The traffic is outrageous, and I'm almost concerned there won't be anywhere to park.

When we get closer to the inn, the field is already full of vehicles.

Oakley looks over at me with wide eyes. "You weren't joking about all of Maplewood Falls being here."

While I expected this, I'm somewhat shocked too.

"We might need to park out here. We can carry the painting and stuff up with us. Later, we'll grab the small one."

She glances down at it. "That's probably a good idea."

We park on the opposite side of the bakery, and before we get out, I turn to Oakley. "Ready?"

"Yep, let's go have some fun, fake boyfriend," she says with a big smile.

I grab her painting. Oakley explains it's not completely cured yet, so it needs to be handled with care and to hold it on the edges. She takes the easel and cloth covering, then leaves the other one in the truck.

"I can't wait to surprise your grandma with the other painting after the big reveal."

"She'll probably cry," I warn. "Grandma is like a leaky faucet when she's overwhelmed and happy. The woman sometimes laughs and cries at the same time."

"And that's why she needs to be protected at all costs," Oakley says as we make our way toward the inn.

It's not even nine in the morning, yet people eat pumpkin pie and candied apples. Kids run past us wearing fairy wings and superhero capes with painted faces. The smell of sugar wafts through the air, and there isn't a person without a smile on their face.

"This is so cool." Oakley smiles as we make our way through the crowd toward the large stage where the band is currently setting up. At the front, there is an area roped off for the painting.

"I don't want anyone to see it yet," she tells me as we make our way up the stairs. I hold it close to my body so no one can steal a glimpse.

"Grandma saved that spot for you." I nod my head toward the velvet ropes. Set up your easel first and then we'll cover the canvas before carrying it over."

"Great idea."

Oakley quickly brings the wooden legs out and checks to make sure the easel is sturdy. Before walking away, she gives it a little push for prosperity's sake before returning to me.

"Do you want to set it up?" I ask.

"No, I trust you," she whispers, carefully draping the thin black material over the canvas.

I lead the way, and she stands close as I cautiously put it in place. Oakley repositions the cover, and we take a step back.

I grab her hand and kiss her knuckles. "I can't wait for everyone to see what you created."

"What time is the reveal again?" she asks nervously.

"One sharp," I remind her, leading her off the stage and through the steadily forming crowd.

I run into Uncle Jack and my dad as we make our way toward the food trucks.

"We saw Levi," Dad tells me.

"Yeah? Where is he?"

"He was in there flirting with Willa." Uncle Jack chuckles.

I shake my head, not at all surprised. "Thanks."

"Ready to meet my best friend?" I ask Oakley.

"Uh. Yeah." She lowers her voice. "And how exactly do I introduce myself?"

I laugh. "As Oakley, the pain in my ass painter who sneaks into my bed. He knows about our *arrangement*."

"Which one?"

I lean in and whisper in her ear, "The fake relationship, not fucking each other's brains out."

She laughs. "Ah. Good to know."

We enter through the back door and pass the common room and fireplace. I can hear my best friend laughing with my grandma in the kitchen.

When I enter, they both turn and look at us.

"There's the happy couple now." Grandma shoots me a wink. We still haven't told her the truth, and though I feel guilty about that, it's easier this way for now.

Levi raises his brows at Oakley and then flashes me a shit-eating smirk as if he knows I'm fucking doomed.

"This is Oakley," I say, then look at her. "And this is my childhood friend, Levi."

"The *girlfriend*," she adds, holding out her hand, but Levi ignores it and pulls her into a bear hug.

"Nice to meet the woman my best friend's gonna marry someday."

I roll my eyes even though I can't deny how I like the sound of that. "I already told you I'm never getting married," I remind Levi, then watch Oakley's back stiffen. I hadn't meant to let that slip out with them here.

"You don't mean that." My grandma waves me off. "I'm still waiting for one of my grandchildren to give me a great-grandbaby."

"Yeah, Finn." Levi smacks my shoulder with a kiss-ass smirk.

When Oakley returns to my side, my arm naturally swings around her, and when our eyes meet, I'm tempted to kiss her. Levi clears his throat, grabbing my attention.

"We were going to enjoy the festivities. Wanna join us?" I ask Levi as Grandma excuses herself to chat with the mayor.

Once we're outside, Levi turns to Oakley. "So how much longer are you here? Gonna stay for the town's fall festival next weekend?"

"Don't ask her twenty questions," I warn.

"It's fine." Oakley waves me off. "No, I fly out Monday."

"Oh." He glances in my direction. "What will you two love birds do?"

I shake my head. "You don't have to answer his nosy questions."

"I asked two things," he protests.

Oakley laughs and reaches for my hand. Her fingers are warm, and I like it when she brushes her thumb over mine.

"Not sure yet." Oakley shrugs. "Finn will have to tell his family once Aspen leaves, I guess?"

"They'll be heartbroken." He frowns. "I have plenty of room at my house if you decide to stay." Levi waggles his brows, knowing it'll piss me off.

"Is that so? Well, I might need to remember that."

"Don't play into his games," I tell Oakley and scowl at Levi.

"What game? I'm being hospitable."

Oakley snickers. "That's more than Finn can say."

"I already like her." Levi smirks. "She's a keeper."

"She's a pain in my ass," I remind him as we pass a few of the craft booths.

Oakley snickers because only she knows the true meaning behind that.

Her gaze zeroes in on the table that has tiny canvases, paints, and brushes. "You never mentioned there was a painting booth."

"Slipped my mind," I admit. "But you should go show those kids who's legit."

Two little girls smear random colors on their canvases and then glance up at us. Oakley walks over and kneels beside them.

Levi and I stand back and chat as Oakley praises the kids' artwork. She's mesmerizing, and I can't take my eyes off her.

"So you wanna tell me what's really going on between you two?" Levi asks, crossing his arms over his broad chest.

"What do you mean?" I furrow my brow.

"Don't play dumb. I've known you way too long."

I shrug him off. "Not sure what you're talking about."

"You like her," he says softly. "Not that I can blame you. She's gorgeous."

"She's too young. And leaves in two days."

After Oakley finishes her painting that's the size of her palm, she strolls toward us. "I painted you something."

"Let me see."

"Hold out your hand and close your eyes."

"Oakley," I warn because I know Levi is eating this shit up, but I can't deny her.

I sigh and do what she asks.

"Alright, you can look now," she tells me after placing it in my hand.

I hold it upward and see it's a heart with an F&O in the middle.

"You two, Jesus." Levi shakes his head. "Get married already."

Right as the words leave his mouth, Aspen prances by.

Levi's laugh slightly fades as Aspen shoots daggers at him. Then when she notices me watching her, she flips a switch.

"Levi!" She shrills in that high-pitched fake voice that's worse than nails scratching down a chalkboard. "How've you been? Almost didn't recognize you without your axe," she says, flashing her cunty smile.

"Aspen," I warn, not wanting to deal with her right now.

Levi chuckles, sweeping hair out of his face. Not much annoys him as he's always had a naturally bubbly personality, but if one person grates on his nerves, it's my ex.

"Aspen…" he says, forced and firm. "I can't believe you found room to park your broom."

Oakley holds back laughter as Aspen blinks fast. She acts like he literally slapped her. "Good seeing ya, *Santa*," she snarls, then flashes her eyes between Oakley and me.

I hold my breath until she's out of sight.

Oakley looks at Levi. "Okay, that was funny. But what did she mean by the axe and Santa comments?"

"My family owns a Christmas tree farm on the outskirts of Maplewood Falls, and I live in a big mountain cabin on the property. She likes to make fun of me for it but forgets I'm the one who knows how to chop wood and use a deadly tool."

Oakley laughs, and I shake my head as he brags about his skills. "That sounds so cool. How fun!"

Levi instantly perks up again. "I think so too. It's the best time of the year."

"You gotta ignore people who don't understand your passions," Oakley tells him.

"Trust me, I'm not worried about Aspen. She has never liked me or *anyone* who had Finn's best interest in mind." He turns to me. "I'm so glad you didn't end up with her."

"Same," Oakley and I both say.

"Geez, you even talk in unison." Levi glances between us, then waves at someone across the way.

"Hey, I'll catch up with you two in a little while. I have to chat with James."

I glare at Levi. "Please tell me you aren't betting on football games with my grandpa again? If my mom finds out you two are back at it, you're *done*."

"Pfft, your mom loves me more than you," he gloats, and that might be true. "Anyway, nice meeting you, Oakley. Hope we can hang out some more before you leave. I'd love to learn more about your art."

"That'd be nice," she admits, then grabs my hand again as Levi jogs through the crowd.

"Thanks for the artwork," I tell Oakley. "I think out of all the paintings you've done this week, this one's the best."

She snorts. "Now, if you want to hang *that* one above your toilet, go for it."

"Oh, I planned on it."

We wait in line for curly fries from one of the food trucks and then share a bag of cotton candy. Afterward, Oakley gets a caramel apple, but I pass. I've eaten enough of them as a kid to last me two lifetimes.

Once we've seen most of the activities, I check the time.

"We need to go get your other painting," I remind her, so we walk hand in hand down the path to my truck.

"Has Aspen always treated Levi that way?" she asks.

"Yeah. I was stupid to ignore it and should've noticed all her red flags."

Oakley squeezes my fingers. "At least he can give it as good as she tries to."

"Levi's not one to back down. He's too nice most of the time, but when it comes to her passive-aggressive comments, he always puts her in her place."

"Must've been uncomfortable for your girlfriend and best friend not to get along."

"It was. Honestly, I should've put a stop to it a long time ago, but it's not my problem anymore."

Once I unlock the truck, she grabs the inn painting, and I set the tiny heart canvas on the dash. When we return to the celebration, we find hay bales in front of the stage to sit and wait.

The band warms up and opens with a Beatles cover. I check my watch, realizing we have a little under an hour before it's showtime.

"I like Levi. He seems like a nice guy," Oakley tells me, sitting so damn close, I can feel her body warmth.

"He's always been one of the friendliest, kindest people I've ever known. The man wouldn't harm a fly and would give anyone the shirt off his back in the middle of a snowstorm if they needed it. That's how he's always been."

"Hard to believe he's not married."

Right as I'm about to speak, my cousin Jessa plops down on the other side of me. I nearly knock Oakley off the edge, then hurry and catch her while keeping hold of the canvas.

"Jessa!" I growl, turning toward her.

"Oops, sorry," Jessa hurries to help Oakley, who's laughing at her antics. "I didn't realize I had so much oomph in my trunk."

"It's fine. I think I need to find a bathroom, though," Oakley admits, and I can tell she's growing more nervous.

"The inn will be your best bet," I tell her. "Do you want me to walk you?"

"No, it's fine. I'll be right back."

I watch as she walks away, then when I turn to Jessa, she's grinning like a fool.

"You're in love with her."

I make a face. "What?"

"Dude, it's so ridiculously obvious. Tell me…is this girlfriend act real or fake?"

"Shush," I say, looking around, making sure no one is within earshot because she's being loud as fuck. "It's whatever you want it to be since you're apparently the expert."

"I knew it."

I groan. "Sometimes you're overly annoying."

"And sometimes you're extremely transparent. I need the real story. Did you set this fake dating scheme up on purpose?"

"Give me a break. None of this was planned. I didn't know Aspen's spaceship was invading the farm this week."

She snorts. "And they say you'll meet the love of your life when you least expect it."

"It's not like those books you read. Trust me." Then I

remember Oakley's audiobook and almost take it back. It's *exactly* like that.

"We'll see. I'd almost be willing to make a bet you two end up together," she muses.

"A bet?"

"Yeah. When is Oakley leaving again?"

"Monday."

"Well, I'm betting she *doesn't*," Jessa states with confidence rolling off her, and I can't stand it when she acts like a know-it-all.

"She already has her plane ticket booked, Jessa. Don't shake on things you'll lose."

"If you're so confident, then let's shake on it. Two hundred bucks."

"Two hundred? Pfft. Double it and you have a deal."

"Double *that* and then we do. Unless you're too scared." Jessa holds out her hand and waits for me to take it.

"You're being way too cocky." I shake it. "She's not staying."

"You better pay up when I win." Jessa grins confidently.

I see Sebastian waving her over, and she nods.

"I should feel guilty for taking your money, but I'll be too busy swimming in fifties," I gloat before she walks away.

"We'll see," she calls out over her shoulder.

A few minutes later, Oakley returns. "Sometimes when I get nervous, my bladder rebels."

I grab her hand and thread my fingers through hers. "Good to know. Hey, what time does your flight leave on Monday? Don't think you've told me."

She frowns. "Seven. I'm supposed to be there at five. I'm sorry."

"Nah, it's fine. Happy to take you." I smile, knowing Jessa is fucked and will have to pay up.

Oakley looks around as more people take the empty seats. I

hand her the painting she made for my grandmother and wrap my arm around her shoulder.

Fifteen minutes later, the band finishes their first set and my aunt and uncle, parents, and grandparents walk up on stage. My mother taps the microphone.

"Hello? Whoa. *Wow.* Hot mic. We wanted to thank you from the bottom of our hearts for coming to our family's centennial celebration. It's our honor to be able to thank you for one hundred years of business." Mom waves over my aunt, who shakes her head, so Grandma steps up.

"Yes, thank you so very much. My parents had always dreamed of owning an apple orchard, and my father hand planted the first trees himself. Without the decades of support from the community, we wouldn't have lasted this long." She continues with more history about the farm, and although she's repeated it dozens of times, I still enjoy hearing her describe the hardships and successes.

I turn around and take pictures of everyone who's here. At least eight hundred people are in attendance, maybe even more. While Grandma speaks, kids play in the field, chasing one another.

"While you're all here and enjoying yourselves, I wanted to share something I've dreamed of having for years. It's something that we can all cherish. Oakley?" Grandma calls out, scanning through the crowd. She blocks her eyes from the sun with her hand, and Oakley stands and waves. "Come up here, sweetheart. I'd like for you to do the honors."

I grin. "Go ahead."

She makes her way up and meets my grandma on stage.

"I first learned about Oakley Benson's work online. Yes, before any of you say anything, I know how to use a computer," Grandma adds, and laughter breaks out. "Anyway, I emailed her and nearly begged for her to come out and paint a scene for the farm. She's also dating my grandson."

My cheeks heat. This is not what I expected her to do.

"Stand up, Finn! Wave at everyone."

I force a smile and do as she says. Oakley beams as she moves closer to the microphone. She clears her throat, and I can see her blood pumping hard by the pulse in her neck. It's adorable to see her so nervous.

"Mrs. Bennett. Before the big reveal, I'd like to give you a small gift, a thank you for giving me a chance."

Grandma looks surprised as Oakley hands her the small canvas. Instant tears roll down her face, as I expected. As my aunt and Mom surrounded Grandma, Oakley takes the opportunity to pull the sheet from the large painting.

The audience breaks out in applause and gives her a standing ovation. Oakley's overwhelmed by everyone's reaction as she wipes her cheeks. My entire family grows emotional as they admire the painting. Even my grandpa has tears rolling down his face. The fact that she was able to paint something so realistic in such a short amount of time proves how incredible of an artist she is.

"I'm speechless," Grandma says, and the crowd laughs. She thanks everyone for coming again and hordes of people move closer to the stage to look at Oakley's masterpiece.

Several people ask her for business cards as she makes her way toward me, but she directs them to her Instagram page for all her contact information. After Oakley fights her way to me, she smiles and falls into my arms.

"They loved it."

"I'm so happy they did."

"Me too," I admit.

"Ready for that hayride I promised earlier?"

She reaches for my hand. "Let's do it!"

As we make our way past the crowd, chatting about Grandma telling everyone we were dating, we're interrupted.

"Oakley Benson?" a voice I recognize shouts above the chatter.

We both turn, and I realize it's Mayor Myers running toward us.

"Apologies for yelling your name like that, but I wanted to catch you before you left." He sucks in air, then continues, "We're having a town fall festival next weekend to commemorate autumn. We held an emergency board meeting since everyone was here, and we'd like you to paint for us next weekend."

Oakley's eyes widen, and for a moment, she's speechless.

"Please. Money isn't an issue," he adds as he waits.

That's when I remember that damn bet I made with Jessa and know she's somehow behind this. *Fucking cheater.*

Oakley looks at me, and I hope with every inch of my being that she'll say yes even though I'll be in the hole eight hundred bucks. But I don't care. I'd empty my savings for another week with her. Call me selfish, but I'm not ready for her to leave yet. Not when each time I look at her, my heart skips a damn beat.

A few seconds pass as the mayor and I wait with bated breath for her answer. And for a moment, when she hesitates, I'm afraid she'll say no.

CHAPTER THIRTEEN
OAKLEY

THE MAYOR's question catches me off guard because I've been mentally preparing to leave this whole time on Monday. Though it'd be a huge honor.

"I'd love to take the job, but I don't have a place to stay, and my flight leaves on Monday," I answer. The last thing I'd want to do is impose on Finn's space because I've already done that enough over the past ten days. He doesn't seem to mind, but I can't assume he'd be okay with me prolonging my trip by another week.

Finn furrows his brow at me, but I'm not sure how to read him. My fate is in his hands.

"There's room for you here if your schedule allows it," Finn tells me, his signature boyish grin sweeping across his handsome face.

"Are you sure?" I ask with uncertainty, hoping he's not being nice for the sake of it. Aspen will be leaving, so I could move back into the cottage if needed.

"I'll cover the cost of changing your return flight. Oh, pardon my manners. I'm Edward Myers, and I've been leading

Maplewood Falls for the past fifteen years. Willa spoke so highly of you, and I can't get over how amazing the farm painting is. You're truly talented. Of course, I'd give you full creative liberties to paint whatever you'd like. It will be hung in the entryway of the town hall for everyone to enjoy."

I look between him and Finn, swallowing hard. "That sounds perfect. I'd be happy to paint it for you."

Edward's mouth turns up into a big smile, and he shakes both of our hands. "Thank you. Thank you so much. Here's my card. If you need anything, please do not hesitate to reach out. I'll send you an official contract tonight if you can give me your email address."

Oakley writes it down in a small pocket-size notebook he had tucked in his shirt.

"We'd like the imagery to be centered around the harvest festival. That's the only requirement. Starts on Thursday."

"I can't wait to check it out. Appreciate the opportunity to do the town justice," I tell him, not caring how much they're paying. Spending more time with Finn is worth any dollar amount.

When he walks away, Finn grabs my hand and kisses my knuckles.

"When Aspen leaves, I'll be happy to move my things back to the cottage if you—"

"You're staying with me, Sunshine," he says with a sly grin. "The last thing I'm doing is moving all that shit again."

I snort. "Don't blame you. Now I'm glad I haven't packed anything."

We laugh as Finn leads me toward the wagon taking people on an orchard tour. When I turn my head, I notice Aspen watching us from the perimeter of the area. I give her a smile, but she turns her head and pretends she wasn't watching us.

Finn helps me take the step up, and it feels like an eternity has passed since we took the first tour together. When he sits, I use his lap instead of taking a seat next to him. He wraps his strong arms around my waist, and I turn my body so I can easily chat with him. I like the way he holds me, but it doesn't feel like it's for show anymore.

"Aspen's watching," I whisper in his ear.

"I swear she's stalking us."

Once the wagon is full, the tractor takes us around the orchard. Finn points out the different trees, and I love listening to him talk about the farm. Some were cross-pollinated to make new species, and others came from the original harvest a hundred years ago.

Finn keeps me in place as the tractor takes a turn down another bumpy road. I can feel him growing hard under my ass, and it's taking me back to the first time we did this. I slightly turn my body, creating a little more friction, and he digs his thumbs in my hips.

Turning my head, I whisper in his ear, "We should leave after this."

"Not sure we'll make it off this wagon if you keep making me hard." He nibbles on my earlobe, and I squeeze my legs together.

After everyone's picked a few apples, we get back on the wagon and make our way back. As we offload, I miss a step and fall into his arms, laughing. He catches me and spins me around.

"Sure am glad you were there," I admit.

Finn sets me down and tucks loose strands behind my ear. "I'm glad you're here and are staying longer."

"Yeah? I thought you'd be sick of me," I tease.

"You're starting to grow on me." Then he leans in and whispers, "Truthfully, I can't get enough of you."

We pass by kids bobbing for apples. There's a timer and the one who gets the most wins a prize. I love how they have different activities for the little ones, most of whom carry at least one prized stuffed animal.

"I've never done that before," I tell Finn as we watch.

"Do you know where it originates?" Finn asks.

"No idea."

He steps close. "It started in Europe and was used to figure out if two people were meant to be lovers."

I narrow my eyes. "You're *totally* making this up."

"I swear, I'm not. It's how they determined their soulmates. They'd put several apples in a bucket, each one representing a potential partner. Women would bob for their crush's apple. If she accomplished it on her first try, it meant they were soulmates and were destined to be together forever. If it took her two tries, it was known that they'd date for a while, but it wouldn't work out. Three tries? Forget it."

I chuckle. "Can you imagine building your entire relationship on crunching into an apple on the first try. That's hilarious and seems ridiculously hard."

"It *is* hard, and it's a true story. At some point, they changed it to figure out who'd get married first. There also used to be an old superstition that if you slept with the first apple you bobbed under your pillow, that night, you'd see the love of your life in your dreams."

This makes me snort. "That's wild."

"I know. Wanna try it?"

"Nah, I think I'm gonna pass on that one. But wait, that looks fun." I point at the children a few tables down with fishing poles. Each has a rod with a magnet attached and is trying to catch apples in a field. Each fruit has a number written on the side of it.

"What's the objective?" I ask.

"They let people *fish* for two minutes, and the person who racks up the most points wins a prize."

"Cute."

"You wanna play? Unless you're scared of getting your ass kicked."

I playfully gasp. "Never. You're on."

After the current participants finish and a little girl chooses a teddy bear, Finn and I step up.

"Thanks, Charlotte," Finn says to the woman who explains the rules. She looks like his mother's age and has a kind smile.

Charlotte counts down, starts the timer, then Finn and I get to work. Right off the bat, he snags three points. I've never wanted to win so badly at something, but I've never been the competitive type, hence the painting. When I glance over and see his pile stacked next to him, I know it's a losing battle, but I don't give up.

I didn't realize how heavy apples are to pull in. I'd have better luck *actually* fishing.

The timer buzzes, and my three points look ridiculous compared to his fourteen.

"You're well practiced." I pout with a hand on my hip. "Probably were doing this in the womb."

"Guess I'll stick with apples, and you stick with painting." He shoots me a wink, then leads me to the prize table. "Lady's choice."

There's a stuffed apple with a heart embroidered on it, and I pick it up and squeeze it. "Thank you."

"Anything for my girl." He brushes his lips to mine. I melt into his kiss, and when he lightly slides his tongue against mine, a burst of heat rushes through me. I grab the hem of his shirt with my free hand, wanting to get lost in him.

"Okay, I gotta use the bathroom, then we can get outta here if you want," I tell him when we break apart.

Finn walks with me to the inn, and I hand him my stuffed apple before going inside. I have to maneuver around a crowd of people talking, then wait ten minutes for a turn.

Once I've washed my hands, I walk back outside but stop in my tracks when I see Finn talking to Aspen. He looks less than pleased, as if she cornered him when she found him alone.

I wait in the distance and hate that I'm jealous when Aspen places her hand on Finn's arm.

She looks like she's pleading with him, but he keeps a straight face. It's obvious that whatever she's saying is important to her, but he's brushing it off. After another minute passes, I make my way over.

Finn leans down and plants a kiss on my lips. "Thank God," he murmurs so only I can hear.

"You ready?" I ask loudly.

"Yep. Are we finished here?" he barks at Aspen. I remember when he used to act that way toward me. That's him building an unscalable wall around himself.

"Finn, *please*," she urges. "You can't deny what we shared for five years. *No one* can change that." As she emphasizes her words, she glances at me. Then she bravely takes a step and reaches out for him. He leans back, avoiding her touch.

His tone grows colder. "It's over. It's *been* over, Aspen. I'm in love with Oakley, so go back to your fiancé."

My heart thuds at how easy that spewed from his mouth.

It's not real. It's not real. It's not real.

I remind myself over and over.

"I can't believe this." She looks like she's trying to cry, but nothing comes out. She wipes fake tears before storming away. I'm so confused about what the hell happened.

When we're alone, I turn to him. "Did she seriously try to get you back with me standing right next to you?" The nerve of this chick.

He leads me away from the crowd, and I can see his heart rate is elevated. "She told me she made a mistake and wanted me to give us another chance."

My face scrunches. "She's *engaged*."

"I know. She said she realized how much she still loved me. Even asked if I'd meet her later tonight outside the bakery."

"For what?"

He waggles his brows. "What do you think?"

I cover my mouth, shocked that she was going to cheat on Austin. What kind of person does that? A piece of shit, that's who. I hardly know her fiancé, but he seemed nice enough and obviously deserves way better.

"I told her the only reason she wants me is because I've moved on. She saw how happy we were and couldn't stand it. She kept pleading with me, and eventually, I told her she needed to stop begging like a dog because I wasn't giving in to her manipulation."

"I can't imagine she liked that comparison."

He shrugs. "It went over her head. She went on and on about how we're soulmates, and I'm the love of her life."

I hate that I wonder if she's right.

"Finn. If you're feeling any doubt that—"

"Hell no. I'm *not*." His voice softens. "Nothing she says or does will ever let me unsee who she is on the inside. She's an ugly, jealous person who wants to use me as a pawn in her game. Only I'm not playing this time. She threw a fit, begging me to take her back, all with her fiancé a hundred yards away talking to my aunt. I won't allow Aspen to bamboozle her way back into my life after she hurt me the way she did. If you'd asked me a few months ago if I'd have taken her back, I probably would've said yes. But now? There's no way."

"Why the change of heart?"

He smiles. "You helped me see I didn't deserve the way she treated me and that I deserved better."

"I did?"

"Yeah." He lets out a shaky breath. "You made me realize there's more to a relationship than being a human doormat. It's supposed to be fun and full of passion, and well, I never had any of that with her. I was going through the motions of having a girlfriend, but it always felt like something was missing. You made me realize a lot. I can safely say I was never in love with her, but rather, in love with the idea of being with someone. I made up this scenario in my head of having a family and raising our kids on the farm, and she never imagined that with me. Bottom line: Aspen and I aren't compatible and never were."

My heart slams against my chest, and I'm so proud of him for knowing his worth.

"You deserve true happiness and to be with someone who loves you for you. She obviously has no respect for relationships, and I'm glad you're not spending the rest of your life with a selfish twat."

He pulls me into a hug and inhales the scent of my shampoo. We stay like this for a moment before breaking apart. "If she hadn't broken up with me, we'd still be together. I would've never left her and would've kept trying to repair something that wasn't fixable. I owe you my life, Oakley."

His genuine tone has my heart breaking.

I wish I were that person to give him everything he deserves.

He takes my hand, and as we walk past the apple-tossing game, we hear high-pitched shouting. Finn and I turn right as Aspen stomps over to her fiancé, screaming at the top of her lungs. Most are watching the scene as she throws her hands up in the air and acts like a psycho. She's so angry and needs to take it out on someone.

"Poor guy. That could've been you."

"Happy to have dodged a bullet." He shakes his head. "Wanna get out of here?"

"Absolutely," I tell him, and we quickly make our way to the truck. The excitement of staying an extra week is overwhelming, but I'm excited about it.

"I need to change my flight before I forget."

When he pulls out of the parking lot, I call the airline and reschedule.

"Alright, it's official. You have a roommate for another week."

He grins. "Good, I'm glad you're not going anywhere yet."

"Weren't ready for me to leave?" I arch a brow.

"Honestly? No."

My stomach flutters with butterflies at his words.

He turns onto one of the gravel roads that leads to another part of the orchard, one I haven't visited yet.

When he parks, we get out of the truck.

"Where are we?" I look at the trees planted in a line and take in the fresh autumn air.

"You'll see." Finn grabs a large blanket from behind the seat and then leads me through the trees. Sunlight streams through the branches, and he reaches out and grabs my hand.

Leaves crunch as we walk, and when we come to a clearing, he fans out the blanket. Once he sits and pats the empty spot next to him, I kneel beside him.

"What are we doing here?"

"Enjoying the quiet."

I chuckle. "It is eerily quiet out here."

Lying back, I watch the clouds pass by, and Finn does the same.

"When I was a kid, I used to ride my bike out here," he breaks the silence.

"Alone?" I look at him and his gaze is already on mine.

Our mouths are inches apart, and I can smell the spicy scent of his bodywash drifting through the air.

"Yeah. But sometimes Sebastian and Jessa would come too. We were inseparable as kids. Growing up on the farm meant there was always an adventure."

"I can imagine. You're lucky to have had this."

We stare at each other for a moment, but then he leans in and cups my cheek before his mouth collides with mine.

He kisses me passionately, slow and sensual, a tenderness I'm not used to from him.

I fist his shirt as his free hand slides up mine. My nipples are

136

hard, and when he pinches one with his fingers, a jolt of electricity shoots through me.

We're breathless as we greedily devour each other's mouths. I straighten up and push Finn down on his back and straddle him. He's so hard, it creates friction between my legs as I rock against him.

Not waiting, I unzip his jeans, and his cock springs out of his boxers. I pull them down below his ass, ready to take what we both need. However, I want a taste of him first. I pump him a few times, loving how his hips buck with each stroke. His deep moans echo through the trees when I take him in my warm mouth.

"Fuck, Oakley," Finn growls, and I love how much control I have over him at this moment. He's putty in my hands as I suck and lick his balls, then trace the large vein that leads up to his crown.

"I need you so fucking bad."

I take off my boots but then hesitate as I grab the button of my jeans.

"It's only us out here. We're alone," he promises, and I appreciate that he knew what I was worried about.

I swallow hard, pushing down my jeans and panties, then step out of them. A chill sweeps down my body at how cold it is. Finn strokes himself a few times before I impale myself on his length. I unbutton my flannel, giving him full access to my breasts as I ride him.

We grind against each other in a quick rhythm, but when I look into his brown eyes, there's electricity between us that's different than before. Our movements grow slow, lips and tongues tenderly tasting each other. Soft pants escape me as Finn cups my ass, adding more friction as our hips meet.

"You're so goddamn sexy." He pulls one of my nipples into his mouth. "I could devour you for the rest of my life."

Our bodies move so perfectly together.

"*Yesyesyes*. Right there…" I moan, my head falling back as the buildup threatens to push me over the edge.

"Come all over my cock, Sunshine," Finn demands, digging his fingers into me harder.

"Mm…I'm so close."

Finn buries his face in my neck and sucks.

"I have a confession to make," he whispers in my ear.

Oh God, I'm about to topple over.

"I'm not pretending with you."

Those five words are all it takes to have me crying out.

"I have a confession of my own," I say once I catch my breath. "I stayed for you."

"Fuck. I hoped you would," he mutters as my pussy squeezes him again.

"I know it doesn't change our arrangement, but at least it gives us more time."

"I'll take whatever I can get with you, Oakley."

I increase my pace until he fills me with his warmth. We stay connected, and I lie on his chest with his arms wrapped around me. The sounds of leaves rustle around us as I listen to his steady heartbeat.

Ten minutes pass, and we both shiver, although my entire body feels like it's on fire.

"Guess I can mark fucking in an apple orchard off my bucket list." I smirk as I button my flannel.

"That was on your bucket list?" he asks as he zips his jeans.

"Nope, but it should've been."

Finn laughs, slapping my ass with his big palm. "Ready?"

"Not yet." I sit on the blanket and admire the incredible view.

"Okay, okay. I won't rush you *this* time," he says, joining me.

He sits behind me with his legs on either side of mine, wrapping me in his arms to keep me warm. I rest my head back on his chest and think about what's happening between us. It was unexpected but not entirely surprising. Things have been escalating, but I didn't anticipate him admitting that.

I swallow hard as he kisses my neck, enjoying the warmth of his lips. Though I know I'm risking a broken heart, it might be inevitable.

But it also might be worth it for this extra time together.

CHAPTER FOURTEEN
FINN

DAY 12

Waking up with Oakley in my arms is something I'm getting too comfortable doing. I have to constantly remind myself it's only temporary. It's a fling, an itch to scratch, someone I most definitely cannot fall in love with.

But that doesn't mean I won't enjoy her while I can.

We made plans to go into town today so she can take pictures and get an idea for the mayor's painting. But when she climbs on top of me naked, I no longer have the desire to rush us out the door.

"If you don't stop being so fucking perfect, I'm gonna put my baby inside you." I palm her tits as she grinds against me.

"Does an old man like you still have good swimmers?" she taunts, her messy hair flying everywhere.

I lower my hand to her backside and give her ass a hard smack. "Keep doubting me, and I'll prove it, you little temptress."

Wrapping an arm around her waist, I quickly flip us over

until I'm on top. Then I slide back inside her wet pussy and thrust hard.

"Sounds like you wanna keep me?" she teases, crossing her ankles behind my back as I drive in deeper.

"I think your smart-ass attitude would put me in a nursing home or an early grave. Not sure I wanna risk it."

She moans as I pinch her nipple, something I've learned she loves. The rougher, the better, but she also likes it when I'm sweet and gentle.

"Well, as soon as I'm gone, you can always go back to your hand."

I slide out and kneel between her thighs, my eyes narrowing on her. "Turn over, Oakley. You're gonna pay for that one."

She licks her lips, knowing damn well what she's doing. Seductively, she sticks out her ass and shakes it in my face. I give both ass cheeks hard slaps, watching as her pale skin turns red. With each smack, Oakley moans and begs for more.

I fist her hair and pull her head back slightly before crashing my mouth to hers. "We're about to break our record, Sunshine. You better hang on."

As I fuck her sweet cunt, driving her to the edge over and over, I realize she's crawled so far under my skin that I can't imagine being with anyone else.

And how once she's gone, there's going to be a bigger hole in my heart. Something I'm not ready to admit.

We spend the next hour tangled in bed, and by the time we crawl out, I'm covered in sweat. We're on a time crunch, so we shower together, but it leads to more fucking, and we end up running late anyway.

Since everyone already thinks we're dating, being close isn't a hardship. Not like it ever was. It's undeniable how perfectly she'd fit into this small-town lifestyle, but I keep those thoughts tucked deep inside. I'd never want to be the one to hold her back. There aren't too many commission jobs for her to pursue, and I understand how important her career is. California has a variety of opportunities for artists, and Vermont can't compete.

Not to mention, we're at two different places in our lives. I was ready to settle down, get married and start a family, and spend the rest of my life with one woman.

Oakley's only twenty-three and has her entire life ahead of her. As far as I know, she's not looking for some old guy to slow her down. The more I think about it, the more I realize that this being temporary is for the best. It gives us time to have some fun, then move on with our lives.

But if she wanted the same, I'd take back my *never getting married* mantra for her.

I park my truck in front of the diner and open Oakley's door. She grabs her sketch pad as she gets out, and we hold hands while strolling down the sidewalk. Since we skipped breakfast, we eat before walking around.

"Well, if it isn't the newest couple in Maplewood Falls," Greta singsongs as she hands us menus. "You two are adorable."

"Thanks," I say, flipping through the pages.

Everyone saw us at the centennial celebration, and Grandma announced it during the painting reveal, so there's no point denying it. Once Oakley's gone and the dust settles, they'll figure we broke up and will move on to some other gossip.

We place our order, and while we wait, she flips open to a blank page in her book. She moves the pencil from one side to another, and I admire her focus. Watching her work is mesmerizing because she makes it look easy.

"Here you go." Greta quickly returns with our drinks. "Food should be ready soon."

"Downtown during fall looks like it fell straight out of a Hallmark movie," Oakley tells me. She said the same thing when she first saw the inn, and I give her a look. "I know, I know. Every tourist says that."

I shrug.

"I wish I could paint a series of landscapes in Maplewood Falls. Every canvas would be vibrant with colors but also different."

"Too bad you won't be around to see it during the winter. It looks like a wonderland when there's a fresh coat of snow on the ground and the sun is high in the sky. The views are like nothing else. Ski tourists travel from all over to experience it."

"You're making me want to start a Christmas landscape." She playfully pouts. "I bet it's gorgeous here."

Greta delivers our plates and we make small talk while we eat. I chat about the festival and some of our traditions. Then she shares her plans as I promise to show her my favorite parts of downtown. Her excitement is contagious as she scribbles down her ideas.

Once we clear our plates and I pay, we make our way down the street.

"There are so many shops!" She sounds amazed. "The town I grew up in has mostly vacant buildings. After the recession, a lot of local businesses went under. It was sad to see," Oakley tells me.

"Nearly happened here too, but the mayor gave grants to help them stay afloat until the economy picked up."

"Wow, that's amazing. I can tell it's a tight-knit community here."

"Always has been," I admit. "Everyone knows everyone. We all have a lot of history here too. In fact, that candy store on the corner is where I had my first kiss." I point at Kari's Kandy Korner.

She laughs. "Do you remember her name?"

"Gabby Jameson. The owner's daughter."

Oakley's mouth drops open, and she bursts out laughing. "Scandalous."

"Oh, it was. At the time, I was dating her older sister, Madeline."

"Finn!" She smacks my chest. "You were *that* guy in high school?"

"No! To be fair, I was thirteen, and we were playing spin the bottle in the back office when Madeline was closing the shop."

"With a whole bunch of other kids or what?"

I scratch my cheek and purse my lips. "Uh, no. It was only Gabby and me…"

"Spin the bottle with two people?" She gives me a knowing look.

"Like I said, I was thirteen. And mostly horny."

She snorts as we move closer to the candy shop. "Small-town shenanigans. Guess I can't be that shocked. My friends and I used to have weed circles in the middle of fields."

"Jesus. Here I am getting scolded for a kiss and my fake girlfriend's a pothead."

Oakley rolls her eyes with a grin. "We lived very different small-town lives. Never mind I was a teenager only like five years ago. Don't act like it's *illegal*. Has tons of medicinal purposes!"

"Your parents didn't smell it on you?"

"Nah, I always carried a bottle of body spray and some breath mints. As long as I wasn't being escorted home by the sheriff, they let me do whatever I wanted. Mostly, I sketched and painted. When I was seventeen, I got a job at the local sub place. It smelled like feet and hadn't seen a health inspector in years, but the owner let me draw when it was slow."

"Got paid to draw before your job commissions, then?" I tease.

"Ha! Pretty much. I love my parents, but I didn't want to stay in my hometown. Way too small."

"And no opportunities for a brilliant artist like you," I confirm.

"Right. I couldn't wait to go to college. Now I'm twenty-three with a master's degree and have to figure out my living situation before I'm on the street. Living the dream!"

"What do you mean?" I ask as we cross the road. The movie theater is a block away, and I can't wait to show her the inside.

"I'd been living with a roommate for the past two years, and when the landlord announced the rent was increasing, she bailed and moved in with her boyfriend. Claimed it was cheaper. So my lease ends on November fifteenth, and I have to decide if I'll renew or not. Another option is finding a one-bedroom that I can afford," she tells me, and I can hear the stress in her voice.

"I had no idea you were facing that," I say, somewhat disappointed she hadn't mentioned it sooner.

"Honestly, I've been trying not to think about it. Tiernan told me to move to Florida and live with them until I found my own place. It would give me an opportunity to save some money and be there when the baby's born. And I could probably help out too. I'm not sure if it's a good idea, considering I have so many contacts in California, but if I can't find another apartment, I might not have a choice."

I almost suggest Vermont as an option, but I'm not stupid enough to think she'd pick me over her sister and niece. It would force us into a conversation I'm not sure we're ready to have.

"For what it's worth, I'm sorry you're dealing with all that. I can't even imagine what the cost of living is there."

"It's more expensive than Florida, that's for sure."

As we walk under the marquee with the times and latest releases displayed, I slow down and open the door to the theater. "I want you to see this."

"Whoa…" She glances around, taking it all in.

The smell of buttered popcorn fills the foyer as kids play on the old pinball machines in the game room.

"I worked here one summer before I decided I'd rather be outside in the orchards than deal with customers." I chuckle.

"This puts my hometown theater to shame." She spins around in awe.

"It was remodeled last year. The orchard held a fundraiser for the owner, who was undergoing cancer treatments. She was so focused on maintaining her health that this place was in disarray and on the verge of closing. Everyone in Maplewood Falls came together and rallied to bring it back to its original state. Not only did we raise enough to replace the carpet, seating, and concession equipment but all her medical bills were covered too. A bunch of local carpenters volunteered to fully remodel it, and since it reopened, it's been nonstop busy. She even hired ten new employees to help run it properly."

"Oh my gosh, that's amazing! I love hearing stories with happy endings like that."

"Yeah, what's even better is that her cancer is in remission."

We continue walking around, and Oakley's eyes light up when she spots a large mural that fills an entire wall.

"Incredible, isn't it?" I say behind her as she stares at the portraits interlaced with embellishments of bright colors.

"That's an understatement. I bet this was a dream piece to create. I can tell it was painted with care and respect. The shading is incredible." She slides her hand over the wall, feeling the layer of paint on the bricks.

"No one knew about it until we showed up at the grand opening. A Vermont artist heard about the theater and asked the owner if she could paint the faces of different business owners and leaders in the community. One day, this will be a part of our Maplewood Fall's history." I smile wide.

"It must've been rewarding to be part of something so special," she tells me. "Without the generosity of the orchard, this might've never happened. You should all be so proud to have helped make this place what it is today."

"My family does what they can and treats others how they'd

want to be treated. All the townspeople look out for each other. It's the way of life around here."

She beams, interlocking her fingers with mine. "I can see why everyone loves Maplewood Falls so much. I'm even more honored that Mayor Myers asked me. How lucky am I to get to paint something that will be admired for years?"

"We're the lucky ones, trust me." I wrap my other hand around our fingers and kiss her knuckles. Damn, I'm going to miss her when she's gone.

We make our way to the town square, and I hold her sketchbook as she takes pictures. People say hello and ask how we are as Oakley takes in the buildings and scenery. It's the perfect time of year for tourists to experience fall and enjoy the autumn foliage.

"I could paint at least twenty landscapes of this place. There's literally no part of Maplewood Falls that wouldn't be a great attraction. The architecture, cute shops, and street design are an artist's dream."

"Wait until you see it this weekend. Tents, booths, pumpkins galore. You'll be living inside your Hallmark movie."

She laughs. "Do you mind if we sit for a minute so I can sketch an idea?"

"Go ahead. I'll grab us some coffee from the café while you get started."

I lean in and brush my lips against hers for no other reason than because I want to. The lines between what's real and fake are so blurred I don't know where it started.

She positions herself on a bench that overlooks the town hall, and I head toward the café a few blocks away.

While I wait to place our orders, I pull out my phone and see an unread text from Levi.

LEVI

A little birdy told me that you owe Jessa $800!

I roll my eyes. Of course he's heard about that.

FINN

> She tricked me into betting her, and I stupidly took the bait. I'm gonna pay up the next time I see her. Just been busy.

LEVI

Ha! Oh, I also heard Austin and Aspen broke off their engagement. Who's even surprised?!

FINN

> We should invite Austin to hang out so we can make sure he never goes back to her. Help him find someone less crazy.

LEVI

Yeah, we should. He seemed cool. Not sure how he got caught up in Aspen's evil web.

FINN

> She has a way of doing that.

LEVI

So how's the "fake" girlfriend? I couldn't go more than ten feet at the celebration without hearing about the "perfect new couple!"

FINN

> Oh, shut up. And it's going fine. We're in town now so she can get some ideas for her next project.

LEVI

And she's still leaving after the festival?

FINN

> Yeah.

LEVI

And you're just going to let her?

FINN

She has a life to get back to. I won't be the one to make her choose between me and her dreams.

LEVI

Seems like she could get plenty of commissions here. She's got two already. Plus, there's a little thing called the internet.

FINN

It's not the same. She already told me she has tons of connections for jobs on the West Coast.

LEVI

And she can't fly there every once in a while for work? I mean, honestly...she could.

FINN

It's not only that. Our lives are in different places, too. I was ready to settle down, and she's just getting hers started.

Now that she's finished with grad school, she can focus on her career.

LEVI

I don't know, man. Sounds like lame excuses to me.

FINN

Too bad I didn't ask you.

LEVI

I'm your best friend, so you know I'm gonna give you my advice and opinions regardless.

FINN

Keep it to yourself for once.

LEVI

Ha! You're in way deeper than I thought.

I roll my eyes and pocket my phone, leaving him on read. Once I give Marcia my order, I wait at the pickup counter and think about what he said. Levi has a long dating history and still hasn't found *the one*, so I hardly consider him an expert.

But I can't deny there's truth to what he said.

I *am* in deep. *Too deep.*

And I'm fucking screwed.

Fifteen minutes pass, and I make my way back to Oakley, who's deep in thought. Her pencil moves quickly over the page, and I could watch her like this for hours. Her blond hair blows in the wind as she squints her eyes and nibbles on her bottom lip.

"Here ya go," I say quietly, not wanting to interrupt her concentration.

"Oh, thank you. Such a perfect fake boyfriend." She smiles wide over the rim of the cup before taking a sip.

"I'm well practiced," I reply.

"Wanna see what I have so far?" she asks, setting down her cup.

"Absolutely." I sit next to her.

She flips her book around to show me. "I'm thinking of painting downtown from this angle to capture the buildings on each side of the street and the cute little businesses here. Then once I see how everything is set up for the festival, I can add in all the small details of the decorations and booths."

"I love it," I tell her genuinely. "At the end of the block, a stage for the band will be set up, and the middle of the square will have lots of games, food, and activities for kids."

"That's gonna look so cool," she exclaims, closing her sketchbook. "I can't wait to go home and get started!"

I wrap my arm around her and pull her in for a kiss. "I can't wait to see what it looks like when you're finished. I'm sure it will be incredible."

CHAPTER FIFTEEN
OAKLEY

DAY 15

I'VE BEEN ANTICIPATING the festival all week and am so excited it's
here. Though each passing day means I'm closer to leaving, and
my time here is quickly coming to an end. Even if Finn were to
ask me to stay, I'd have to go back and figure out my apartment
situation. The more I try not to think about it, the more it will
slap me in the face when I get home.

For the past few days, I've been going on more Maplewood
Falls tours with Finn and working on the painting. I drew my
original sketch onto the canvas to get the foundation of the
buildings' layout beforehand. The sidewalk and road are
finished, and I'll fill in the festivities once I see them. Afterward,
I'll add in small details for each local business.

Needless to say, I'm feeling the pressure to make it perfect. I
have until Sunday to finish since I fly out on Tuesday.

"Levi's on his way over, then we'll go set up."

Last night, Finn told me Levi volunteered to help set up the
orchard's caramel apple booth. It's tradition, something they've
hosted each year since the beginning. Willa asked Levi, who

could never tell that woman no—since Paisley and Poppy are working at the bakery until five.

"I think it's sweet how Levi helps your family like that," I say, brushing my hair. "I only get updates from my childhood friends on social media. We're all so busy living different lives that it's hard to keep up with everyone."

"Yeah." There's sadness in his response.

I'm tempted to ask him what's wrong, but I know we don't have time for a deep conversation right now.

As I finish getting ready, Finn cleans the mess in the kitchen from the breakfast he made this morning. While he busies himself, I shoot my sister a quick text. After I told her about my extended stay, she asked if I'd made a decision about moving to Florida. I'm still undecided, and while I'd love to be closer to her, too much is going on in my head right now.

OAKLEY

We're leaving for the festival soon! I'll send pics later!

TIERNAN

Awesome, can't wait to see! Your painting is gonna turn out so good.

OAKLEY

I hope so! I don't want to let them down.

TIERNAN

You don't ever have to worry about that. You're so meticulous. I'm sure it will look like the real thing.

OAKLEY

Fingers crossed.

TIERNAN

How's everything else going? You and Finn still "pretending"?

OAKLEY

Until I leave, we are. It's easier.

TIERNAN

But?

OAKLEY

But what?

TIERNAN

You've been hooking up. So that's not really "pretending."

OAKLEY

We agreed that it was just a fling. Nothing serious.

TIERNAN

And that's still the case?

OAKLEY

As far as I know, yeah. We both know I'm leaving in a few days.

TIERNAN

Maybe you should tell him how you feel?

OAKLEY

What difference would it make?

TIERNAN

You never know. It could change your life. But at least you'd know and not have to wonder. Maybe he'll even offer to visit you in California.

OAKLEY

What'd be the point? He'll never permanently leave his family's farm. I doubt long distance would work.

And I wouldn't want to ever make him feel like he had to choose between me and his family or change who he is. The orchard means the world to him.

TIERNAN
I think you're both setting yourselves up for heartbreak.

OAKLEY
Sis, I'll be okay. I agreed to this arrangement, and I'm not going to make it more complicated by turning it into something it's not. His path is to work here and start a family.

TIERNAN
And would starting a family be so bad?

OAKLEY
Maybe when I'm old, like 30.

TIERNAN
Excuse me!

I burst out laughing because that always gets a rise out of her.

"Levi's here. You ready?" Finn pokes his head into the bathroom.

"Yep." I set my brush down, realizing I'll need to pack my shit soon. Right now, it's scattered all over his house.

"You look beautiful." He scans his eyes down my body before pulling me into his arms. "Not sure how I'm supposed to keep my hands off you all day."

Before I can respond, Levi stalks inside. "Well, you're gonna have to because I'm not third-wheeling."

I snort as Finn shakes his head.

"You better close your eyes because I'm about to kiss her."

"Ooh, a free ride *and* a show?"

Finn presses his mouth to mine, but I can't stop laughing. Every word Levi says agitates Finn more.

"We better go. I'll grab your stuff."

I cup his face and smack my lips to his. "Thanks."

"I'm not sitting bitch!" Levi calls out, opening the door and strutting out.

"Thank God," Finn shouts when I realize I'll be squished in the middle of them. I don't mind, though. Levi cracks me up as he helps Finn carry my art supplies to the truck. He's well over six feet and is built like a lumberjack yet is so bubbly. They're complete opposites that it's a wonder they're even friends.

"So, California, have you met any movie stars?" Levi asks, and I snort at his new nickname for me.

"A few but not super famous ones. You need to have connections to get invited to the big events. I pursue a lot of local and independent galleries, and not a lot of A-listers go to those. However, I interned at a highly reputable gallery in LA for a semester, and Trent Hugo came in with his entourage. It was *wild*."

"What was he looking for?" Levi asks as Finn drives us into town.

"From what I gathered, a gift for someone. He only said a few words to me, but once he found something he liked, he bought it and left." I shrug. "There have been a few others, like lingerie model, Meghan Bailey, but I don't get starstruck easily, so I stopped paying attention."

"I would literally shit myself if I saw a supermodel," Levi exclaims.

"Jesus Christ," Finn mutters, shaking his head as he focuses on the road.

I glance over at Finn. "Oh yeah. She's gorgeous. I'd put her on my free pass list."

Levi chuckles, slapping a hand on his leg. "Maybe we should take a trip to LA? Let Oakley give us the proper Cali tour."

"They'd eat you up and spit you out," I tease.

Finn's clenches his jaw, clearly not enjoying this conversation. "But I only go into the city when I have a commission or an interview. Normally, I'm at home painting and listening to audiobooks."

"Yeah, Finn told me you like very spicy books." Levi waggles his brows.

I playfully roll my eyes as Finn chuckles. "That's not how I described them," Finn says.

"He called them audio pornos," Levi admits.

"You laugh but don't knock it till you try it. I'll send you some recs. I bet you could learn a thing or two," I throw at Levi.

"Pfft."

"Levi's dated almost every girl in our graduating class," Finn tells me.

"Oh, so you're *that* type of guy. Got it."

"Dude." Levi scoffs. "Give her some context at least."

"What?" I ask, confused.

Finn glances over at me, smirking. "There were only eight girls total."

"*Eight*?"

"Yep."

"And thirty boys," Levi adds.

"Jesus. But still...you dated all eight?" I pop a brow.

"No, only five. I was related to the other three."

I burst out laughing. "Oh my God. What a small-town cliché."

Once we're closer to the festival, I see cars lined up along every road. Main Street is blocked off, and all the parking lots for the small businesses are full.

"I'll drop you and Levi off by the entrance so we don't have to lug your supplies around. Levi can help you set up while I find a spot a few blocks away."

"Okay, that works," I tell him as he slows and shifts the truck into park.

"Levi, be good," Finn warns.

Levi puts his hands up in surrender. "What'd I do?"

"I know you."

Levi chuckles as he grabs my stuff from the bed.

"Be right back." Finn pulls me in for a kiss. "And don't believe *anything* he says."

I snicker. "Well, now I'm curious."

Levi carries my easel while I carefully hold my canvas and paints. Mayor Myers secured a spot for me out of the way so I can work.

"He's crazy about you, ya know?" Levi speaks up once Finn drives off. "In case he hasn't told you, he's sad you're leaving."

I frown. "Yeah, I'm sad too."

"You can't stay?"

"My job kinda requires me to be close to a large city. I mean, I could technically live anywhere, but if I want to do this professionally with higher-paid commissions, I need to meet people in the industry. Be present at events."

"I bet you could open your own gallery," he points out. "Just a thought. But I know people would love to see your work and would purchase whatever you created."

"It's not a business model that makes a lot of money on its own. Most of them have sponsors or funding from universities. There's *a lot* of networking involved."

"Sounds like it's more complicated than just selling art."

"It is. A lot of shit goes on behind the scenes. Most times, we don't even meet the clients. They hire people to find what they want, and it's their job to track down the right pieces."

"That seems so weird. Art is personal and should be something you connect with before hanging it in your home."

I smile. "I agree. That's why I prefer to freelance. It allows me to work with the clients on a more intimate level. But it's not always easy finding work. I was lucky with this one and even luckier with Mayor Myers."

"Do you have jobs lined up when you get home?"

I frown as I set up and organize my paints by hue. "No. I was waiting until I had my apartment situation figured out first. I can do some small paid projects to cover expenses, but finding bigger jobs takes a while. I wish it was more stable, but hardly anything in the creative field is. I'm still new to the game, so I gotta do my time. Hopefully, one day, it will be more consistent. The Bennetts' project and this one will be great for my portfolio. I'm hoping to use it to get larger ones."

"Maybe you can do one for me? We have a gift shop in one of our barns, and a nice canvas of the farm would look great in there."

"You're just trying to find ways to keep me here, aren't you?" I taunt.

"I like seeing my best friend happy," he says somberly. "I haven't seen him smile and joke so much in months."

I swallow hard, pushing back the tears threatening to spill over. "Will you keep an eye on him after I leave?"

"Already planned on it."

I nod, silently thanking him for understanding. This will be hard on us both.

"What about you?" he asks.

"I'll bury myself in my work like I do with every other life inconvenience."

"Ahh, art therapy," he muses.

"Pretty much the coping mechanism I've used my whole life." I shrug.

Before he can respond, Finn appears. "Sorry it took me so long. I parked a mile away." He comes to my side and kisses my cheek. "Can I get you some coffee?"

"Sure, that'd be great." I look up at him and smile. "I'll

probably work on this for a while if you two wanna walk around."

"Alright, I'll deliver your caffeine first."

As Finn and Levi walk away, I do my best to gain control of my emotions. I need to focus on this piece. Since it's chilly outside, I can only paint for a couple of hours each day before my fingers freeze.

As promised, Finn returns with a hot latte. I thank him and tell him I'll shoot him a text when I'm done. It's hard to work with someone hovering over me, so it's best he enjoys himself while I paint.

Jessa and Sebastian are already at the caramel apple booth, and I wave when they spot me. They're across the street, but I almost have a bird's-eye view from where I'm standing. It's the perfect vantage point for the painting.

After two and a half hours, my fingers are like icicles. I have enough outlined and started that I can work on the rest back at Finn's.

"Wow, it looks so good already," he tells me as he carefully lifts it into the truck. We'll keep it there while we walk around the festival.

"Thanks! Where's Levi?"

"He found some friends and said he'd hitch a ride back with them."

"How was the booth?"

"Bombarded with kids."

I laugh. "The entire street is."

"So you wanna tell me what you and Levi talked about earlier?" Finn asks, taking my hand as we walk toward the downtown area.

"A whole lot of *none of your business*."

He glowers. "I know my best friend likes to talk."

"And we had a good conversation. That's all you need to know."

He sighs. "Great."

"What are you so worried about?"

"He has a big mouth."

"You think he shared embarrassing stories about you or something? Because if those exist, I need to hear them."

"Hell no."

I giggle. "Pull that stick outta your ass, and let's go have some fun."

"Excuse me?" he warns, yanking me into one of the alleys and pressing me against the exposed brick. "Are we back to that?"

"You tell me, Mr. Grumpy."

He buries his face in my neck, and his warm breath feels good against my cold skin. "I have to ask you something."

"Hmm?" My heart hammers as he keeps me waiting.

"Will you come to my family's dinner tonight?"

"What?" I wasn't expecting that at all.

He leans back to meet my confused eyes. "My grandparents are hosting a big get-together tonight and demanded I invite you. You don't have to, so don't feel obligated. It's going to be a lot, and I know how they can be sometimes. I can make up an excuse that you're working or too tired, if you prefer."

I give him a puzzled look. "Do you not want me to?"

"Of course I do, but they'll ask a ton of questions. I didn't want to put any more pressure on you."

"I think I can handle them." I wrap my arms around his neck. "I survived Levi's inquisition, so I think I'm prepared for anything at this point."

"God," he grumbles, leaning his forehead against mine. "I knew he would."

Smirking, I cup his face. "Your friends and family love you. I don't mind the questions. I'm good at winging it." I shrug proudly.

"Not sure if I should be proud or scared of that."

I laugh. "Come on, fake boyfriend. Let's parade our relationship all over Maplewood Falls, then have dinner with your parents."

This day has been one of the most fun I've had in months. After I warmed up, we walked all through town, greeted everyone who smiled our way, and tried all the sweets.

At five, we drove back to Finn's to get ready to go to his grandparents. He dressed in nice black slacks, and I wore the same dress Jessa let me borrow.

As soon as I'm ready, Finn takes my hand and kisses me. "I can't wait to peel this off you later."

"Mm...no dirty talk before dinner, or I won't be able to think about anything else."

He grins, brushing a thumb over my cheek. "Ready to do this?"

"Yep. Let's go."

I've met most of Finn's immediate family, but Willa and James invited over their other siblings, who brought their kids. The house is jam-packed, and there's so much going on, I can hardly keep up.

Everyone I've met has been kind—with the exception of Finn's jealous ex—and it's honestly a nice change from what I'm used to. Since I have no family in California, I never get to experience this. It's something I'll miss when I'm gone.

"Did you have fun at the festival?" Willa asks as she finds me after dessert.

"Oh, it was incredible. I've never experienced anything like it."

"I'm glad to hear it. Trick-or-treating is a fun time too. You'll have to make sure to go down there on Monday."

"Oh, I will. That's when I'm presenting the painting for the town hall."

"I bet everyone loves it."

The self-doubt and pressure never go away, no matter how much experience I have, and this time is no different. "Thanks, I hope so."

"It's a shame you have to leave so soon."

I frown. "I know. I've loved being here. I can't thank you enough for the opportunity."

"I know about your little…*arrangement*," Willa whispers.

"What do you mean?"

"With my grandson."

I swallow hard. "Oh."

"I may be getting older, but I see fine."

"I still don't understand."

"He's in love with you, Oakley. I know you two were pretending to date."

"You did?"

"Of course. I'm aware it happened because his ex was here, but I also know you can't fake real feelings."

"I-I'm not sure about that."

She pats my shoulder. "Trust me, dear. He's smitten with you."

Something more *is* brewing between us, but we agreed to make the most of our time together until I had to leave. That's all it could be.

"I very much feel the same," I admit. "Maybe it's a *right person, wrong time* kind of situation."

"I know you live far away, but I hope you'll at least come back to visit. You're basically a part of our family now."

"I hope so too," I tell her honestly, though I'm not sure that'll be possible. She shoots me a wink, and we join everyone in the living room.

After an hour of chatting, Finn and I leave. After my text conversation with my sister this morning, and then Levi, and now his grandmother, my head is spinning. I hate that everyone knows I'll be the reason for his heartbreak.

It won't be easy for me, either. But what choice do I have?

"You okay?" Finn glances over at me as he drives us to his house.

"Can you pull over?" I ask.

We're only a few minutes away, but this can't wait.

"Sure. Is everything okay?"

As soon as he puts the truck in park, I climb over and straddle him. He quickly moves his seat back to give us more room.

I crash my lips to his, he braces my hips, and together we rock against each other.

"Pull your pants down," I order, lifting my skirt as he does.

Then he moves my panties to the side and lines up our centers before I impale myself on him. We moan in unison as we frantically make love.

I can't get enough and can already feel him slipping away. I'm going to miss him more than I want to admit.

"Fuck, that was hot," he murmurs after we come down from our highs.

"We steamed up the windows." I laugh as I shimmy my dress down and sit next to him.

He waggles his brows. "Now, let's go home and steam up the shower."

I snort at his joke. "Lead the way, Country Boy."

CHAPTER SIXTEEN

FINN

DAY 17

TOMORROW IS the last day of the harvest festival, and Oakley has been painting her ass off, trying to finish in time. After she worked on it for a couple of hours this morning, we strolled through the pumpkin patch.

Once it got too crowded, we grabbed coffee, then left. Oakley's deadline is looming, and all finishing touches have to be added so it can dry.

When we walk into my house, she immediately grabs her brushes and gets to work.

"Am I bothering you?" I ask, standing behind her and admiring her delicate brushstrokes.

"No, not at all. You're the only person I don't mind watching," she admits, looking over her shoulder. "Grab a seat if you want. I'm just adding a few tiny details."

"Wish I could, but I have some work to do today."

She smiles. "I understand. You know where I'll be."

It's taken us all week to clean up after the centennial celebration. The stage had to be torn down, and all the picnic

tables, chairs, and hay bales had to be put away. The main
storage barn is a disaster, and I promised my grandfather I'd
have it organized before Monday—which is tomorrow. I've been
procrastinating, but I'm a man of my word.

When I arrive, I immediately start moving things around to
make room to walk. I appreciate the task because it keeps my
mind busy. Oakley's leaving on Tuesday, something I've been
dreading for too long. And I know there won't be anyone who
can convince her to stay, not even me.

Spending time with her this past week has been incredible,
but I feel like we've just gotten started. When she wasn't
working, we hung out, and when she was, she'd let me watch
her paint while we chatted.

I'm completely and utterly entranced by her. Even though
I'm older, she's the brilliant one who teaches me more than I
could ever teach her.

We haven't talked about what will happen when she leaves—
it's the elephant in the room that we've avoided. I'm not sure
what I'd even say anyway.

Stay here?

Don't get on that plane?

Sounds ridiculous.

"What's up?" I hear a voice say from behind and nearly jump
out of my skin.

"Fuck," I cuss at my cousin Sebastian. "How about you *not*
give me a heart attack?"

"Too jumpy for my liking," he says with a chuckle. "Have
some more chairs for ya."

He turns and points at his truck. Metal chairs are
haphazardly stacked, and I'm uncertain how he made it here
without losing some. Wouldn't be surprised if I found a few on
the side of the road.

"Great," I deadpan. "Lend me a hand, will ya?"

Sebastian and I take several trips and set them next to the others that need to be put into the storage loft.

"So what's been going on?" he asks.

"Nothing."

He gives me an incredulous look. "After seeing you at dinner together, I gotta ask. Are you two hooking up?"

"None of your damn business."

He shakes his head, chuckling.

"What?" I ask.

"It's obvious you *are*. I heard Aspen begged you for a second chance and then broke up with her fiancé."

"News travels fast around here," I say. Makes me thankful Oakley was here to rescue me from making that mistake twice. Who knows what would've happened.

He pats me on the shoulder. "Well, guess I better get going and leave you to it."

I chuckle. "Ya bored? Want to help me put all this shit up?"

"I'm good. Have fun with that." Sebastian laughs as he heads to his truck. He honks twice and then waves as he drives off.

Hours pass, and I'm already sore from the constant lifting. After a quick break, I neatly stack the tables in the loft next to the chairs. They aren't heavy, but the repetitive motions are exhausting. I push through it because I want to spend all tomorrow with Oakley—something I'll need to chat with my grandmother about.

Before I go home, I stop at my grandparents' house. As soon as I walk in, the smell of fresh-baked cookies hits me.

"Grandma? Grandpa?" I holler.

"In here, dear!"

When I enter the kitchen, Grandpa's rinsing dishes in the sink as Grandma reads the Sunday paper at the table. They still refuse to get their news electronically.

I snag a few cookies that are still warm. Making myself at

home, I open the fridge and pour a glass of milk, then Grandma invites me to join her at the table.

"So what's on your mind?" she asks as I sit across from her.

"I'd like to take tomorrow off for Oakley's painting presentation and spend some time with her before she leaves on Tuesday."

"Aw." Grandma beams, and I resist the urge to roll my eyes.

Grandpa looks at me over his shoulder and grins.

"Don't you start too."

"I said nothing," he muses.

"Consider it done," Grandma tells me. "She's a nice girl. Going to be very sad to see her go."

"Yeah," I mutter, not wanting to talk about it.

"Will she come back and visit?" she asks with a twinkle in her eye.

"Yeah, we'll try the long-distance thing and see how it goes."

I hate lying, but I have to keep up the act until Oakley's gone. Although, my grandma looks at me like she knows something I don't. Either way, I ignore it.

"That's nice. I hope it works out. You two seem very happy," Grandma says, but her eyes don't leave mine.

"Thanks."

Before she can continue, I thank them for the cookies and see myself out.

I make it home in record time, and when I enter, Oakley's sitting on the couch with her phone. She's wearing nothing but a towel.

I grin and plop down next to her. "Did you finish?"

"Yep. Check it out." She stands and leads me over to the canvas.

My eyes scan over the town square decorated for the harvest festival, and I'm amazed by how she continually captures all the small and important details.

"Oakley," I say, pulling her close. "You're so talented."

"Thank you," she says. "I'm happy with it. The colors complement each other so well, but then again, I painted it just as it was. Vermont is beautiful."

"The townspeople are going to lose their shit over this. Mayor Myers might not let you leave without painting ten more." I look closer and see the back of a couple holding hands as they stroll down the street. "Is that *us*?"

"Yes." She chuckles. "How'd you know?"

"The flannel gave it away," I admit. "And your hair."

"It's our little secret." Her gaze lingers on my lips.

"I love it," I say, pressing my mouth to hers. "I thought we'd do something fun tonight."

"Oh, I love the sound of that now that I don't have the weight of the project on my shoulders."

I inhale the sweetness of her bodywash and am tempted to lick her from head to toe.

"Are you hungry?"

"Starving."

"That's all I needed to hear." I flash her a wink, then make my way to the kitchen. Digging in the freezer, I grab the homemade lasagna my mom made a few weeks ago and pop it into the oven.

As Oakley gets dressed in a hoodie and leggings, I let her know I'm stepping outside. She follows me as I grab large pieces of wood from the stack on the side of my house, then chop them into smaller pieces.

"I'm enjoying the lumberjack vibes. My only regret is that I didn't grab my phone."

"It's not too late." I lift a brow, then swing the handle over my shoulder and smash the blade on the wood. It cracks and splits.

Oakley runs inside and returns with her phone. She smirks as she takes pictures and videos while making me laugh at her vocal antics. It brings me joy knowing she'll look at them later.

Once I have plenty of logs and have rounded up some kindling, I carry them over to the firepit.

I move the two patio chairs close to one another. It's already in the lower forties, and I wouldn't be surprised if we got our first snowfall soon.

"This view…" She sighs happily, and I turn and look over my shoulder at the rolling hills. The sun hangs lazily in the distance, and everything that surrounds us is splashed in burnt yellow.

"It's the best time of the day to take pictures. Golden hour— when everything is covered in a warm hue. I'd consider it one of my favorite times of day, especially during fall."

Her eyes meet mine. "This time, I was talking about you."

I smirk and move closer. "Maybe I can be the subject of your next painting? You do portraits?"

Oakley chuckles. "I've not done many. But I'd consider it if you'd be willing to pose for hours…*while naked*." She barely gets the words out before she bursts into laughter.

"Sure, but I doubt you'd be able to focus." I flash her a smug grin.

"You're right. I'd get no painting done. Just a lot of dicking down."

I snort.

The timer on the oven blares, so we go inside to eat. The hearty aromas waft through the air. I pull out the pan and place it on top of the oven. While the lasagna slightly cools, I pop in some garlic bread.

As I do this, Oakley grabs some plates, and I love how she moves around my place like it's her own. It basically has been.

"Want to eat outside?" I ask once the bread is done.

"Yeah, I'd like that if we can start the fire first."

I grab a lighter as she carries our plates. Once it's lit, we sit and eat.

"This is amazing." She moans around a mouthful. "Good

food and company. Can't tell you the last time I've done anything like this."

"When I was remodeling this place, installing this pit was one of the first things I did before moving in. Levi and I have spent many nights shooting the shit out here. But I've also enjoyed it plenty of times alone. It's quiet and peaceful."

She wipes her mouth with her napkin. "I think pure silence is one of the things I'll miss the most. I'd never get that living in my apartment. If sirens aren't blaring, it's my loud-ass neighbors."

"I couldn't handle that. However, it's not always like this, though. In the summer, the crickets are loud as hell."

After we finish eating and put our dishes in the sink, I join Oakley with a box of graham crackers, chocolate bars, and marshmallows.

"S'mores?" Her eyes light up with excitement as she scoots to the edge of her chair.

"Hope you saved room." I hand her a retractable roasting stick that automatically spins when a button is pushed.

"This is cheating." She watches the two prongs at the end twirl in a circle.

I make a face, and she giggles. "Then don't press the button and do it the old-fashioned way. I prefer mine to be roasted evenly."

"A s'more connoisseur. Honestly, that's a good thing. Burning it to a crisp creates carcinogens, which aren't healthy."

I burst into laughter. "You and your random facts."

"Everyone knows that, right?"

"No."

She shrugs. "I was in Girl Scouts for like two weeks when I was seven, and my mom quickly realized outdoorsy things weren't for me. Same with sports. Basically, if you needed a smart kid who could draw and paint, I was your girl. Everything else, forget it. Funny enough, as an adult, not much has changed."

"At least she knew your strengths and encouraged that. Otherwise, we might've never met." I shoot her a wink.

"That's very true. I'll have to thank her for that the next time we chat," Oakley says as she carefully places a marshmallow on the end of the stick.

"You have to prepare your cracker and chocolate before you start roasting. Otherwise, it's a sticky disaster."

She chuckles. "I'm following your lead, Country Boy. Show me how it's done."

I hand her all the supplies and do the same for myself. We place our sticks in the fire and let them do the work.

"If there was a contest for marshmallow roasting, you'd win." She states it as a fact.

"You pull it out when it's lightly toasted like this." I show her and then walk her through the process of building the perfect s'more.

I use the top of the graham cracker to smoosh the gooey marshmallow onto the chocolate and pull out the stick, then set it to the side. She follows my lead, then takes her first bite. When she moans, my cock springs to life.

"This is *orgasmic*."

I chuckle as I eat mine.

"Sticky, but I don't mind that," she says, placing her finger in her mouth and sucking it off. Now she's teasing me.

After we've finished eating, I hold her as she sits on my lap. We don't say much as we watch the flames lick and devour the remaining wood. As the sun sets, the temperature drops, and Oakley shivers.

"Let's go inside," I mutter, and she happily leads the way.

Oakley sits on the couch. Reaching for the remote, she flicks on the TV. I go to the kitchen and dig around in the fridge.

"Want some cider?" I ask.

"Hell yeah!"

When I hand hers over, she studies the logo and reads the words on the back of the can. "This is from the distillery?"

"Yep. It's my favorite flavor, too. Sour apple."

She takes a sip, and her eyes widen. "Whoa. This stuff is *dangerous.*"

"Very. It sneaks up on ya because it's sweet and smooth but has a high alcohol content. Took years to perfect."

She takes another sip. "How many do you have left?"

"More than you can handle in one night."

"We'll see about that. Tonight, I'm celebrating finishing that painting and getting to show the mayor tomorrow."

She lifts her drink, and we cheers.

"Now that's something I can drink to."

She chugs it down, and I lift my brows when she crunches the aluminum with her hand, then burps.

"What? I'm from Nebraska. All we had were pot circles and booze for entertainment, remember? So you better try to keep up, old man." She grabs my drink and happily claims it as her own.

"It's gonna be like that, huh?"

She nods, and I make my way to the fridge and pick up the box that's over half full. I set it on the coffee table, and she gives me an approving look.

"Better catch up. I'm already halfway into this one."

"Well, shit." I crack a new one open and down it.

"Ever shotgunned one of these?" she asks.

"Of course, but it's been over a decade. Also, don't get too cocky. This cider will kick your ass. Keep drinking like a fish, and I'm gonna have to carry you to bed."

"Thankfully, you're big and strong." She stands and pulls me up with her. "Let's do one."

I pull the truck keys from my pocket and hand them to her. "After you."

Like a pro, Oakley turns the can sideways and slams the key into it. Liquid slightly sprays, but she pops the tab and drinks it down. I watch her finish it in a couple of gulps, and my eyes widen.

"*Damn, woman.* Maybe *I am* too old for this." I chuckle.

She smirks as she releases another burp. "Your turn."

I mimic her actions, but I don't spill a drop.

Oakley's brows rise as if she's impressed. "Nice job."

Then she turns her attention toward the TV. "Oh my gosh. *Halloweentown* is on. This was one of my favorite movies as a kid!"

"I've never seen it."

Her mouth falls open, and she gasps. "Never? *How?*"

"Maybe bits and pieces, but never all the way through. Guess I was too *old* for it." I shrug.

"That ends tonight. We're about to play a *Halloweentown* drinking game unless you're too chicken."

"Pfft." I open another can. "Tell me the rules so I can destroy you."

"Now who's getting cocky?"

"It's reality, babe. I'm larger and can hold my booze better. It's all about anatomy with drinking."

Her head falls back on her shoulders as she laughs. "We'll see about that. Now, the rules are simple. Anytime someone says Halloween—even when talking about the town—or if they try to do magic, if someone is in costume, or the word human is said, you take a sip."

"Sounds easy enough. Though I have a feeling that's going to be like every other word."

"Take two sips if Sophie uses her intuition or if someone says witch or warlock. Oh, and when Marnie complains."

"Jesus. Anything else?"

"Nope. For now."

In the first twenty minutes of the movie, we've opened

several cans each. At some point, Oakley pauses it for a bathroom break. She stands and walks as if she hasn't drunk a drop.

"Color me impressed," I say when she returns, and instead of unpausing it, she places a hand on her hip.

"Told you I could hold my booze."

I can't help but laugh. She lifts a brow but instead of sitting beside me, she straddles my lap. Immediately, she cups my cheeks, and our lips magnetize to one another. I'm hard as hell for her already. She rocks her hips, knowing I want her just as bad, then grabs my shirt with her fists.

"Take me, Finn. All of me."

I crash my mouth to hers. She undoes my jeans and frees me, then stands and slides her shorts and panties down.

Oakley takes all of me in with one swift movement, and I cup my hands under her ass. With my feet planted on the floor, I lift my hips, slamming up into her.

"God, yes," she whisper-hisses as she removes her shirt. I take one of her nipples into my mouth as I pinch the other.

We fuck hard and fast, greedily racing toward the edge.

At this moment, nothing matters but her.

I selfishly wish I could freeze time so we could stay like this forever. When Oakley Benson entered my life, I couldn't wait for her to leave. Now I'm dreading the moment she does.

Our movements slow, and I can tell she's close. I kiss her and tell her how gorgeous she is before she completely loses herself. I can't hold back any longer and spill inside her. She leans her forehead against mine, and I wrap my arms around her, holding her tight.

My heart gallops as we catch our breaths and come back down to reality. She kisses me one more time, and her lips linger a little longer than usual.

After we've cleaned up, Oakley yawns, and I know she's beyond exhausted.

"Let's go to bed." I reach for the remote and turn off the TV.

She stands, and I grab her hand, then lead her upstairs. I'm honestly shocked she's not hovering over a toilet right now.

Oakley slides under the comforter in only her panties, and I smile, loving it when she sleeps practically naked. I join her in only my boxers.

As I roll over and spoon her, I whisper, "Guess what?"

Oakley hums in response.

"I've still never seen *Halloweentown* from beginning to end."

"Dammit," she mumbles with a laugh.

"Don't worry, I've never seen *Elf* all the way through either," I admit.

"What am I gonna do with you, Finn? Those are classic holiday movies."

I hold her a little tighter. "Maybe one day we can watch them together."

"Deal," she whispers right before we drift off to sleep. And I know deep down that'll probably never happen.

CHAPTER SEVENTEEN

OAKLEY

DAY 19

I WAKE up with a heaviness in my heart, and I'm full of dread as this is the day I leave for good. Yesterday, I experienced one of the best Halloweens I've had as an adult. I was especially glad I woke up without a hangover, considering how much cider I had.

The Maplewood Falls festival was incredible, and the reaction from the crowd when my painting was presented was even better. When everyone applauded and gushed over it, I nearly burst into tears but somehow kept it together. Afterward, the city council and mayor thanked me so many times, I lost count. I made Finn promise he'd send me a picture once it was hung in the town hall.

Although Finn and I didn't dress up, the kids in costume were adorable. Watching the winner of the pumpkin-carving contest accept their trophy was one of the highlights. Hundreds were carved and set out for people to vote on as well as a panel of judges. All I have to say is Vermont takes their pumpkin carving very seriously, and I don't know how half of these designs were humanly possible.

Most importantly, I spent the day with Finn. We held hands and kissed, and being together felt right. I ate so many caramel apples, my stomach hurt, but I didn't care. That evening, Finn took me around the farm so I could say goodbye to everyone. Hugging his grandma was the hardest.

Once we got home, we made love and held each other until we fell asleep.

However, all of that is making today that much harder.

After we wake up and devour each other—which felt more like a final goodbye than a good morning—Finn kisses the softness of my neck as he holds me. I try to take in every second with him and cherish every moment we have left. I breathe in his musky scent, trying to remember the softness of his sheets and comforter, and how warm his body feels pressed against mine while I sleep.

We lie in each other's arms until we're forced to get up and get dressed. Reality calls, and I can't miss my flight. He wouldn't let me anyway.

Finn puts my luggage in the truck as I make us some coffee. I try to keep the mood light, but it's obvious neither of us is enthusiastic about my departure. A black cloud floats over us, and I'm sure it'll follow me back to California.

I've avoided thinking about what I'd say and do when our fling ended. Now, it feels like it snuck up and is smothering me.

"Thank you," Finn says when I offer him his to-go mug. He wraps his strong arms around my waist and slides his tongue inside my mouth.

I moan against him, wishing things could be different.

"Welcome." I take a sip of mine, and it nearly burns the roof of my mouth.

"We should get going," he reminds me as if he knows I'm stalling.

"Yeah, guess so." I breathe out slowly.

"I'll get all your supplies shipped this week, so you should have them in a few days." He gives me a sad smile.

I look at the boxes stacked by his front door. "One more task from this pain in the ass, and you're in the clear."

"Ha! Loading them might break my old back," he says, and I laugh at him being able to make a joke at his own expense.

He locks up and grabs my hand as we move to the truck. Quickly, he opens my door, and I hop inside. I yawn at how early it is. The sun hasn't even come out, so fog hovers above the road.

"So how would one go about ordering some of that cider?"

"On the website," he explains. "You liked it, huh?"

"Hell yeah. Might have to make it a tradition after I finish up a project," I offer.

"Sounds like a good tradition," he tells me. We're making small talk about nothing because I don't know what to say after the time we've spent together. I didn't expect it to hurt like this.

When he turns onto the main road, I clear my throat. "Have you decided what you'll tell everyone when they ask about us?"

He nods. "I'm gonna tell them that we broke up. Make up some excuse that neither of us wanted to do the long-distance thing and that you couldn't uproot your life to move here."

"Sounds reasonable," I tell him and glance out the window. "I'm sure they'll all forget about me once you start dating someone else."

He laughs. "Oh, sure. Because handfuls of women are waiting on the sidelines to swoop in once you leave."

I shrug. "Hey, you never know."

Finn reaches over and grabs my hand. "Oakley, no one is going to forget you. Especially not me. I had a lot of fun."

"Yeah, I did too." I'm sure he can hear the sadness in my voice. But we do what we do best and avoid discussing it.

Soon, the airport appears in the distance, and I swallow hard. I try to hold in my emotions, not wanting to deal with how I feel right now. Finn owes me nothing and has already given me every part of him while I was here. Especially a glimpse into a life I don't currently have.

Finn slowly stops and looks at me once he's parked.

"I'm going to miss you," I tell him.

"I'm going to miss you too, Sunshine. Probably won't sleep for weeks after you leave. I'm so used to your ass rubbing on me."

I chuckle to prevent myself from tearing up. "Why did we do this to ourselves?"

"We couldn't stay away from each other even through the arguing."

I meet his heated gaze and nod.

"Do you regret it?" he asks.

"Never," I admit without pause. "I'd do this a million times over, even knowing I had to leave at the end, if it meant meeting and spending time with you. But I still wish things could be different, Finn."

His mouth tilts up into a sad smile as he leans toward me and cups my face. "I feel the same. You changed me, and I'm forever grateful to have met you. I know you'll continue to do amazing things with your art, Oakley. It touches so many lives, and you should be proud of that."

As soon as I feel the tears spill, I go to wipe my cheeks, but he catches them before I can. There are a million things I wish I could say, but nothing would change our situation. This is what we agreed to.

My heart feels lodged in my throat as blood rushes through me. It's cold outside, but my entire body feels as if it's on fire and nothing in the world could extinguish it. The electrical current that's always buzzed between us nearly electrocutes me as my feet touch the pavement.

He gets out as well and grabs my two suitcases and duffel bag from the back.

"Let me walk you in," he offers, his biceps flexing from the weight. I can't help but admire how good he always looks.

With his free hand, he grabs mine, and I know this is the final time we'll do this. I walk closer to him and squeeze his fingers as I carry my other bag.

After I've checked my two large bags, I follow him into the secluded area before the security line. When we stop, Finn meets my eyes.

"Text me when you get home so I know you made it safely."

"I will," I tell him, my heart hammering with sadness.

He tangles his fingers in my hair, gripping my head and pulling me closer. "Can I kiss you goodbye?"

"You better."

He brushes his mouth over mine, soft and gentle at first before sliding his tongue between my parted lips. The kiss turns deeper as I fist his shirt, tugging him impossibly closer. People walk around us as we fuck each other's mouths, but I don't care. I selfishly want every last millisecond with him.

When we pull away, our breathing is ragged with swollen lips.

He places his palm on my cheek and rubs the pad of his thumb against my face. I lean into him, staring into his chestnut-brown eyes. "I hope everything works out with your apartment."

"Thanks, me too."

Then he leans in and kisses my forehead, his lips lingering a second longer than usual. I suck in a deep breath and let it out, feeling the tears threatening to spill again.

"Bye, Mr. Grumpy."

"See ya, Sunshine." He gently smiles and watches until I walk toward the long line.

Once I've passed security, I try to stop my heart from racing. The tears welling in the corner of my eyes won't fall, and it makes them burn. This fucking hurts more than I ever expected it would.

Once I've found my gate, I go to the bathroom and find a stall, then give myself permission to cry. I quietly sob in my hands, replaying all the memories we shared, knowing this is how it *has* to be. Still, I hate that it feels like I'll never see him again.

"Are you okay?" I hear a woman ask from the other side.

"Yeah," I tell her, sniffling. I grab some toilet paper and blow my nose, trying to compose myself as heartbreak washes over me. A fling shouldn't feel like this, like I'm mourning a soulmate I was never meant to meet.

Once I've cried all the tears, I wait for my flight by the large windows. A few planes land as others move toward the main runway, but I'm numb as images of Finn's final expression linger in my mind. I hope Levi keeps an eye on him as promised.

What is Finn thinking right now? Is he feeling just as shitty as me?

Needing a distraction from my thoughts, I pull my phone from my pocket and text Tiernan. She's always been able to make me laugh or take my mind off things.

OAKLEY

Wanted to let you know I'm at the airport.

That's all I can type. I can't seem to pull words from my tangled web of emotions and explain the turmoil I'm experiencing.

TIERNAN

Great! How'd leaving the farm go?

OAKLEY

It was a goodbye. How do you think it went?

It's a rude response, but I don't know what she expects me to say. *Great?*

It wasn't. It was awful.

My phone rings and it takes every bit of strength I have to answer because I don't feel like talking.

"Are you okay?" my sister asks in the tone she uses when she's handling me with care.

"No," I admit. "I feel sick and my heart hurts."

"Lovesick?" she asks, and I don't answer. "Are you sure you're not pregnant?"

She knew that would make me speak up. "No, I'm anxious and emotional. I'm going to miss Finn and his family. Plus, all the shit I need to take care of when I get home is weighing on me, and I'm already overwhelmed by it. My life is dangling by a thread and about to unravel all at once."

"Talk me through it. Save yourself a call with a therapist," she offers.

I chuckle, even if I want to sulk. "I don't know what I want. My career is the most important thing in my life, but I also know Finn and I connected on a deep level that I've never experienced with anyone before. He made several comments about how our lives are in two different places and why it made sense that we were only together while I was there. He's probably right about that, but it still doesn't make it easy."

"Did you talk to him about any of this?"

"No. It'd only make it harder to confess our feelings when we can't be together. There are too many obstacles keeping us apart. Neither of us seems to be a fan of long distance, and if neither of us will move away from our homes to be with the other, what's the point?"

"Hmm. Well, we both know I'm not the best when it comes to relationships, so take my advice with a grain of salt. But I truly believe that if something is meant to be, it'll find a way. Remove the outside bullshit and ask yourself if you'll regret not being with him."

"I don't know. It was supposed to be a fling. But it felt like… *more*."

"If it feels like a breakup, it *wasn't* a fling."

Her words stab me directly in the heart, and although she's right, I'm too stubborn to admit it. How can it be a breakup when we both knew it would end when I left?

"Now you do sound like a therapist."

"I'm giving you a different perspective from the outside. Only you know how you truly feel and what you and Finn experienced. Regardless of your *fling*, you were hired for a great commission job, received some nice exposure online, built your portfolio, and met a bunch of new people. If you weren't sad about leaving after having an amazing new experience, I'd be worried that you were a psycho with no emotions," she tells me.

I can hear the smile in her voice. My sister is logical and thinks differently than I do, so I always appreciate her insight.

"You're right about that. It was an experience of a lifetime. Maybe I need some good quality sleep. It's been a long time since I've been in my own bed, and on top of all that, I'm mentally exhausted."

"That's very true. You have a lot of decisions to make. You just completed two huge projects back-to-back that took a lot of mental and physical work. Gotta give yourself some grace, Oakley."

"Yes, *mother*," I say with love, knowing she's going to be an amazing parent with good advice. My niece will be so lucky to have Tiernan as her mom.

"Go home and rest for a few days, then see how you feel once you're not exhausted. Promise me, okay?"

"I promise."

Tiernan chuckles. "You know they say distance makes the heart grow fonder. And if it doesn't, no big deal. You're young, beautiful, and talented, so there's no rush on who you'll spend forever with."

"Before you called me, I broke down in the bathroom. I've never done that before." I laugh at myself. "But I'm already starting to feel a lot better after chatting with you and letting it all out."

"Good. Cheer up because it's all going to work out. It always does. Try to remember to take baby steps so you don't overwhelm yourself. I know you, Oakley. You go, go, go nonstop. You always have."

"I can't help it, but I'll try. Thanks for talking me off the ledge."

"Of course. What are big sisters for?"

I chuckle. "Conversations like this."

After I'm much calmer, we talk about the baby and the surf shop. I'm happy to have the distraction.

Once it's time to board my flight, I let her know I have to go.

"Thank you again," I graciously say. "Seriously."

"You're welcome, sis. Text me when you get home, okay?"

"I will. Love you!"

"Love you, too."

I board the plane, and as we lift off into the air, I watch the autumn colors disappear below the clouds. A few tears roll down my cheeks, and I wipe them away before closing the window blind.

I have no idea what the future holds, but my heart will forever be in Vermont with Finn. We might've only been together for a short time, but the pain will last a long time.

CHAPTER EIGHTEEN
FINN

TWO WEEKS LATER

"You look like shit," Jessa tells me when I enter the inn.

I glare, huffing in response.

She's not wrong. I can't fucking sleep.

It's been two grueling weeks since I dropped Oakley off at the airport, and it feels like I haven't slept since then. I got used to holding her and us snuggling through the night. Now my bed is cold and lonely.

As I grab a plate, Jessa walks over. "Need a tranq? I'm sure I can find you one. Knock your ass out for a few days."

"I'm not in the mood," I growl, trying my hardest to ignore her, but she keeps following me around the buffet.

"Let me help you. What's on your schedule today? I can get someone else to take care of it so you can rest."

"No."

"Well, you're going to get yourself killed if you work while exhausted. You shouldn't even be driving."

"Operations don't stop because I'm having a hard time. I've

done it before, and I'll work through it again. Don't make it a big deal."

After Aspen and I broke up, I was fucking miserable for weeks. I was barely functional but powered through it for the sake of the orchard.

However, this feels different.

It's so much worse.

"Have you two spoken?" She follows me to a table, helping herself to the chair across from me.

"Not since she told me she landed in LA."

Two weeks ago. Might as well be an eternity because that's what it feels like.

"Why not?" She snags a piece of my bacon, and I scowl.

"She needed time to get settled in and figure shit out with her apartment."

Not being able to touch and kiss her while we talked would hurt too much.

Jessa purses her lips, then grabs her phone. She types something, then sets it down.

"There."

"There, what?"

"I texted her."

I pop a brow. "Why?"

"Why not? We're friends. I can check on her."

I stab my fork into my eggs and sausage, then shovel both into my mouth so I can get the hell out of here quicker.

When her phone vibrates, my heart rate increases.

"Hmm…"

I want to ask her what Oakley said, but I know Jessa's baiting me, so I stay quiet. After she sends another message, she sets her phone down again.

"You know, she's not Aspen."

"Of course she's not," I grind out. "I've *never* thought that."

"I'm just saying, if you stopped acting so jaded after one bad relationship, you'd see that you and Oakley are perfect for each other."

"Doesn't stop the fact that she lives across the fucking country, Jessa. It's not even the same."

"Did you ask her to stay?" Jessa asks, and when she goes for another piece of my food, I smack her hand. "*Ow!*"

"No. I knew she couldn't anyway."

"You sure about that?"

"Positive. She mentioned several times that she needed to network and make connections in big cities to build her career. Considering we're in a small-ass town, this place wouldn't be ideal for a professional artist."

"So you're gonna let her slip away because of *geography*?"

I roll my eyes. "Wow, I didn't realize you were a relationship expert."

"I'm a woman, and I can read you like a book. You're miserable and miss her."

Of course I fucking do. She invaded my space for nearly three weeks, and we had more sex than I can count. But Oakley meant much more to me than that.

She had me wanting to rip out my hair one second and fuck her the next.

But the tender and vulnerable moments together are what made the difference.

"I'll get over it...eventually," I say harshly, wanting this conversation to be over.

"Well, in case you wondered, she's just as sad as you and decided she's moving out of her apartment."

"To where?" I blurt out.

"She hasn't responded yet."

I shipped her boxes the same week she flew out, so she should've gotten them a while ago. There was so much I wanted to say before she left, but I couldn't get the words out. Instead, I wrote her a letter and put it in one of her boxes.

But who knows when she'll see it.

And if she's already read it, she hasn't texted or called.

I finish my food and put my dishes in the kitchen. When I come out, Jessa's in my face again.

"You want me to tell you when I find out?" she asks.

"No."

If Oakley wanted me to know, she has my number.

Once I escape her, I head to my truck. Even that has too many memories of her. Along with every inch of my house. I can't go anywhere on the farm or in Maplewood Falls without thinking about her.

It's fucking torture.

After a long-ass day, I call it quits. I worked nonstop, but it did nothing to clear my head like I hoped. If anything, it reminded me of the tours I gave her and when we made love in the orchard.

I'm tempted as hell to call her, but I'm not sure it'd help either of us. We never discussed keeping in contact after she went home. What would be the point? To stay friends? It'd hurt too much to hear about her moving on or dating someone else. I wouldn't be able to handle it.

As soon as I walk into my house, something's different. The lamp upstairs is on, and I know I turned it off. I'm tired as fuck, so I might've forgotten.

Shrugging off my jacket and kicking off my boots, I make my way to the fridge to grab a beer. If anything, maybe booze can numb me long enough to pass out for a bit.

God knows I need sleep more than anything right now.

I make my way to my room and stop dead in my tracks when I hear sheets rustling.

Someone's in my bed.

My heart pounds as I stomp up the remaining stairs, and I grow anxious at the possibility of Oakley being here. But when my bed comes into view, my anger shoots through the roof.

"What the fuck are you doing, Aspen?"

She's sprawled out on the covers in nothing but a tiny piece of lingerie.

"*Get out,*" I bark before she can respond.

"I'm here for you, Finn. Use me to feel better. I know you still have feelings for me. We can get through this little mishap and start over."

I blink hard, wondering if I'm really seeing and hearing this bullshit or if I'm having a nightmare. Standing in front of the bed, I cross my arms and stare her down.

"You've crossed the line this time, Aspen. Get the fuck out of my house!"

"Finn!" She rises on her knees. "We used to make love in this bed, too. You can try to replace me with some twentysomething bimbo, but we had something real. You can't forget that after a few weeks of being with someone else."

"I don't know what it's gonna take for you to understand I don't want you. My feelings for you are long gone, and nothing you can do or say will change that. What we had is over."

She lays on the fake tears, and her bottom lip quivers.

"You don't mean that."

I throw off my T-shirt and toss it to her. "Cover yourself."

She lets it fall and doesn't move to put it on. I roll my eyes as she wipes her dry cheeks. The fake crying is pathetic, even if the old me used to fall for it.

"Finn, *please*. Give me another chance. We'll fall back in love like we were if you tried. Remember all the amazing memories we shared? All the hot sex we had?"

"You ruined every memory I had of us when you broke my heart."

"I hate that I did that, Finn. I'm sorry. Please let me make it up to you."

I shake my head, knowing she won't be reasonable no matter

what I say. Instead of dealing with her shit, I take the stairs down to the bathroom.

"You better be gone by the time I'm out of the shower," I warn.

"I'm not going anywhere. I had a friend drop me off because I'm staying here with you, Finn. Stop fighting your true feelings."

I glare at her and finish my thought. "I won't think twice about calling the sheriff to come throw your sorry ass out if you're still here. You've got fifteen minutes."

"You sure you don't want some company in there?" She follows me, ignoring everything I said.

"Jesus fucking Christ!" I turn around and yell. "You need some goddamn help, Aspen. I don't know how to make myself any clearer. *I. Don't. Want. You.*"

"If you'd let me make you feel good, I know you'd change your mind."

My blood boils as my frustration rises. I'm too tired for this.

"Just please...consider it. What we had—"

"*I'm in love with Oakley!*" I blurt out, my voice booming against the walls. It's the first time I've said those words aloud. Though I wrote in my letter that I'd fallen for her and that there'd always be a place for her here if she decided to come back.

It hasn't been acknowledged.

Even after two weeks.

"She's not here, Finn!" Aspen shouts in my face, looking around at my empty house. "If she loved you, she'd be here begging for a chance, but she's not. I am!"

My breathing grows ragged as I attempt to calm down.

"If you'd come crawling back to me six months ago, there's no doubt I would've taken you back. But not anymore."

"What's changed?"

"Me," I confess. "I've changed. Realized I deserved so much better."

Oakley helped me realize that.

Before she can respond, there's a knock on the door. *Fucking great.*

When I whip it open and see my best friend, I shake my head. "Now's not a good time, man."

Aspen comes up behind me, and Levi's eyes go wide. "Dude...*no.*"

I brush a hand through my hair, blowing out a stressed breath. "It's not what it looks like."

"Then why are you both half naked?" He eyes my bare chest and Aspen's lack of clothing.

"We're in the middle of something, *Levi.*" Aspen scowls as she comes to my side.

"No, we're *not*," I snap.

"This isn't good." Levi shakes his head, headlights shining in my eyes.

"Who's that?" I furrow my brow.

"Jessa," he explains.

"God. Not her again."

I can't catch a fucking break.

"Yeah, but she's not alone."

"What do you mean?"

"I was coming over to make sure you were home. If I'd known you were in the *middle* of something, I would've given her a heads-up."

"Who?"

The passenger side door opens, and out steps Oakley. *What the hell?*

"You better pray she doesn't knee you in the nuts, man. She flew three thousand miles to see you."

I push my best friend to the side and walk onto the porch. It's really her.

She meets my eyes and smiles.

Jessa steps out and rounds her truck. She looks like she's ready to fight. "Why the fuck is she here?"

I blink out of my trance and realize Aspen's standing next to me.

Fuck me.

Oakley's jaw drops as her eyes widen in horror.

"We're back together," Aspen happily announces.

Oakley's face cracks as her chest rises and falls. There's no telling what she's thinking, given that I'm shirtless and Aspen's in her bra and panties.

"We're not!" I shout so everyone can hear and face Aspen. "You have lost your goddamn mind. For the hundredth time—"

Before I can finish, Levi appears next to her and grabs her arm. "Let's go."

"Get your hands off me!" she squeals, trying like hell to fight against him, but it's pointless. He's bigger and stronger than her. He pulls her down the steps and toward his truck.

"Finn! Tell them! Tell them we're in love and getting married!" she shouts over her shoulder.

"Shut up," Levi snaps, opening the door and making her get inside. Once he slams it shut, he points at me. "You owe me, dude. You know how much I despise being anywhere near her."

"I'll go with him and make sure she doesn't kick his ass," Jessa says, rushing over to Levi's truck and squeezing in. Once he shifts it into gear, gravel flies up, and they speed off.

"Oakley," I say her name in disbelief that she's here.

She meets me on the porch.

"What...what are you doing here?"

"Apparently witnessing The Housewives of Vermont in action."

"I swear, she was here when I got home. I didn't invite her."

"I know, Finn." She says it with so much certainty that I want to pull her in for a hug for not thinking the worst of me. "Might want to change those locks when you get a chance."

Breathing out a sigh of relief, I invite her inside. "But that doesn't answer my question. What are you really doing here?"

She smirks. "I read your letter and wanted to respond…*in person.*"

"Oh." I scratch my cheek, gazing down her body, tempted as hell to kiss her.

"But first, I have to ask…" She tilts her head at me in amusement. "Can I crash here tonight?"

CHAPTER NINETEEN
OAKLEY

TWO HOURS PRIOR

THE PLANE RATTLES as it lands on the runway. The late-evening view from above is as stunning as it is in person. An immediate chill hits me as I deplane, and though it's only been two weeks since I was here, it already feels colder than before. Good thing I packed the right clothes this time.

Jessa waves frantically at me when she finds me at baggage claim. She rushes over and hugs me tight. "I'm so glad you're back."

I laugh, letting her squeeze me. "Me too. Though I'm second-guessing this weather."

"Oh shush. It grows on you, and you'll be used to it in no time." She waves me off, grabbing my large suitcase while I take the other.

Returning to California after being here for three weeks was a big adjustment, and not because of the weather. The time zone difference and being without Finn sucked.

"He's going to flip out when he sees you."

"I hope he doesn't mind me showing up unannounced."

"Are you kidding? He's been wallowing for weeks. You're doing us all a favor, trust me." She groans, and I chuckle.

Finn wasn't the only miserable one.

From the first moment I walked into my apartment, it felt wrong. The loud city noises and my neighbors yelling at each other in the middle of the night drove me nuts. Not to mention how cold and lonely my bed was. I felt like a stranger in my own home. But I figured it was because I'd been gone so long.

I'd convinced myself that once I got on schedule and unpacked my stuff, my life would return to normal.

However, days later, it didn't. My boxes from Vermont arrived, and I had no desire to unload them. I told my landlord I wasn't renewing my lease and would be out by the fifteenth.

For days, I packed, with no place to go other than Florida. Tiernan was excited and so was I, but the hole in my heart was nagging at me. In only a few short weeks, I'd somehow gotten used to the farm, and surprisingly, found myself missing it.

Missing *him* more than anything.

One night while I was chatting with Tiernan, I remembered my favorite palette was in one of the boxes Finn shipped back. We were talking about baby stuff as I unpacked it, and I found an envelope with my name on the front. It was in Finn's handwriting. I hadn't realized he'd written a letter, and tears welled in my eyes as soon as I opened it.

I'd read it aloud to my sister, and by the end of it, she demanded I go to him. We were both in tears, and I could no longer contain my emotions. I told her it was crazy to drop everything without a plan, so she helped me make one.

Step one: sell everything I didn't need, then put what was left in storage.

Step two: book a one-way ticket to Vermont.

Step three: ask Jessa to pick me up at the airport so I can surprise Finn at his house.

That was a week ago.

I needed time to get rid of my furniture and pack my art supplies. Jessa kept me updated and kept an eye on Finn for me. As did Levi. Both of them were on board.

A part of me wanted to reach out and make sure it was okay to show up, but I wanted to talk face-to-face about what he wrote in that letter. It wasn't something to nonchalantly discuss over the phone.

"Levi's on his way to Finn's house now to make sure he's home. I tried like hell to get him to take the day off to rest, but he wouldn't budge. He's been a grumpy ass," Jessa tells me.

I snort. "Sounds like him."

We continue making small talk as we drive closer to the farm. Nervous butterflies swarm my stomach, and I mentally rehearse what I want to say to Finn.

"Grandma's gonna be excited to see you too," she says, then adds, "The whole family will be."

"You don't think I'm crazy for doing this, do you?" I ask warily.

"Huh? What do you mean?"

"I put my entire life—that I had no intention of leaving—in boxes and flew across the country for a *man* because he wrote me a love letter. Doesn't that make me lose my feminist card or something?"

She bellows a laugh. "Sweetie, if someone poured their heart out to me and meant it without expecting sex afterward, I'd do whatever it took to be with them. I love the orchard, but I'd never pass up a chance for happiness with my soulmate. You're too talented to worry about finding work, anyway. Plus, you have a social media expert at your disposal, so I'll help you market yourself online. I have no doubt you'll find a way to be successful wherever you live. But finding a love like you have with Finn again? Not likely. You'd search for that again for the rest of your life."

Deep down, I know she's right. I truly believed I had to be in

California to be successful when my career allows me to live anywhere in the world. I might not get huge commissions or be asked to create something for an A-list actor, but that's not why I paint. I do it because it's like oxygen—I *need* it to survive. And no matter what, I'll never stop painting regardless of whether I'm getting paid for it.

So when Finn confessed he'd fallen in love with me, I knew I had to tell him in person that I'd fallen for him too. I didn't want to just tell him. I needed to show him how much he meant to me with action.

Being with the man I love is more important than a career in a big city.

I should've realized that earlier and am kicking myself for not, but I didn't know how he felt until I read his letter. Once I flew home, I assumed it was over.

Turns out, it wasn't, and I couldn't be more excited to see him again.

But I hadn't anticipated him having *company*.

However, I knew not only by his letter but also by witnessing how much he hated being around his ex and the times he stated he'd never take her back. If I know one thing about Finn, it's that he's not a liar.

"Come inside," Finn says. Once the door is shut, he continues, "But that doesn't answer my question. What are you really doing here?"

I smirk, admiring his handsome face. "I read your letter and wanted to respond…*in person.*"

"Oh." He scratches his cheek, and I notice how scruffy his jawline is from not shaving. His gaze lowers down my body like he's ready to eat me alive.

"But first, I have to ask…" I tilt my head in anticipation, gazing at his inked biceps and wanting to lick over his tattoos. "Can I crash here tonight?"

He puffs out a laugh of disbelief. "Sure, but I should warn you, the couch isn't that comfortable."

"Damn." I bite down on my lower lip and step closer. "Guess I'll have to find other arrangements elsewhere."

"Like hell you will." Finn closes the gap between us, cups my face, then crashes his mouth to mine. I melt into him, never wanting him to let me go, and slide my tongue against his.

"Fuck, I've missed you so goddamn much," he mutters against my lips. Before I can respond, he grabs under my thighs and lifts me. My legs instinctively wrap around his waist. Our mouths stay fused together as he carefully walks upstairs.

As soon as he gets to the bed, he lays me down and hovers above me but then stops and sits on the edge of the mattress. "Shit, Aspen was up here. I should strip the bed."

I bolt up and arch a brow. "Excuse me?"

"I found her here, I swear!"

I shouldn't laugh, but I can't help it. She's probably been giving him hell since I left, and tonight, she snapped. Finn looks so conflicted between tearing off my clothes or the sheets.

"Finn, I trust you and don't care that her naked ass was probably on every inch of this bed waiting for you because I know you love me. Not her."

He meets my eyes, and I turn so we're face-to-face. "I should've told you everything I wrote in that letter in person."

"Well…I'm here now."

The corner of his lips twists up as he takes my hand and cups my cheek. "Oakley, when you first came here, I was determined to push you and every dirty thought I had about you away. But you wouldn't let me. You made me face my feelings, and it wasn't until I allowed myself to open up to the idea of being in a relationship again that I realized I'd fallen deeply in love with you. And if you didn't feel the same, then at least you knew, and I wouldn't have had to wonder about the what-ifs for the rest of my life."

"And *what if* I had fallen for you too?" I ask.

He brushes loose strands of my hair behind my ear and drags his thumb over my bottom lip. "Then I'd hope you tell me so I could stop being a miserable bastard."

Chuckling, I crawl onto his lap and straddle him. He quickly grabs my ass and settles me between his thighs. "I came all the way here to tell you that I choose you. I can pursue my career dreams in Vermont and would very much like to be with you because I'm so deeply in love with you, too."

For the first time, Finn's eyes gloss over. He tries so hard to protect himself and not be vulnerable, but it's something he'll have to get used to with me. I wear my heart on my sleeve and want us to be open about everything.

"Wait. Does that mean you're moving here?"

I chuckle with a nod. "I moved out of my apartment. I'm here to stay."

He grabs my face, and our mouths crash together. "Thank God. You were my downfall, Oakley. I couldn't breathe without you."

"That makes two of us."

We scramble to remove our clothing, and when Finn slides inside me, I see stars. His soft touches are a contrast to the roughness of his cock pounding into me.

"Fuck, Sunshine. I missed this so goddamn much." He buries his face in my hair. "You were made for me."

"Yes, yes. All yours." I arch my back as he slams into me. "Fuck. Harder. Just like that."

"Goddamn, baby. You're addictive in the best way possible." He cups my breast, licking over my nipple, and then reaches between us to play with my clit.

"It feels so right with you," I confess.

"We're a perfect fit." He kisses me so damn softly before he leans his forehead against mine. "I'm so in love with you, Oakley."

An overwhelming amount of emotions takes over, and tears fill my eyes. I've never had a man say those words and mean them as deeply as he does.

And he's the only man I ever want to hear those words from.

"I love you too. More than I thought possible, considering you did everything to grate on my nerves."

"Was just returning the favor for you getting under my skin."

I chuckle as the tension between my legs builds. "Come with me," I beg.

"If you think I'm even close to being done with you"—he peppers kisses along my jawline—"you have another thing coming. We have two weeks to make up for."

And for the next several hours, we do.

"So there's something else I wanted to ask," I say as we eat a frozen pizza in bed. It's all that was left in his house since he neglected to go grocery shopping while I was gone.

"What's that?"

"How'd your grandma find out about us fake dating?"

He arches a brow. "You knew about that, huh? I didn't find out until after you left, and she gave me a whole-ass speech about letting you leave."

"Aw…" I smirk. "Willa loves me."

"She's gonna lose her mind when she finds out you're here."

"She told me you were *smitten* with me," I singsong.

He snorts. "I don't know how she knew, but I'm guessing it's because she hears everything."

"Or she knows you better than you realize."

"Probably. That little sneak."

He leans in to brush sauce off my lip. "What'd your sister say when you told her you were coming here?"

"She's the one who pushed for it. I read the letter to her. She said I'd forever regret not seeing where this leads, and the thought had me in tears. I didn't want to live without knowing, so I booked a one-way ticket, and voilà, here I am."

"Can't wait to thank her someday." He grins.

"I was thinking we should fly down there next summer after the baby is born. Then we can do formal introductions."

"Sounds perfect."

After we finish eating, we snuggle in bed, and as he holds me, I stare into his beautiful brown eyes. "So we're doing this, right? No temporary fling or fake labels. We're together?"

I hate how insecure my voice sounds, but the last time we made an arrangement, we were left heartbroken, so I need to be one hundred percent certain this is for real.

"Sunshine." He strokes his thumb over my cheek. "You're mine, and I'm yours. I lost you once, and I don't ever want to lose you again."

I pull him in for a kiss. "Good. Because I'm not letting you go."

CHAPTER TWENTY
FINN

ONE MONTH LATER

WHEN OAKLEY TOLD me she had a lot of art supplies in storage, I thought she was joking until it all showed up on a shipping truck. What she'd sent for her project was only a small fraction of what she had. Never knew a person could own so many easels in different sizes, colors, or materials. Large, small, cherry wood, or metal—the options seem unlimited.

Since Oakley has been super busy and has several online orders to fulfill, my grandmother is allowing her to use the cottage. It's become her own personal art oasis, and it's working out perfectly to give her space to work and store all her stuff.

Since she's such a fast painter, she's been taking and finishing small jobs every few days. When she's bored or needs a change of scenery, she helps at the inn and bakery. My mother and aunt adore her. Hell, the whole family does.

Not one of them was shocked when she returned.

I think I was the only one.

Her being here with me has been a dream come true. I've never slept better in my life than when I have her in my bed next to me. Sometimes I have to pinch myself to make sure I'm not dreaming. Not positive what I did in a past life to deserve someone so kind and caring who still tries to be a pain in my ass, but I'm thankful for how things turned out.

"Almost ready?" I ask as Oakley slides a beanie over her head and then puts on some gloves. Although she's dressed in double layers, she's still convinced it won't be enough to keep her warm.

Moving closer, I lean in and steal a kiss. "You're adorable."

"It's negative degrees out there right now," she explains, pointing at the window. "It's nothing but white."

"Would be easy to paint, though."

Now she's laughing. "Might have to test out that theory."

I walk over to a blank canvas and point at it. "See, I created this yesterday."

She playfully rolls her eyes and comes closer. "Wow, the shading and detail. I should put this online and sell it."

"How much do you think I could make?"

She snorts. "About twelve bucks."

"Is that how much this size canvas cost?"

Oakley nods and wraps her arms around my neck, pulling me close to her. "Sometimes you're goofy as hell." She slides her tongue between my lips, and I'm tempted to take her upstairs and say fuck it. Although Levi would probably be pissed since we've been promising to visit the Christmas tree farm since Oakley moved here.

"Might have to unwrap you like a present if you keep that up," I mutter, pressing a soft kiss on her nose.

"Not happening, Country Boy. Do you know how hard it was to pull my jeans over my thermals, then to put ski pants on top of that?"

"Your pussy is gonna be on fire later, babe. The ski pants are enough."

She chuckles. "Just warming up your snack."

"Mm, tempting. But we should get going so we can hurry up and come back home before more snow falls."

Oakley walks to the window and watches the flurries fall. "You're sure it's safe to drive in this?"

"Yeah, it's nothing. I have chains on the tires anyway. Trust me?"

"Of course, but you better go start the truck so it's warm and toasty for me when I get in."

"It's already waiting for ya," I tell her with a wink, and her smile widens.

"And this is why I love you."

I lead the way to the truck and open Oakley's door. She rushes in, coughing from the cold.

"My lungs don't know how to handle this air. I think California weather ruined me."

"You'll acclimate, and before it's all over, I'm determined to have you love a true New England winter."

"We'll see about that," she murmurs as we slowly drive down the old country road toward Levi's place.

We've been so busy that we haven't had a chance to put up a tree yet, and since I had a day off, I didn't want to pass up the opportunity. It's our first Christmas as a couple, and I want it to be extra special. Plus, Oakley's been dying to visit his farm.

"Prepare to be amazed," I say as we turn toward Levi's. This is the busiest time of the year for him and his family, and it might be the only time I'll get to see him until after the holidays. Christmas is only two weeks away, so the place is jam-packed.

When we arrive at the parking lot, there are no free spaces, and the overflow is a long walk. So I improvise by driving onto the curb and hope no one says anything. I glance over at Oakley, and she's shaking her head.

"We could've walked."

"Being a rebel is more fun, though."

Before I can say anything else, there's a knock on my window. I smile wide when I see Levi.

"Sir, this isn't a parking spot. It's a sidewalk."

I chuckle. "I'd like to order a double cheeseburger and fries. Want anything, babe?"

"This isn't a Wendy's either." He rolls his eyes at me but then smiles at Oakley. "Hey, Oakley. How've you been? Enjoying our weather?"

I give him a look. "Back with the twenty questions again?"

He laughs, and Oakley speaks up. "I'm better now that I'm back in Vermont! Let's not talk about the snow. There aren't enough layers I can wear to stay warm."

"Eh. You'll get used to it," he confirms. "Finn treating you okay? Or do you need a real man?"

I smack his arm. "Dude, I'm right here."

Oakley cracks up. "Don't worry. He treats me like a queen and even worships the ground I walk on."

"He better," Levi playfully warns. "Anyway, can you park in the field up front? The sleigh ride will be back from the tour in about five minutes and can pick you two up then."

"I guess," I tell him.

"Great, I'll chat with ya when you return." He taps the top of the truck, shoots Oakley a wink, then we head to the overflow area.

"How is he still single?" Oakley asks as we wait.

"He hasn't met the right woman," I tell her. "Have any friends for him?"

She shakes her head. "Nope and my only sister is married to the love of her life."

I look out the windshield, searching for the horse-drawn carriage.

"That's too bad. Maybe some annoying-ass woman will show up at his property, and she'll sneak into his bed."

Oakley lifts a brow. "Wouldn't he be so lucky?"

I flash her a wink. "He'd be the luckiest man alive."

We unbuckle, and I see our ride in the distance. Oakley's eyes light up when she sees the Clydesdale horses.

"They're gigantic," she says, eager to get out of the truck. We wait for the sleigh to come to a stop and the people to unload, and then we step on. It's big enough to fit eight people, but we're the only ones waiting for it now. The midmorning rush is coming, though, especially now that the main lot is full.

"So is Levi Santa?" she whispers in my ear, and I let out a hearty laugh.

"If he is, he knows you've been *very* naughty."

Once we take off, the bells on the horses jingle as they trot. The driver gives us a quick hello, and we make our way to the main area.

"This is a real wood sleigh. Been in Levi's family for decades. I think his great-grandpa built it."

"Seriously? Wow," she says, enjoying the sweeping views of the snow-covered hills as the sun greets us up above. We take a small trail that runs perpendicular with the road, and I think Oakley's disappointed when it comes to a stop by the gift shop because she was enjoying the ride.

I tip the driver, and when we step off, Levi greets us.

"So where do you keep the reindeer?" Oakley asks him, and he gives her his best belly laugh. He's way too good at that, and of course, she eats it up.

"Ready to pick your tree?" he asks her, then hands me the axe.

"Wait! We're cutting it down on our own like the freaking Griswolds?"

"That's right, City Girl." I swing the axe over my shoulder. "Lead us to the best ones," I tell Levi, and he takes off.

I hold Oakley's gloved hand and glance at her with a grin. She waggles her brows, and Levi shakes his head.

"I knew I'd be third-wheeling it."

Soon we're in an area full of beautiful evergreens. "You can pick," I tell Oakley. "Any size you want."

"This is incredible. I almost feel bad chopping one down. But then I feel bad for the ones that don't get picked."

She walks by different ones, holding her hand out to brush it across the needles. Oakley's like a kid in a candy store and keeps up her pace as Levi and I trail her.

"I forgot to tell you what happened with Aspen," he says, lowering his voice.

"Oh yeah." I totally forgot that he and Jessa hauled her ass away the day Oakley came back to me.

"She kept talking shit to Jessa. So you know what your cousin did?"

I shake my head. "I can only imagine."

"There was duct tape on the back seat of the truck, and she literally took a strip and slapped it over Aspen's mouth. Then she told her if she dared to rip it off, she would make me pull over and leave her on the side of the road in the snow or she'd stuff her dirty sock in her mouth."

"Fuck," I whisper-hiss. "Jessa never told me any of this."

"She made me swear I'd keep it to myself." He chuckles. "*Whoops.* But also pretend you don't know because she's scary."

I laugh. "Apparently."

"Anyway, Jessa forced me to drop Aspen off at her parents' house in her bra and panties, and her mother lost her shit. Jessa politely explained Aspen broke into your house and refused to leave."

My eyes go wide, knowing how strict her parents are, even at her age. "Yikes."

"Don't think you'll be hearing from her *ever* again. Not after that. I felt sorry for her, and that's saying a fuck ton."

I don't even know what to say. Aspen's parents were always very religious, and their daughter lied a lot to appease them. Can't imagine that went over well at all.

"This is the one," Oakley announces, looking up at a tree that towers over Levi.

My mouth falls open as I realize how tall it is.

"What?" Oakley places a hand on her hip.

"Nothing, babe. If this is the one…"

"It is. Size matters," she purrs. "Even when it comes to Christmas trees."

"Please don't talk about my best friend's dick with me right here."

Oakley snorts at Levi, and I walk over with the axe and get to work. Teenagers on four-wheelers drive around to tag the cut trees. They also pick them up and take them up front.

"Timber," I say as it falls over with a thud. Oakley interlocks her fingers with mine as one of the teenagers who works on the farm loads it.

"Bennett, right?" he asks me, putting it on a candy-cane-striped tag and plopping it on the back rack of his ride.

I nod. "That's right."

"That one's on me," Levi tells him, and the kid nods before driving away.

"Ya didn't have to do that." I smack his shoulder.

"You're family," he explains. "Your money's no good here."

"What are they doing with it?" Oakley asks.

"We wrap them for travel and send you away with care instructions," Levi explains.

"Wow, that's fancy," she says. "You know, the scenery has me itching to go to my art oasis and paint," she tells Levi and me on the way back.

"My offer still stands. The gift shop could use your magical artwork. You'll see what I'm talking about when you go in there. The wall behind the front counter is bland and has a big spot waiting for it," he says.

"I'll do it on one condition," Oakley offers, and Levi waits for her to continue. "I need a sleigh ride that lasts longer than ten minutes."

"Shit, that's easy. Consider it done."

Oakley beams wide, and I wrap my arm around her as we squeeze through the crowd. We go to the pickup area, and once our tree is loaded, Levi thanks us for coming.

"Sorry, it's hectic." His walkie-talkie keeps going off because they're so damn busy.

"Your farm is beautiful," Oakley explains, giving Levi a big hug. "It was good seeing you, and thanks so much for the tree. We're gonna decorate the hell out of it."

He chuckles. "Hope you have a lot of decorations."

"If not, we'll make some." She turns to me. "Art project style."

"Yay!" I say sarcastically. "As long as no glitter is involved."

"There will be piles of it," she mocks.

Levi tells us goodbye and excuses himself before we make our way into the gift shop.

Christmas music plays as soon as we enter, and I immediately smell gingerbread cookies. It's as hectic inside as it is outside. I keep a tight hold on Oakley for no reason other than I like her close, and we grab two cups of hot cocoa.

"We should get this," she says, holding up a turtle dove ornament that says our first Christmas.

"Our first Christmas and first ornament. Lots of firsts together." I smile. "I love it."

"Me too," she tells me as we finish our cocoa and make our way to the counter. As we wait in line, Oakley stands on her tiptoes to get a look at the wall behind the counter, and she gasps.

"They wrapped the wall in Christmas paper. No wonder he wants something there. It's horrendous."

I laugh. "His mom did it, and I think the only way she'd

remove it is for one of your paintings. He's begged her for years to tear it down. She's refused."

Her face squishes. "I better start on it tomorrow, then."

After we pay for our ornament, we stand in the flurries, waiting for the sleigh ride to return. After we hop on, I press a kiss on her warm lips.

"Thank you for taking me here. I loved every minute of it."

"Even in the cold?"

She chuckles. "I'm pretty sure my ass is sweating."

"Told you!" I say with a laugh as she leans into my side and takes in her surroundings.

"So after we decorate this tree, we're watching *Elf* from beginning to end, right?" She lifts her brow, and I laugh because she remembered.

"Does it include hard apple cider?"

"Not a chance. You're not getting out of finishing it like you did with *Halloweentown*."

"Alright, deal." I kiss her cold cheek and inhale the sweet smell of her shampoo.

I can't remember a time I was ever this happy and am so damn grateful to call Oakley my girlfriend, but one day, I plan to make her my wife.

CHAPTER TWENTY-ONE
OAKLEY

SIX MONTHS LATER

I've been bouncing in my seat for the past three hours, but I can't help it.

I'm so damn excited to officially meet my niece and see my sister again. It's been way too long. Although we FaceTime and text regularly, it's not the same.

"Babe, you're shaking the whole plane," Finn teases as he puts his hand on my knee. "We're about to land."

"I should warn you, Auntie Oakley is about to activate. Don't get in the way of me holding my niece."

"You're going to scare that poor child," he teases.

My jaw drops, and I playfully elbow him. "You're just mad I introduced you as Uncle Grumpy."

He rolls his eyes.

We make it to baggage claim, and when I spot Everett, I bolt for him.

"Jesus Christ, you nearly toppled me over." He wraps an arm around me.

"Aren't you happy to see me?"

"Of course. You've grown since the last time I saw you."

I smack his chest. "I'm not a child! You're only a few years older than me, remember?"

"More like seven, but who's counting?"

Finn catches up to me with our bags. "Don't worry, I got 'em."

I smirk, pulling Finn toward me. "Babe, officially meet my brother-in-law, Everett."

"Nice to meet you, man."

They shake hands.

Tiernan's kept the baby on a strict eating and feeding schedule, which means she couldn't come pick me up. But that's okay because Everett and Finn can spend some time bonding while we drive to their beach house.

Once Everett parks, I dart out like I'm on fire and rush inside. Tiernan waits for me in the foyer and quickly wraps me in a tight hug.

"Oh my God!" I squeal. "I've missed you *so* much!"

"Shh, she's sleeping," she whispers.

"Oh, come on, let's wake her up."

"Oakley, no. You never wake a sleeping baby."

I pout with my arms on my hips. "She wants to meet her aunt."

"She will in an hour."

I scoff. "Fine. I'll introduce you to my boyfriend, I suppose."

She laughs as Everett and Finn walk in with our luggage. "Oops, sorry. I forgot to grab my bag."

Everett smirks as if he knows better than to say anything.

"Finn, meet my sister, Tiernan."

Tiernan immediately gives him a hug. Finn looks at me over her head, and I snicker. "I told her you gave the best bear hugs and she wanted to see for herself."

"I'm right here." Everett playfully clears his throat.

"Aw, feeling left out? I gave you a hug earlier!" I exclaim, then open my arms. "Do you want another?"

Tiernan chuckles, releasing her hold on Finn. "It's nice to see you in person. From the times we've talked and everything I've heard about you, it's like I already know you."

"Same," Finn agrees.

The past six months have been wild. While finding my new normal living with Finn, I worked with Jessa a lot to build my social media presence. I started painting during live streams and let strangers on the internet ask questions about my techniques. On top of that, Jessa helped me make a professional-looking website where I can show off my pieces. There's also a tab with my contact information so people can easily reach out to me. Everything she's done has been a game changer for my career, and I don't think I could've done it without her help. Instead of feeling this overwhelming stress about finding new clients, I now have a waiting list.

Between all of that, I've been keeping up with my sister and their surrogate since she was due a couple of months ago. I've never cried so hard in my life when they FaceTimed me and I saw my niece for the very first time.

"Are you hungry? I can make us something," Tiernan offers.

"I'm giving it thirty minutes before I go in there and steal her," I say. "But yes, I could eat."

Everett pats my back. "Sit tight. I'll go check and see if she's still snoozing."

I can hardly stand the wait and am ready to climb the stairs two at a time to see her. This baby will be glued to my arms for the next five days.

"Grilled cheese with pickles. Is that still your favorite?" Tiernan asks as she looks in the fridge.

"Yeah, when I was nine." I laugh, and Finn makes a face. "Sounds delicious."

Ten minutes later, Everett walks downstairs, and I nearly scream in excitement.

"She's still sleepy," he tells me.

My eyes well up as soon as he places her in my arms. "Oh my gosh," I whisper, rubbing her soft cheek. "Bluebell Rayne, you are the most beautiful thing I've ever seen."

Finn stands next to me with his hand on my shoulder. "She's precious."

"Did you know I named her?" I beam with pride as I tell Finn the whole story of how it came about.

"But we call her Belle for short," Everett says.

"No, *we* don't," I argue. "She looks like a Bluebell."

"She does," Tiernan agrees. "But Belle is cute, too."

"Sweet Bluebell, you better come to me with all your boy problems, okay? When your dad's embarrassing you or won't give you money, you call your auntie Oakley."

Everett shoots me a glare at the mention of boyfriends, and I laugh. Then I glance over at Tiernan.

"So when are you having the next one?"

Five days pass by way too fast, and I'm in tears when we have to say goodbye. It won't be easy for them to travel for a while, so I promised we'd visit again as soon as we can.

"Would joining the mile-high club put you in a better mood?" Finn whispers in my ear as we board the plane.

I burst out laughing, and the other passengers stare at me in annoyance.

"Don't offer something you can't deliver."

He smacks my ass as I slide into our row of seats.

"Would this be a good time to have the future talk?" he asks once we're in the sky.

"Seriously? You want to have this conversation right now?" I smirk.

It's not like we haven't discussed what we eventually want, but we've only been together for six months, so it's not a subject I've rushed to bring up.

He shrugs unapologetically. "I'm not getting any younger, babe."

I roll my eyes. "You're thirty-five. Plenty of male actors have had kids in their fifties. Some in their sixties!"

Finn pops a brow. "I'm not an actor nor do I plan to hire nannies to raise my kids. But I might have to if we're starting a family when I'm that old."

Chuckling, I lean into him and wait for his mouth to meet me halfway. "You're too easy."

He presses his lips to mine. "I saw how you were with Bluebell and figured you'd have baby fever by the time we landed in Vermont. So figured I'd ask so I could prepare."

"Prepare?"

"Yeah, like wearing loose boxers and buying baby stuff."

"Wait. Are *you* having baby fever?" My mouth falls open.

The corner of his lips curve up. "I warned you that I was ready to settle down. But I'm waiting, don't worry. I'm content with you in my bed every night...*for now*. Eventually, I want us to discuss other future things, too. Maybe build a bigger house so we have room for a nursery. And a place for you to paint without leaving. I know inspiration calls at all hours of the day."

"Okay, fair enough. How about I tell you when I'm at that stage, and then you can decide when it's time to...*do all that stuff*." I wave my hand in the air.

"All that stuff, as in...marriage and babies?"

My heart flutters because it sounds sexy when he says it.

"Yeah, you know, grown-up stuff."

He chuckles, pulling me closer and kissing my forehead. "Oh, Sunshine. You sure do keep me young."

I snicker, leaning into him. "That's my job, Country Boy."

Though I may not be ready to walk down the aisle tomorrow, I know without a doubt that Finn's the man I'm going to marry, and I honestly can't wait to have his babies.

CHAPTER TWENTY-TWO

FINN

FOUR MONTHS LATER

I walk through the front door of the cottage and smell something burning.

"Oakley?" I shout, quickly removing my dirty work boots and then walking toward the kitchen. "Is there a reason the oven's on?"

Noticing the red light indicating the surface is hot, I grab an oven mitt and look inside. It smells like burnt meat and cheese.

For the past few months, she's been trying to teach herself how to cook. Watching videos online, reading cookbooks, and looking up recipes. She says it's a good distraction when she's creatively blocked with painting and uses it as another outlet.

But as much as I love the thought of coming home to a hot meal, I've had to use the fire extinguisher twice already. After the day I've had, I'd love not to have to use it again.

Quickly removing the pan, I set it on top of the stove and then turn off the oven.

"Oakley?" I shout louder this time.

"Up here!" she calls from the loft.

I make my way upstairs two steps at a time, ready to scold her for not setting a timer *again*. "Babe, you can't—"

Stopping in my tracks as soon as I see her on our bed, I swallow hard.

"Uh..." I chuckle under my breath, scrubbing a hand through my hair.

Oakley's in a lacy black lingerie piece I've never seen her in before. She's laid out on the bed like my favorite dessert ready to be devoured.

"What're you doing?" I step closer, admiring every luscious inch of her exposed skin.

"I thought we'd celebrate tonight," she says seductively. Getting to her knees, she slowly crawls to the edge of the bed.

"Baby, I'm gonna need you to tell me what's going on. You had something burning in the oven and now I find you up here half naked—not that I'm complaining—but—"

"Oh, shit!" She smacks a palm to her forehead. "My lasagna!"

"Is that what that was?"

"I forgot." She winces. "I came up here to shave and get ready, and well, I got distracted."

Reaching for her, I wrap my arms around her and pull her to my chest. "Maybe we stick to me doing the cooking."

"Hey, I'm trying!" She swats my chest. "I wanted tonight to be special."

I rack my brain, trying to remember what today is.

"You don't know, do you?" Her hands go to her hips as she scolds me with a narrowed gaze.

Now it's my turn to wince. "It's October fourteenth."

"Mm-hmm." She nods slowly as if she's waiting for me to remember.

I know it's not her birthday or mine.

"Just tell me, babe."

She sighs. "It's the one-year anniversary of when we first met."

"Is it?" My brows rise, trying to remember when she arrived last year. "Shit, I think you're right."

"One year since I fell for you." She grins, wrapping her arms around my neck. "Well-*ish*. Pretty sure we didn't get along that first week, and I wasn't sure what date would be our official anniversary, so we'll say, almost one year."

I chuckle, tilting her chin and dipping down to press my lips to hers. "Happy one-year-ish anniversary."

She giggles. "What date do you think it should it be on? The first time we kissed? Slept together? When I returned and moved in?"

"Nah, today's date is perfect. It was the day you burst into my life and flipped it upside down. I knew my life would never be the same again and that's something to celebrate."

"We did fake date for a bit, so that obviously counts, too."

"*Obviously*," I taunt, smirking. "The best three hundred and sixty-five days I've ever had."

"Don't make fun of me." She pokes my sides, and I squeal embarrassingly loud.

"Okay, enough." I step back out of her reach, but she's quick to her feet and chases me downstairs until I'm in the bathroom. "Let me take a shower and then I'll make us some dinner."

"Or…" She brings her hands up to her breasts that are nearly busting out of the thin fabric. "We could go right to dessert."

"Oakley…" I growl, grabbing the back of my shirt and tearing it over my head. "Give me ten minutes to get cleaned up and then I'm tearing that little thing off you with my teeth."

She watches as I remove my jeans and boxers. "Or let's start with an appetizer." She parks her ass up on the countertop. "Give me a show while you're in there."

I reach into the shower and turn on the hot water. "You think you'll be able to keep your hands off me?"

"I spent an hour doing my hair, so I'm not getting it wet."

The corner of my lips tilts up. "Hmm…care to make it interesting?"

"Such as?" She crosses her legs with an arched brow.

"You play with yourself where I can see you from the shower and try not to come before me while you watch me touch myself. Whoever loses has to do whatever the other says, *all night long*."

She licks her lips, contemplating my offer. "You sure you wanna wager with me? I can hold out much longer than you…"

Bending down, I remove my socks and then stalk toward her. "That's what you like to think, baby." I tilt her chin, inching close enough to brush her mouth. "But as soon as you hear me talking you through your pleasure, you'll be a goner."

"That's cheating!" she hisses.

"Says who?" I cock a brow. "The only rule is you stay up here, and I stay in there."

"Fine." She beams. "As soon as you hear me moaning your name, you'll drop to your knees, begging to finish me off with your tongue."

I chuckle at how well she knows me. But not tonight—I have plans to make *her* do the begging.

"We'll see, baby. Good luck." I wink and then get into the shower.

Soaking my hair, I thread my fingers through it before grabbing the shampoo and lathering it in my palms. By the time I'm rinsing it out, Oakley's moans grab my attention.

Glancing over, I find her legs spread over the sink and her little thong shoved to the side, giving me the perfect view of her pretty pussy.

Fuck.

"Well, are you gonna join me or stare the whole time?"

Biting my lip, I palm my cock and stroke it as I watch her rub her clit.

"Such a good boy," she coos, and fuck that turns me on. She knows what she's doing and she's damn good at it.

221

"Oakley," I hiss in warning. "Put your fingers inside and tell me how wet you are."

She obeys, shoving two between her thighs. "Mm…so wet. I can feel my arousal leaking out already."

I squeeze my shaft tighter, and when I'm hard and throbbing, I bite back the urge to drag her ass in here with me.

"Fuck yourself nice and deep, baby. Let me see and hear how turned on you are…"

"You wish you were inside me right now, don't you?" Her taunting voice has my balls drawing up. "Thrusting deep and hard in my cunt until I moan your name."

"Goddammit, woman…" My head falls back as I swallow hard, fisting myself harder.

Oakley's dirty talk always works on me, but I'm about to uno reverse her strategy.

"Pinch your nipples, love," I order. "And use your thumb to rub your clit."

Her senses are about to go crazy.

Oakley reaches up and squeezes a nipple through the thin lace. She shifts her hand until she can add pressure to her sensitive nub. And as soon as the pleasure teases her nerves, she's breathless and moaning.

"That's my good girl. Making me watch how you get yourself off when I can't touch you…such a dirty little slut."

Her eyes roll back at my words, and I smirk when she moans.

But my dick reacts the same, and soon, I'm fighting back the urge to come all over the shower door. Shivers roll down my spine and my thighs tense at how close I am to losing.

"Sunshine, I need you to come…" I plead.

"Not until you do," she taunts, moving her hand to the other breast.

"I can't. It feels wrong to get off before you do."

Which is the truth. I never come before I've made sure she has, sometimes twice.

"Not this time, Country Boy. I'm not losing this bet." She sucks her lower lip in between her teeth. "You wish your mouth and hands were on me, don't you? I know your fist doesn't feel half as good as my tight pussy does. Imagine I'm on my knees in front of you...waiting for you to fill it with your cum."

Fucking hell, she's not backing down. Her words nearly have me losing it, but I loosen my grip in time before I do.

Though I should let her win, if not to give myself the relief, but I love taunting her too much not to give it one last shot.

"I'd rather come inside you so I can practice knocking you up. Fill your pussy with my cum and then when it tries to slide out of you, I'd shove it back in with my tongue."

We both want to have a baby someday, although I'd rather wait until we're married so we're not planning a wedding and for a baby at the same time, but I'd honestly be happy whenever it happens.

"Oh my God. *Fuck...*" Oakley's mouth falls open, gloriously moaning through her release, and it only takes seconds later before I'm spilling out in my palm.

"You're a filthy little cheater," she grumbles between clenched teeth. "You knew that'd work."

I chuckle, rinsing off under the stream of water.

"Get in here, love. I wanna kiss my prize." I open the door and give her a come-hither motion.

Oakley tortures me by slowly removing her lingerie. Then she rubs her hands across her soft skin, taunting me further until I reach out of the shower and drag her to my chest.

"Such a little temptress, aren't you?" I dip down and capture her mouth, moving us into the shower.

"You're ruining my hair." She pretends to pout.

I tilt up her chin, smirking. "I plan to ruin a lot more than your hair tonight."

"You better appreciate my wax job."

Sliding my hand between her thighs, I groan when I feel how smooth and soft her skin is. "Christ. You did a good job, baby."

"Did you mean what you said before about knocking me up?" she asks.

"Of course," I reply, moving wet strands of hair off her face. "I can't wait to start a family with you."

"Me too." She grins wide. "And anything more with you, I want. Just in case you wondered…"

Biting back a laugh, I know exactly what she's referring to.

But she has nothing to worry about because I have every intention of making her my wife and the mother of my children.

"Duly noted, my love." I wink. "Now…on your knees and open that filthy mouth so I can feed you my cock before I feast on your sweet pussy for dinner."

EPILOGUE
FINN

TWO MONTHS LATER

THE SNOW-COVERED landscapes on the farm are as beautiful as ever. We got hit hard with a blizzard, and now everyone's trying to clean up the mess. The sun reflects off the snow and shines bright in the sky, giving the illusion of a perfect clear day when in reality, all of our vehicles are buried, and people are scrambling to find cell service.

"Finn!" Oakley shouts from the bedroom, and I rush upstairs from the kitchen, where I was staring out the window.

"What? Are you okay?"

"Levi's looking for you. My phone just turned on, and he's messaged me like ten times."

"Oh shit. Is he okay?" I grab my cell off the nightstand and see I have a couple of bars. Levi also left a few voice messages and half a dozen texts.

Instead of listening to each one, I call and put him on speaker.

"Hey, man. You alright?" I ask as soon as he picks up.

"Dude. A strange woman is in my house."

"Are you j-joking?" I choke on my words because there's no way he said what he said.

"Hell no. Her name is Fallon, and she's a journalist from Seattle."

Oakley chimes in. "How'd she end up there?"

Levi explains the whole situation about how Fallon was scammed by an online rental company that wasn't legitimate. Apparently, someone posted his cabin on this phishing site and claimed it was for rent. They took her money, and when she showed up, the door was open, so she made herself at home thinking it was her rental.

"I was outside chopping wood, and when I walked inside, I started taking off my clothes and making my way to the shower," Levi explains. "So I'm walking upstairs toward the bathroom when I find her in my bed."

Oakley's jaw drops. "Oh my God, *no*…"

"Yep, showed her *all* my goods. Scared the living shit out of me because I thought she was robbing me or something. Meanwhile, she thought I was breaking in to harm her. In the midst of me trying to cover my junk, she sprayed me with pepper spray, and I tripped over her suitcase. Made a complete ass out of myself as I tried to explain she was in *my* house."

"Jesus fucking Christ," I bellow out, imagining the entire scene in my head as I die with laughter.

Oakley's in a fit of giggles as she covers her mouth.

"When was this?" I ask.

"Three days ago, right as the blizzard hit."

"Shit. I'm surprised you're still alive at this rate."

"Honestly, me too. When she showed up, the roads were already bad. So I told her she could stay in the guest room for the night, but then by the morning, all the roads were closed. Right after I got a weather alert, I lost service."

"So she's living with you?" Oakley asks.

"Yep. I called the inn and all the hotels in town this morning. They're all booked."

No surprise there since it's the holiday ski season.

"How long is she in town?"

"Two weeks."

"Is she pretty?" Oakley asks.

"Yeah, she's drop-dead gorgeous, but she's rude as fuck. I swear she's the Grinch's twin sister."

Oakley snickers, giving me an incredulous look.

"Huh?" I ask.

"She hates Christmas, man."

My eyes widen. "What? Who *hates* Christmas?"

"*This chick.* Like seriously, she's here on some job to write an article about Maplewood Falls, and based on her shitty attitude, I feel like it's a smear piece. I don't want her to say anything bad. If she does, it could be detrimental for all the small businesses who rely on winter tourists to stay open."

"Well, then perhaps you better show her a good time so she has nothing but positive things to say," Oakley suggests, waggling her brows at me, and I know she's up to something. "How'd she even end up on a Christmas tree farm?"

"It's such a long-ass story. But anyway, I wanted to let you know what was going on because you'll be meeting her soon. She's supposed to visit all the farms and stay through the winter festival."

"*Great.* Can't wait," I deadpan.

"Maybe I should talk to her. Out-of-towner to out-of-towner."

Levi scoffs. "Doubt it would matter, but we've gotta do something. First, I have to figure out how to pull that entitled stick out of her ass, then help her realize how charming and amazing our town is."

"I know of one way…" I taunt, staring at Oakley's bare chest.

"If flashing her your dick didn't work, I don't know if there's hope." Oakley giggles.

"Ugh." He groans as if he's been frustrated nonstop for the past three days. "Thanks a lot for all your help, guys. Super appreciate it."

I bark out a laugh. "We'll come to your rescue as soon as we plow ourselves out of here."

"Yeah, I gotta do the same. Little Miss Seattle needs some fancy coffee beans that I don't and won't ever have. She's been complaining about it since she arrived."

"Good luck!" Oakley yells before he ends the call. "Poor Levi."

I snuggle back in bed with my fiancée and cup her breast. "I didn't even get a chance to tell him we got engaged last night."

Oakley moans at my touch.

"We'll fill him in later when his head isn't ready to explode," she says.

We've basically been locked in the house for three days straight since the blizzard hit. I intended to propose on Christmas Eve, but I couldn't wait any longer. I needed her to say yes to being my wife.

"Don't start something you can't finish," she warns as I suck the softness of her neck.

Before my call with Levi, I was planning to go snow plow the parking lots and gravel roads.

"Fuck." I lick her hollow throat. "Screw it. What's another twenty minutes?"

She giggles as she claws at my boxers, and we end up tangled between the sheets.

"I can't wait to tell my sister and your family," she admits once we come down from our high and lie in bed.

"Me too, Sunshine." I kiss the tip of her nose, then get up to find my jeans and boots. "I better go before they come looking for me."

"Okay, be careful, please. Love you," she says while she pulls the sheet up and snuggles back in bed.

I lean over and press my lips to hers. "I will."

OAKLEY

After Finn leaves, I manage to take a hot shower and scrub myself from top to bottom. As I stand under the stream, I hold out my left hand, still in shock.

I knew he'd propose soon, but I didn't know when. When we were celebrating our one-year anniversary, I'd made it known that I was ready for the next step in our relationship. And although it wasn't anything over the top, it was the perfect proposal.

We were watching my favorite holiday movie and drinking hot cocoa when he dropped to one knee and asked me to be his wife. I was so surprised that I could only stare at him in shock. He then asked if I was okay before I blurted out *yes*. Then I laughed because I couldn't believe it was happening.

Of course, we spent the rest of the night celebrating.

But now there's a lot of cleanup to do. The snow is great for ski businesses but not for agricultural farms. There isn't much I can do since the walkway to the cottage hasn't been shoveled yet, and all my supplies are there. So for now, I'll wait until Finn returns so I can go help at the inn or bakery.

My phone rings, and when I look at the screen, I see it's Jessa.

"Hey! You guys okay?"

"Yeah, finally have service." She groans. "Finn's plowing us out now and told me a little about Levi but said to get the full story from you."

I laugh thinking about it.

Once I recap everything, I share the news about our engagement.

"Oh my God! About time!" she squeals.

I smile wide at how excited she is. "I know it's early, but would you be in my wedding party?"

"Duh! I'm going to help you plan it, too. But please, do I have to wear a dress?"

I snort. "Yes."

"Damn, fine. Nothing pastel, though."

"Okay, deal."

She recaps the past few days of being snowed in with her girlfriend, Layla. They started dating five months ago, and when the storm hit, Layla was staying at Jessa's. I adore them together and have enjoyed getting to know her when she visits. The two of them were made for one another. She's a creative like me but on the introverted side. Doesn't matter, though, because Jessa's loud enough for both of them. Layla's a novelist and spends most of her time penning thrillers. I've listened to all her audiobooks already.

Four hours go by before Finn returns, and he looks frozen from head to toe.

"Allow me to warm you up…" I tease, tearing off his clothes. Next, I lead him into the shower and keep it on hot.

"Fuck, that feels like needles," he hisses as the water pounds hard on his cold skin.

Once he's acclimated, it'll be much better, but until then, I kneel between his feet. "Let me distract you."

I pull him into my mouth and enjoy the way he hisses out a moan.

"Goddamn." He fists my wet hair, clenching his teeth. "Get up so I can put a baby inside you."

I immediately do as he says and position myself in front of him with my palms against the wall, then spread my legs.

We've not been actively trying to get pregnant but not taking extra precautions either. I take birth control, but we don't use condoms. I know we have time, and now that we're engaged, I wouldn't mind waiting until after the wedding. But I still love hearing him talk about knocking me up.

"Thatta girl." He smacks my ass, encouraging me to lean over farther.

As soon as he enters me from behind, I gasp in pleasure.

Our bodies move in perfect rhythm, and when Finn whispers in my ear how much he loves me, I explode. Moments later, he fills me up with his hot cum.

"I can't wait to see your swollen belly," he confesses as he washes every inch of my body.

"I already have names picked out."

The corner of his lips knowingly rises. "Why am I not surprised?"

I wrap my arms around his neck, pulling him as close as I can. "Because you know me better than anyone."

"Do I?"

"Yep, and I wouldn't have it any other way."

"Same here, love," he mutters as he kisses my forehead. "Now let me devour my future wife's cunt so we can go watch another one of your Christmas movies."

"How do you manage to make that sound so damn sexy? If I hadn't already said *yes* to your proposal, that would've done it for me."

"Glad to know that's all it would've taken."

"What can I say? I'm easy to please," I singsong.

Finn nearly chokes on some water. "Sunshine, you are anything but easy, but I love you regardless."

I shrug because he's not wrong. "As long as you know what you're getting yourself into."

He cups my face, smiling so sweetly. "I already know I'm one of the lucky ones who gets to marry their best friend. You made falling in love with you so goddamn effortless."

"Okay, I lied. *That* would've done it for me, hands down."
My face cracks in two as he fuses our mouths together. "I love you."

"Love you too, my forever pain in the ass."

"Forever and always."

Keep reading for a never-before-released bonus scene

Curious about Levi and Fallon?

Find their story next in *My Greatest Joy*

BONUS SCENE
OAKLEY

"WHAT DO you mean you can't button up my dress?" I say to the girl who's helping me with my final wedding dress fitting. "It fit fine two months ago."

"It's a smidge too tight. Inhale and hold it, and I'll try again."

She's gotta be kidding me.

But I'm three days away from walking down the aisle, so I do as she says and suck in as much as I can.

By the time she gets it done, I'm lightheaded and ready to collapse.

"There, got it."

"Great. So as long as I don't breathe, move, eat, or drink it'll stay buttoned," I deadpan.

Jessa comes up beside me. "Maybe a few hours in a sauna will help you sweat off any extra weight and by Saturday, you'll slip right into it."

"What do you mean *extra* weight? I've been working out for months."

Jessa grins, waving it off. "It's probably muscle, then."

I shoot her a glare because I know she's full of shit.

It's not my fault Finn's family serves me cookies and sweet

treats nonstop. It's hard to say no when they smell so damn good.

But I swear, I've been working out for months to get in tiptop wedding shape and this dress fit like a glove at the end of summer.

"I'll do what I can to fix it, okay? Come back in two days." The girl flashes a sympathetic expression.

Considering I'm getting married in three, I don't have any other option.

"Okay, thank you."

Once she helps me out of it, Jessa and I walk down to the café where we meet her girlfriend, Layla. She spent the morning writing here while we ran errands and agreed to meet up once we were done. They're both in the wedding party with my sister and brother-in-law along with Finn's best friend, Levi, and his very pregnant wife, Fallon.

Jessa and Layla have been helping us plan the whole ordeal and keep me on track in between Finn's and my work schedules. Since we met in October and love fall, it only made sense to have an October fall-themed orchard wedding.

Tiernan, Everett, and Bluebell are flying in tomorrow evening, and I can't wait to see them. Bluebell's over a year old now and will walk down the aisle as the flower girl, *hopefully*. I haven't seen them since last summer when she was born, but we FaceTime and text almost every day.

"Hey, where's the dress?" Layla stands when she notices us walking in empty-handed.

"My fat ass can't fit into it," I deadpan.

Layla glances at Jessa. "Uh, what'd you mean?"

"She put on like two pounds. It's no biggie," Jessa explains.

"Tell that to the button that won't reach unless I stop breathing."

Layla grins. "All this fuss over one button? That's not a big deal."

"Um...hello? My wedding is in three days!" I pout, taking the chair across from Layla.

I watch as Jessa and Layla share a look.

"What?"

Jessa releases a slow breath. "Okay, don't take offense about what I'm about to ask."

"This can't be good..." I murmur. "Go ahead."

She fidgets with her hands for a moment. "Is there any chance you could be pregnant?"

"Oh my God. I look *pregnant*?"

"Oakley, no! But pregnancy can make you bloated more than usual, especially in the first trimester. So it's something to consider as a possibility..."

"Do you use protection?" Layla asks.

"I'm on the pill, but we don't use condoms," I explain.

Oh wait.

I smack myself in the forehead. "When Finn surprised me with that weekend trip up north a month ago, he packed my bags for me since he didn't tell me until we were in the truck, and he forgot to pack my birth control. I only missed two days, so I took three as soon as I got home to make up for it."

"Can you do that?" Jessa asks at the same time Layla says, "I don't think it works that way."

"If you were ovulating and having sex, taking those late did nothing to prevent conception," Layla explains.

"Did you get your period?" Jessa continues.

"Yes!" I exclaim, but then remember... "Wait. I remember thinking I got it, but it was just spotting. I figured the stress of the wedding was messing up my cycles."

"When?" Layla asks.

"Like two-ish weeks ago."

"Could've been implantation bleeding. Some women experience that ten to fourteen days after conception."

Jessa gives her a suspicious look.

"So if we had unprotected sex four weeks ago—"

"You could already be having symptoms," Layla explains, and when Jessa gives her another confused expression, Layla continues, "I do a lot of weird and random book research."

I'd laugh at their antics if I wasn't internally freaking out.

"I threw up two days ago, but I thought it was something I ate," I admit. "Oh my God, what if I am, and I've been taking my pills this whole time?"

"You're fine." Layla reaches over, covering my hand with hers. "Once conception happens, it's not gonna hurt the baby. But I'd obviously stop taking them now."

"Guess there's only one way to find out…" Jessa grins. "Let's get you a test."

My heart pounds at the realization that I could be pregnant. Something Finn and I have talked about, something I've *dreamed* about, and now it could be our reality.

"Yeah, I need to know before I drink alcohol. But also, so I can throw it in that judgmental lady's face that the button not reaching isn't *my* fault. It's Finn's."

"She wasn't judging you." Jessa laughs, standing with me. She leans down toward Layla, kisses her, and then tells her we'll meet her at their house later.

"Good luck, Oakley! Text me the results."

"I will."

Jessa and I walk to the pharmacy a couple blocks down and my mind won't shut off as I think about what these next nine months will consist of if I am pregnant.

"How will you tell Finn if you are?" Jessa asks.

"Well, considering the wedding is this weekend and my sister comes tomorrow, I'm gonna tell him when I get home. I won't be able to hide it from Tiernan anyway and I want Finn to be the first to know—besides you and Layla."

"Maybe we can find a cute onesie at the boutique across from the theater. We can pull something cute together in a pinch." She links her arm through mine and smiles.

"Thanks, Jessa."

Maplewood Falls is beautiful any time of year, but especially during October. Each storefront is decorated with pumpkins and Halloween décor. There's a crisp feel in the air that feels so cozy, and I can't get enough of it.

"Alright, do you want the digital or lines one?" Jessa scans the aisle with all the tests.

"Hell if I know. Which one's the best kind?"

"No clue. They all claim to be ninety-nine percent accurate."

"Let's grab one of each, then." I shrug.

"So glad I don't have to worry about this," she mutters. "Twenty bucks for one test?"

I snort. "I dunno. From the sounds of it, I think Layla wants a baby."

"Because of her book research?"

"Is it actually research? Isn't she a thriller writer? What kind of thriller goes into that much detail about pregnancy?"

Considering I've listened to her entire backlist of books on audio, I can confirm none of them have ever mentioned it.

"Well...I don't know," she admits, leading us toward the checkout. "Wouldn't she tell me if she wanted to have a baby?"

"Maybe she's warming up to the idea first before she says anything."

"Oh my God." She spins around until she faces me. "I saw a sperm center website on her laptop a few weeks ago. I didn't think anything about it since her history is always questionable."

"Hm, there ya go. So who's carrying it?"

She bursts out laughing. "If you're not pregnant, can we rent out your womb?"

I nudge her with my elbow. "Nice try. I think you two would be great parents."

"I do, too." She smiles before adding, "As will you and Finn."

Once I've paid for the overpriced tests, we head to Belle's Boutique and find a cute pair of baby booties and a onesie with a pumpkin print over it.

"If I'm not pregnant, whoever gets knocked up first gets to keep this," I tease Jessa.

She smirks. "Deal."

We drive to Jessa's where I chug some water and wait until I have to use the bathroom. Luckily, it doesn't take long until I feel the urge to go.

The digital test took less than a minute to flash the word *pregnant* on the screen.

The other one had two lines appearing before I even finished peeing.

Excitement fills me from head to toe, and I can't wait to surprise Finn tonight with the news. I'm probably supposed to wait until it's confirmed with a blood test or something, but I'm not waiting. He'd know I was keeping something from him anyway.

FINN

When I walk into the cottage, my heart warms at the familiar setting.

Soft music playing. A fall-themed scented candle burns on the coffee table. There's a fire going in the new electric fireplace I installed a couple months ago. Oakley's been so excited to use it, and even though we're not in freezing temps, I enjoy it, too.

She must be painting.

But then the aroma of fettuccini alfredo and chicken grabs my attention and the fact that it smells good.

"Oakley?" I call out once I've removed my work boots. This

is our busiest time of the year, which has made it extra difficult to get the last-minute wedding prep done.

"In the kitchen," she replies.

As soon as I find her in front of the stove, I arch a brow. "You're cooking?"

"I'm warming it up," she clarifies. "And thanks for the confidence."

Her cute scowl causes me to laugh. "Can you blame me?"

"Funny. I wanted us to eat your favorite tonight."

"It looks and smells great in here." I tilt up her chin until I press my lips to hers. "How was your day?"

"Well, um…that'll be better explained once you open the gift I have for you."

"You got me a gift? For what?"

She turns off the stovetop, moves the pan off the burner, and then turns toward the table where a small box is placed.

"You'll see…" The devious smirk on her face has me curious as to what's going on.

She hands the gift to me, and I set it back down so I can open it.

Two pregnancy tests followed by a white onesie and baby shoes.

Correction—two *positive* pregnancy tests.

Holy. Shit.

I blink a few times, my chest tightening at the realization.

My breaths come out in pants as I blink toward her, holding up the tests in one hand and the onesie in another.

"You're pregnant?"

She nods, sucking in her lips to hold back her beautiful smile.

"Oh my God, baby! That's…" I set the items down and then pull her into my chest. "I can't believe it."

She curls herself into me, and I kiss the top of her head.

When I hear her crying, I pull back slightly until I find her eyes. "Are you happy?"

She nods, wiping her cheeks. "Shocked, but yes, so happy."

Cupping her face, I crash my mouth to hers and slide my tongue between her soft lips. "Me too, love. Getting to become your husband and now a father...thank you."

Her confused gaze meets mine. "For what?"

"For making me the happiest I've ever been. For agreeing to be my wife and starting a family with me."

"Well, I'll have you know...getting pregnant is your fault."

"*Mine*? Pretty sure you were an active participant each time, sweetheart."

She playfully swats my chest. "You forgetting my birth control last month."

"Oh...shit."

My palm lowers to her stomach. "I'd say I'm sorry, but I'm not."

Her hand covers mine. "Me neither."

I kiss her again and this time I don't stop until she's breathless underneath me on the couch.

"I can't wait to see your belly big and round."

"Excuse me?" She arches a brow, grabbing my hand and getting to her feet.

"With my baby, of course."

"Yeah, well, your gigantic baby is the reason I can't fit into my wedding dress. I have to get the buttons adjusted."

I can't help the bubble of laughter that spills out of my mouth at her serious and agitated tone.

"It's not funny, Finn! I couldn't breathe."

"Sweetheart, relax." I press my lips to her knuckles. "You could walk down in a black trash bag, and I'd still marry you."

"Good, because that might be what happens if the lady can't fix it."

Chuckling, I lead her back into the kitchen. "Let's get you and my baby fed. We have a busy few days ahead."

Luckily, I'm off work starting now. I took ten days off and

now I'll get to enjoy them with my pregnant wife on our honeymoon.

"You're gonna fatten me up even more." She takes a seat when I pull out the chair for her.

"Good. Now who cooked this?"

"Pretty bold of you to assume I didn't…"

"No…but I know my woman's cooking ability, and this is a smidge above yours."

"Rude. And it was Jessa."

"So I guess that means she knows, huh?" I grab two plates and serve us both a heaping amount of pasta.

"And Layla."

"Are you gonna tell your sister right away?" I ask, setting the plates down on the table.

"Yeah, she'd figure it out anyway. I'll call my doctor tomorrow and set up an appointment for when we get back."

I sit across from her and as I dive into my pasta, a burning smell lingers.

"Oh shit, the garlic bread!" Oakley flies out of her chair and yanks open the oven door.

"Babe, let me take care of it."

I carefully nudge her out of the way so she doesn't burn herself, grab a pot holder, and pull out the tray of burnt bread. Once it's on the stovetop and the oven's turned off, I look at her and smirk.

"Don't even say it…" She points a finger at me. "You distracted me with your tongue."

Laughing, I can't even be upset because if there's one thing Oakley's going to do, it's keep me on my toes.

Pulling her into me, I wrap my arms around her. "Go sit, I'll put some more in."

"Are you sure? Your food's gonna get cold."

"Positive. My woman and baby need to eat."

"You know, I could get used to this possessive daddy side."

I growl at her choice of words, knowing she's purposely taunting me. "Oakley Jane..."

She giggles, then goes back to the table.

Once the second round of garlic bread is done, I grab two and come up behind her chair to set them down on her plate.

"Eat your food like a good girl, and I'll eat you like a naughty one later," I whisper in her ear. "Preferably with you sitting on my face."

She nearly chokes on her pasta and has to take a drink to clear her throat.

The rest of the evening goes exactly as planned—Oakley fully sated and nearly passed out in my arms.

"You know, since I named Tiernan's baby, she's gonna demand she gets to name ours," she says.

I clench my jaw. "Not happening."

She chuckle. "Fair is fair."

"She's gonna pick something weird like...Sunset Paradise or Apple Delight."

Oakley perks up, her gaze meeting mine. "I love those! And how perfect would Apple be for the orchard? Plus, it gives fall vibes."

"Not happening," I repeat. Oakley loves strange names, but I have to draw the line at fruit.

"Oh, come on...we can wager for it?" A devilish smirk spreads across her face and she waggles her brows.

"Sunshine," I offer instead.

She's silent, and I assume she hates it.

"Wait, are you suggesting that as a name or calling me that?"

"A name."

Her eyes widen in excitement. "Immediately yes."

I grin at her eagerness.

"And for a boy?" she asks.

"Not sure on the first name, but I'd love to have James be his middle name."

"In honor of your grandpa, of course." She beams. "Maple James would be the coolest name."

"*Maple*? That's straight-up child abuse."

She scowls. "Fine, hold on."

When she grabs her phone and types, I ask what she's doing.

"I'm looking up fall-themed baby boy names…" She scrolls a bit. "Archer, Rory, Cedar…ooh, I like that one. Hunter, Forrester, Ash."

She continues rambling off names, but I already know she's going to fixate on that one she likes.

"Cedar James?"

"You like it?" She sets down her phone.

I shrug. "I could get used to it. But"—I place my hand on her belly—"it's gonna be a girl."

"How can you be so sure?"

"I just am."

"Maybe it's twins and we'll get one of each—Sunshine and Cedar."

Smiling wide at that idea, I dip down and kiss her stomach. "Sounds perfect to me."

Curious about Levi and Fallon?
Find their story next in *My Greatest Joy*

MY GREATEST JOY
LEVI & FALLON'S BOOK

There's a reason I hate the holidays, but nothing could've prepared me for the literal nightmare of flying three thousand miles in the middle of December.

When my coworker gets the flu, I reluctantly volunteer to take their assignment to write a piece on Vermont's most famous Christmas small town.

After a delayed flight and driving through a blizzard in a minivan to a mountain cabin in the middle of nowhere, I find myself mixed up in a rental scam.

It's bad enough the owner walks into my room naked and accuses me of breaking in, but then he tells me all the roads into town are closed. Even if I could leave, all the hotels are booked with tourists for the winter festival.

Even worse, his house is decorated like the North Pole.

Like I said, a nightmare.

The only perk about being snowed in with a lumberjack is that he's accustomed to the cold and lets me steal his body heat in the middle of the night.

But then that turns into more, and even when I try to resist, I can't help getting attached. It'll never work out because we live on opposite sides of the country and have nothing in common.

Except, maybe we do...

ABOUT THE AUTHOR

Brooke Fox is the alternate pen name for Brooke Montgomery. She lives in the Midwest with her husband, teenage daughter, and four dogs. She survives on iced coffee and afternoon naps.

Find her on her website at
www.brookewritesromance.com
and follow her on social media:

facebook.com/brookemontgomeryauthor
instagram.com/brookewritesromance
threads.net/@brookewritesromance
tiktok.com/@brookewritesromance

Printed in Great Britain
by Amazon

48723701R20148